VALLEY
of
SECRETS

KARI LEE HARMON

OLIVER
HEBER
BOOKS

To all the mothers out there who have loved and lost. You are not alone. And to my mother, Marion Harmon, who is the strongest, most inspiring woman I know. This one's for you, Mom 🌚

1

"Your visions will become clear only when you can look into your own heart. Who looks outside, dreams; who looks inside, awakes."

— *CARL JUNG*

The sun was shining the day Jordan Mills found out she was broken. Syracuse, New York, didn't get much sunshine. When it did, it was considered a gift. But it didn't feel like a gift to Jordan when shiny rays of hope blanketed everything as her whole world fell apart, much like it was doing today. A bright shiny day, six months later in the Spring.

A shiny day when Jordan's life would change forever.

She set down the Sunday newspaper, pushed her untouched wheat toast away, inhaled the warmed lavender essential oil, and strived for calm as she stared out the window of her fully restored landmark historic house, not far from Syracuse University. A lot of the old buildings had been renovated and turned into apartments, but an apartment would never be good enough for her husband. They had the entire building to themselves, which normally she wouldn't mind, but nothing was normal about her life anymore. She felt more alone than ever in a house this big.

The snow had melted. When had that happened? It wouldn't be long before tulips poked their silky heads through the soft earth and bloomed with color. She used to love Spring. Loved the time when everything was fresh and new. When everything started to grow. Life needed sun to grow. Maybe she didn't get enough sun. Maybe that was why she was broken. She blinked and was taken back to the Fall when everything began to die.

"I'm so sorry," Dr. Hamlin said, a genuine look of regret shadowing his haggard features.

He looked thinner than the last time she had seen him, his lab coat now one size too big. He was her husband Erik's age, forty-three, but looked much older with a head full of gray hair and a lot more wrinkles. They'd gone to college together, Matthew graduating with an MD in obstetric gynecology, and Erik with a PhD in literature. They had both chosen to stay in the area and work. They weren't exactly close, but they'd never lost touch completely. Matthew was a top OBGYN doctor at University Hospital, and Erik was a professor at Syracuse University. Erik trusted Matthew, and Jordan had trusted Erik. Trusted him with her heart, her soul, and her future the day he'd swept her off her feet and asked her to marry him, thirteen years ago.

She'd grown up as Jordanna Wilkinson, at Wilkinson's Winery on Cayuga Lake, the second largest of the Central New York glacial Finger Lakes. She was the youngest of six girls. She loved having sisters and her mother was kind, but Jordan had never really been like the rest of them. Her father was about as old-fashioned as they came, believing girls didn't need an education. They were meant to be wives and mothers, pampered and cherished for all of their days.

That's all Jordanna had ever known.

All of her sisters had gone on to happily marry and have children right out of high school, so when three years went by, she was terrified the fairy tale would never happen for her. And then what would she do? She could have sworn she heard someone whisper, *Think for yourself. Get a life. Do whatever the hell you want to*, back in those days, but she'd always laughed off her crazy thoughts and tried to stay positive. Hopeful. That's why when handsome, dashing Erik Mills—nine years her senior —had shown up, he'd seemed like Prince Charming, with golden-blond hair and sky-blue eyes.

Erik came from money. He was the last of the Mills, and desperate to carry on his family's name by having a son. As taken with Jordanna as she was with him, he made her Mrs. Jordan Mills and she couldn't have been happier. They truly had been happy at first. He introduced her to a whole new life in Syracuse, showering her with gifts, pampering her with spa treatments and luxurious vacations, and proudly displaying her about at department parties. All she had to do in return was adore him and give him a son. They'd talked excitedly over names and whether the baby would look like him or have her auburn hair and jade-green eyes. They'd even decorated a nursery, presumptuously assuming it would all be that easy.

Over the years, their happiness began to fade as they tried and tried without success to conceive. The pressure became unbearable, but nothing compared to the disappointment simmering in Erik's eyes. When he suggested they see his longtime friend, Jordan had agreed immediately, desperate to try anything that might help them have a baby. She just never imagined there would be nothing in the world that could possibly help them now.

"Are you sure, Matt?" Erik asked the doctor after clearing his throat.

Erik sat ramrod straight, his sweater vest a perfect fit over his casual cotton pants with matching shirt and tie, not a hair out of place. His usual work attire. Unlike Dr. Hamlin, Erik looked younger than his years and more handsome than ever. He couldn't look at Jordan. Her stomach turned over. Why wouldn't he look at her? She'd made sure she was impeccably dressed in the latest fashion, with her hair artfully styled, her posture perfect, knowing she was a reflection of him. So why wouldn't he look at her? She started to shake in the cold, impersonal exam room. Dr. Matthew Hamlin might be the best in his field, but he wasn't exactly the warm fuzzy type. It was no shock that he wasn't married.

Dr. Hamlin stared at Erik for a long moment and then nodded sadly. "I truly am sorry."

The doctor wouldn't look at Jordan either. She couldn't seem to inhale enough air, the pungent scent of antiseptic making her queasy. Why wouldn't anyone look at her? Her skin itched on the inside, and she wanted to crawl outside of her own body. A body that wasn't a temple anymore, but an empty, useless cage. Oh my God, she was trapped inside an empty, useless cage! She desperately wanted out, but there was nothing anyone could do about it. No one could help her now. Matt was the best. All hope was lost.

"I'm broken," she said on barely more than a whisper, and something inside of her cracked. A sharp pain pierced her heart as the doctor's words sank in.

She was infertile.

Her dream of becoming a mother would never happen now. Not ever. Because she wasn't whole. They'd tried IVF among other things, but nothing ever worked. And now she knew why. It was all her fault. Something about her irregular ovulation and hormone deficiencies. She would never feel the flutter of new life growing inside of her womb. Never give birth to a precious creation that was a part of her. Never hold her child in her arms and look into eyes and see herself. Wasn't that why God created Woman? To give life? That was all she'd ever wanted. *Wasn't it?* Of course it was.

After the shock wore off, the blame set in. She knew she was sounding irrational, but there had to be a reason why she was defective. Her skin was so fair, she'd always been lectured to stay out of the sun. Could that be why? Why had she listened? Everyone knew life needed sunlight to grow. She'd been so stupid to stay out of the sun. Suddenly she couldn't blame Dr. Hamlin or Erik for not looking at her. Couldn't blame her husband when she later found out he'd had an affair with a younger student of his and the woman was pregnant with his child. Couldn't blame him when he filed for divorce and traded her in for something better. Someone whole.

A robin chirped outside Jordan's window, bringing her back to the present. Back to the papers on her table that said her divorce was final. Back to the campus e-mail stating Erik was the proud father of a healthy baby boy. Back to the newspaper article announcing his engagement. Jordan was numb. She hadn't cried or yelled or done anything, really. For six months she'd sat alone, licking her wounds and slowly dying inside, no longer stylish and fashionable. What was the point?

No one wanted a broken woman.

Her parents were disappointed with all that had happened, of course, encouraging her to return to the vineyard and try again. She was only thirty-four, after all. There was still hope she could remarry. She wasn't *that* broken, and she could always adopt. She could start over. Maybe they were right. Six months was long enough to wallow in self-pity. She really should get on with her life, but how could she do anything when all she felt was empty inside?

Jordan couldn't decide what to do because she'd never had

to. Everything had always been decided for her. First by her family and then by Erik. Her mother begged her to at least come for lunch. The sun was shining, and it was a beautiful day. She and Erik had always gone to Sunday dinners at her parents' with her siblings and their families, but Jordan hadn't been back since Erik had left her, and her parents hadn't pressed until now. Doing what she always did, Jordan listened to them, even though she'd come to hate the sun.

A FEW HOURS LATER, Jordan arrived at Wilkinson's Winery on the long, narrow, fingerlike Cayuga Lake. The place where she'd grown up. Her family home. She hadn't appreciated it back then, but she was old enough now to realize how impressive the place really was. She drove her Mercedes down the long driveway past the large barn used to produce wine from several types of grapes. Jordan knew the winemaking process by heart: fermentation of the fruit, blending and aging the juice, then bottling and sealing the wine. She drove past the sophisticated wine cellar that housed the barrels and the charming tasting room, until she reached the ancient two-story colonial house overlooking the lake, that had been in her family for generations. The house might be old, but it was impeccably kept, with class and good taste.

Her father used to be the winemaker, having learned the craft from his father, who'd learned from his father before that, and so on. For generations, a Wilkinson had been at the helm, but Henry Wilkinson didn't have any sons. Six daughters he pampered and adored, but didn't trust to take over. None of them had complained, happy in their roles of wives and mothers. At thirty-four, Jordan had no desire to take over, not that her father would let her. She'd left at twenty-one. Techniques had changed a lot since then, with modern technology improvements she knew nothing about.

Come to think of it, she didn't know much about a lot of things she suddenly realized. Did being pampered and cherished really involve being naïve? Ignorant? She sighed as she shut off the engine and stared at the house. How had she let her life come to this? Shallow emptiness with no depth. She knew how. She'd been so focused on adoring her husband and getting pregnant that she'd lost sight of everything else, including herself. She really should go in. They were all there with their husbands and children, waiting for her.

It was almost too much to bear.

Beyond the house stood rows of grapevines that called to her. Nature had always called to her soul, beckoning for her to do... what, she wasn't exactly sure. Today the urge to follow was stronger than ever. Jordan climbed out of her car and bypassed the house, heading for the vineyard. She tightened her thick sweater coat around her, as March in central NY could be quite chilly still. The snow had melted and the lake thawed out, looking pristine and beautiful in the distance. A calming presence that spoke to her. This place had always had that effect on her. The trees and vines were bare, but would soon sprout leaves and buds now that Spring was upon them. The whole winery had an air of elegance and refinery. In fact, her entire life had been elegant and refined.

Their winery was housed on the southern end of the lake, near Ithaca. The northern end consisted of shallow mudflats and marshes that drew various migratory birds and encompassed a national wildlife refuge, whereas the southern end consisted of boaters and sport fisherman. Jordan and her sisters used to hang out at the marina and the yacht club on the western shore. Their father had a boat, and they'd soon realized the club was an excellent place to meet eligible bachelors who measured up to his standards.

Jordan's sisters had a much easier time of finding a husband than she did. They were all beautiful. Tall and elegant with various shades of blond hair and blue eyes like their mother. Jordan was the only one who looked different. Her father had brown hair back in the day—it was stark white now—and jade-green eyes. She had her father's eyes, but that's where the resemblance ended. She looked much more like her Aunt Annabeth, with her fiery-red hair and sparkling emerald-green eyes, only Jordan's hair was a darker auburn and eyes a paler green.

She smiled fondly as she walked through the rows of vines, running her fingers lightly over the branches, realizing she hadn't thought of her aunt in years. Not since she was ten years old and her aunt passed away. Jordan's smile faded sadly. She missed her aunt. Probably because her mother and sisters were elegant angels who enjoyed being pampered and cherished. Jordan remembered feeling a longing for something more like her aunt. She was the strongest, most independent woman Jordan had ever known. Her father had named her Jordanna, the *anna* part after her aunt Annabeth.

Henry had adored his sister when Jordan was born. Annabeth was ten years younger than Henry, who was thirty-five when Jordan arrived. But as the years went by, Annabeth became fearless. Stubborn and strong-willed, she had no desire to get married, shocking everyone. She'd defiantly changed her name to Anna Wilks as she grew increasingly bold, going on grand adventures and taking unnecessary risks, happy not to settle down. Happy with who she was. Happy to do *whatever she damn well pleased,* Jordan had once heard her say. No matter how much Henry or their father had tried to talk sense into Annabeth, she wouldn't listen.

Jordanna had wanted to be just like her.

When Anna died in a skydiving accident at thirty-five, Jordan was ten. She'd been devastated, but her father cut her grieving short and quickly steered her back on track, where she grew up and forgot what it was like to be adventuresome and fearless. She thought she'd been happy with her role in life, until now. Jordan suddenly realized with the utmost clarity that it was the role of mother that had called to her, not so much the wife part. She'd simply accepted the rest in order to get what she wanted, but now it was all gone, and she was left with no idea who she was or what she wanted out of life. She still hadn't cried. In fact, she didn't remember crying much about anything since she was ten. She couldn't, because she felt hollow and empty, with nothing left inside. Not even tears.

Jordan looked up and realized she hadn't walked this far through the vineyard since she was a child. She sucked in a breath as she looked at the strand of trees before her. The fort she and her aunt had built so many years ago was still there. For the first time in a long time, she felt a spark of the carefree child, full of excitement and wonder, ignite within her. Biting her bottom lip, she looked around, but no one was nearby. She climbed into the circle of trees under the rotting wooden roof and sat on a large boulder. Once the leaves came in, the whole world would be shut out, just the way she and her aunt had liked it. The hideaway had been their secret haven. Their safe space to think and dream and write. Jordan had forgotten about that. She'd forgotten about this place.

She'd forgotten about a lot of things.

A strong desire to be close to her aunt settled over her, and Jordan wondered if the box was still there. Looking around frantically, she spotted the metal box, barely visible beneath layers of old dried leaves, and tucked under the blackberry bush where they used to hide it. Holding the box tight in both hands, she returned to the rock. Her heart started beating harder as she dropped to her knees to expose the precious contents from her youth.

She picked up the box, skimming her fingers along its rusted edges, anxious to rediscover the many hopes and dreams she'd stored inside. Inhaling a deep breath of crisp air that smelled like wet dirt and lake water, she pried the rusted lid open. Her lips parted for a moment, then she swallowed the lump in her throat and stared at her diary. Carefully picking it up, she flipped through the pages. The childish scribbling of a confused ten-year-old scrawled across the pages.

I DON'T LIKE when Daddy gets strict.
  Why is Mommy crying?
  Jill, Jessica, Jasmine, Jennifer, and Jamie are so pretty.
  Why am I so plain? I shouldn't be a "J".
  I wish Aunt Annabeth was my Mommy. Why couldn't I be an "A"?
  Why did you have to go away, Aunt Anna?
  You're the bravest person I know, Aunt Anna.
  I love you, and I promise I won't let you down, Aunt Anna.
  I'll never forget you.

BUT SHE HAD LET her aunt down, Jordan realized. She'd forgotten her. And now her aunt wasn't the only one who was dead. Mrs. Jordan Mills was dead, and Jordanna Wilkinson had died a long time ago. She didn't know who she was anymore. The first tear rolled down her cheek, surprising her, and then the floodgates opened. Sobs wracked her body for her aunt, for herself, for her unborn child that would never be, for who she wasn't, for all she'd lost. Her life was as dead as the trees surrounding her, never destined to bloom. She couldn't catch her breath. It felt like forever that she sat on the rock and cried.

"What am I going to do now?" she finally said out loud, just to hear a voice and not feel so alone.

Whatever you damn well please, came the whisper.

Jordan looked around startled, but no one was there. Her gaze fell down to her lap, and she blinked. Her aunt's diary lay on top of hers now, with the spine flipped open to page one. How had that happened? Jordan swallowed hard. The only rule they had ever created was that their diaries were sacred and meant for their eyes only. They talked about everything, but they never talked about what they wrote. It was somehow more special that way. But now the book lay open like an invitation to read the passages and draw strength from her namesake when she needed it most.

Jordan was about to close the book, knowing it was wrong, but the words on the page grabbed hold of her and refused to let go. As if a force greater than herself was willing her to read on.

WHEN I'M READY, I will die on my own terms, dammit!

THE BREATH WHOOSHED out of Jordan's lungs as she discovered her aunt's secret. She reread the entire passage to be sure her eyes weren't playing a horrible, sick, twisted trick on her.

LIFE IS SO UNFAIR. I waited way too long to start living. I let too many people try to tell me what to do and how to live my life, suppressing what I really wanted in hopes of making everyone happy. For what? One year? I only have one fucking year left to do what I want. A goddamned brain tumor. How is that possible? I don't get sick. I feel

fine. Well, that's it, then. No one can know. I won't allow it. I hate pity.
I know what I'm going to do. I refuse to die. I choose to live.
    When I'm ready, I will die on my own terms, dammit!

HER AUNT WAS her age when she'd found out she had a
cancerous brain tumor. That was when they'd built their fort
and she'd started her journal, never letting on to Jordan or
anyone else what was really going on. Her father kept saying he
thought Anna was losing her mind with how crazy she was
acting. And that if she wasn't careful, she was going to die. But
Jordan knew the truth now. Her aunt hadn't been trying to die;
she'd been trying to live. Jordan had known her aunt was brave,
she'd just never realized *how* brave. They'd said her parachute
never opened the day she went sky diving. The day she'd died.
At least she didn't suffer. She'd died doing something exciting
while she was still full of life.

Flipping through the book, Jordan saw a year's worth of
entries. Her aunt had chosen to do one adventurous thing every
day for the next year, opting to go without chemo or radiation
because she'd wanted to live fully and in the moment. She didn't
want to be sick. She wanted to be free. Jordan didn't realize she
was softly crying again until she turned the last page and read:

TO MY DARLING JORDANNA. You are strong and brave and beautiful.
Don't ever let anyone tell you otherwise. You're special, baby. I can
only hope you grow a mind of your own someday. You can do
anything you set your mind to. Life is too short to live for others. So,
honey, here's my last piece of advice for you. When you are down on
your luck and don't know what to do, remember this...
    Do whatever you damn well please!

2

"You're what?" Henry Wilkinson stared at his youngest daughter in shock one week later.

They'd had a delicious pot-roast dinner prepared by his lovely wife, Mary, with his whole family there. The mouthwatering aromas still lingered, but the feeling of contentment and satisfaction had turned to one of indigestion as he tried to process what his daughter had just said. Everyone had gone home except for Jordanna, who'd been there, yet hadn't really been present the entire time. Mary stood by his side, looking elegant and refined and deeply troubled, as she deferred to him to get to the bottom of all this crazy talk.

Jordanna had never shown up for lunch last Sunday, leaving them all frantic with worry. He'd nearly called the police, but had tried her phone one last time. She'd answered and had said she had been there, but that an emergency had come up so she'd left. She refused to say what the emergency was, remaining suspiciously vague. She'd been acting strange ever since Erik had left her. Henry was furious with Erik for what he'd put his little girl through. He wasn't worthy of Jordan's love, yet Henry could understand how he felt, in a way. After all, he himself had been blessed with six beautiful daughters. Yes, he would have liked to have had at least one son to carry on the winery, but he wasn't complaining.

Children were gifts from God.

If Mary hadn't been able to have children, it would have devastated him, but he wouldn't have had an affair and left her for another woman. He would have simply adopted a baby—with a fine pedigree of course. He would have still had a family. Henry could understand why Jordanna was so upset as well. What woman didn't want to be a wife and mother? He suddenly thought of his sister, Annabeth. He refused to call her Anna. She'd never had children. She'd never married, but she'd had plenty of suitors. He now wondered if maybe she couldn't. His Jordanna was so much like his sister, it would make sense if they were both infertile. Maybe that was why his sister had gone crazy in the end.

And now he was terrified Jordanna was headed for the same fate.

"I'm changing my name to Anna Wilks, selling my house, and moving to a place called Mystic Valley, Vermont," Jordanna repeated, trying to sound firm, but he heard the quake in her voice. There was still hope he could change her mind. And he'd be damned if he would call her Anna, either.

"But why, sweetheart?" Mary finally asked quietly, looking hurt. She smoothed her chicly styled golden-blond hair and adjusted her lavender silk pantsuit.

"What's wrong with your name?" Anger and disappointment surged through Henry. Not for the first time, he regretted letting Jordanna spend so much time with her aunt before she died.

"Nothing is wrong with my name, it's just not who I am anymore. Neither is Mrs. Jordan Mills. Anna Wilks makes me feel inspired, and that's something I need right now."

"Why not move back here with us? We'll set you on the right track. We know plenty of eligible men, many of whom already have children. You could start over," Mary said, softly adding, "You could still be a mother."

"I've accepted my fate, Mother," Jordanna said with resolve. "I need this. I need to get away. It's time I found out who I really am. What makes me happy."

"You're our daughter. You've always known what you wanted. You were meant to be a wife and mother. You just need time. Maybe you should talk to someone. I know a guy," Henry said sternly, feeling every one of his sixty-nine years. She was thirty-four. His opinion didn't carry as much weight as it once did, and for the first time ever he felt helpless. He didn't like not being in control.

"No, Father, *you* always knew what you wanted me to be. Frankly, I don't have a clue."

That much was apparent, he thought. She looked too thin and run down, her hair a little frizzy and her clothes wrinkled. Not at all put-together like she used to be, and nothing like her immaculate sisters. Lord only knew what would happen if she went to a place like that by herself.

"But how will you live?" her mother asked, looking worried.

Jordanna's face hardened stubbornly. "I have plenty of money thanks to Erik's guilt."

Henry felt like he was losing her. "Vermont!" he spat. "Why Vermont? I've never even heard of Mystic Valley. It's sounds so... so..."

"Unrefined?" Jordanna finished his thought, and then added her own, "I think it sounds charming. 'Refined' obviously hasn't worked for me. Maybe it's time I tried something else."

"Like your Aunt Annabeth?" He grasped at any straw he could. "Look how she turned out. Why are you choosing to throw your life away? Because that's exactly what will happen if you follow in her footsteps." He shook his head and felt his perfectly styled hair slip out of its gelled place.

"I *am* following in her footsteps," Jordanna said almost reverently. "I'm choosing to live."

"How?" he asked, desperately adding in a loud voice a bit more harsh than he intended, "What in the hell are you going to do in a place like Mystic Valley, Vermont?"

His baby looked him square in the eye, and for a moment he could swear he was staring at his sister come back from the dead, as she said with raised chin before walking out the door and not looking back, "Whatever I damn well please!"

MYSTIC VALLEY WAS A SMALL, old-fashioned Vermont town, with rustic farmhouses and covered bridges. Worlds apart from a modern city like Syracuse, with its busy streets and high-rise buildings. Located in Maple County in the middle of the Vermont Piedmont, the town was nestled at the foothills of the Green Mountains between several rolling hills and lakes formed by glaciers. The surrounding forests gave off the feeling of being in the middle of nowhere, which was exactly where Anna wanted to be these days.

"Anna Wilks," she tested the name out on her tongue and tried for a tentative smile.

She'd decided to start smiling more, and maybe someday soon it would feel natural again. Normal. She'd decided to do a lot of things on that sunny Spring day two months ago, as she'd sat in the fort she and her aunt had built, feeling her comforting presence all around her. Anna had decided to fulfill her promise to her aunt and not forget her ever again. She'd decided to leave the only home she'd ever known.

She'd decided to start living, no matter how hard it might seem.

After finding the brochure on Mystic Valley beneath the journals in the metal box, Anna had realized that was the next place on her aunt's list to visit before she died. Her aunt had been all about making choices, deciding things for herself, and *acting* instead of being a passive lump of nothing. So Anna had made the choice to take her aunt's name and pick up where she left off, no matter how scary. She would keep her aunt's secret, and she would keep her journal as a guide for inspiration, because one thing was certain.

Anna didn't have a clue how to take care of herself.

People had taken care of her for her entire life. She felt hopeful and even a little excited, yet definitely terrified to try to make it on her own. It would be hard, but if her aunt could do it, then she could too. Anna had already lost herself. What more did she have to lose? She was desperate, and hoped that by learning to be adventuresome and fearless, she just might get lucky and find herself. But that didn't mean it would be easy or that she wasn't scared.

Misty fog from the hills that blanketed the valley every morning began to burn off, revealing gorgeous May flowers in full bloom as Anna drove over a weathered wood-covered bridge into town. She rolled down the window of her Mercedes and breathed in what she hoped was new life. The smell of maple syrup wafted down from the sugar shacks high in the hills, mixing with the scent of pine. She'd done her homework before moving here. Sap was tapped in the spring and boiled into syrup, so the batches were fresh.

According to the brochure, the maple syrup festival took place in April. Even though it was an old pamphlet, she imagined they would still hold these events. She'd been bummed she'd missed it, but next up should be the dairy festival this month, then the wildflower festival in June and the blueberry festival in July. She would participate in those for sure, even though she certainly couldn't milk a cow, wasn't very crafty, and her cooking was hardly mouth-watering, to say the least. The county fair in August sounded like fun, followed by the apple and harvest festivals in September, the fall leaf peepers in October, antique shows in November, and the winter carnival in January.

Anna was really looking forward to living in a town that banded together and celebrated every stage of life. She passed the small police department, followed by a brick building the newspaper was housed in, then the town hall and post office, as well as the only bank. A small gray building with a white-and-red striped pole that served as the sign for Nick's barber shop came into view.

Three middle-aged men sat in folding lawn chairs out in front of the store window. One wore a fishing hat and puffed on his pipe as he studied her. This area had some of the best trout, perch, walleye, bass, and pickerel fishing. At least that's what the brochure had said. Another one huddled in a camo jacket and hat, smiling at her. White-tail deer, coyote, red fox, and snowshoe hare provided an abundance of hunting for those so inclined. And the last one—who had to be Nick since he sported a white barber coat with a long comb and scissors sticking out of the pocket—waved as she drove by.

She smiled—her cheeks already aching—and waved back, thinking, *See, that wasn't so hard*. Maybe it wouldn't be so hard to be happy either.

It would take time to heal her wounds and find herself, but time was exactly what she had plenty of, and quiet was something she craved. Mystic Valley was the epitome of quiet and peaceful and scenic. Glancing at the horizon, a series of isolated mountains called monadnocks dotted the landscape. She'd read about these in her research. The Indians had named these hard igneous rock formations—made of granite that resisted erosion —the island mountain place. The area boasted plenty of rock quarries full of granite, marble, slate, sand, gravel, and stone.

A person could get lost here and never be found, Anna mused with a shiver, but shook off that scary thought, determined to stay positive and find her own way.

The surrounding forests were filled with conifers and northern hardwoods, as well as wildflowers and honeysuckle galore. And in the Fall, the hills would be speckled like paint on a canvas with brilliant red, orange, and gold leaves from the various butternut, white pine, yellow birch, and sugar-maple trees. A regular bird haven for the black ravens, gray Canada jays, saw-whet owls and endangered bald eagles who called this area their home. With Anna having come from a city, Mystic Valley appeared much more low-key with its many lumber mills, construction sites, dairy, grain, and apple farms, as well as a multitude of small shops selling artisan foods and crafts.

Anna could be happy here, she decided. Something about this place called to her in a way that no other ever had. She could see why her aunt had been drawn to it.

She drove past a rustic house with two old women sitting in rocking chairs with colorful quilts over their laps and playing checkers on the front porch. They looked up curiously at Anna with a smile as well. This place was certainly friendly. Anna liked that. She needed friendly. Next she passed an old white Roman Catholic church with a steeple, and a charming country store, before finally arriving at Deb's Diner. That's where she was meeting her realtor, Misty Monroe. Anna's mouth twisted into an amused grin. The place looked like an old train caboose

—both clever and welcoming. She only hoped the patrons inside would be so, as well, she thought as she pulled into a parking space and nervously stepped out of her car.

Heading toward the door, a man came out at the same time she was about to enter. He stopped abruptly before running into her, and then a slow smile spread across his All-American, boy-next-door handsome face. He was tall and muscular, with a sandy-blond buzz cut that looked like he was in the military. He might be intimidating to most people, but his warm hazel eyes gave him away. They crinkled at the corners, making everything about him friendly, as though getting mad would be a struggle for him.

He was a big softie if ever she'd seen one.

"Officer Jones at your service, ma'am, but you can call me Drew. I don't believe I've had the pleasure of meeting you before, so let me be the first one to say welcome to our town." He held out his hand.

Ah, a police officer and not military. She'd been close, she thought, and couldn't help smiling in return. For once it didn't feel forced. "Thank you, Drew. I'm Anna Wilks, and you're right. I'm new in town." She slid her hand into his.

He folded his large palm around hers and gently shook it. Something told her everything about him was gentle. He would make some woman very lucky, not that she was looking for a new man. She'd just noticed the absence of a ring. Though these days, that didn't seem to matter. Sadly, no one seemed to take their vows seriously anymore. She shook off her depressing thoughts and refused to think about Erik.

"Well, Miss Anna Wilks, I look forward to seeing you around." Drew gave a slight bow. "Duty calls, but please don't hesitate to give me a jingle if you need anything at all. You know where to find me."

"I just might take you up on that," Anna shocked herself by

saying, realizing he was surprisingly easy to talk to. Something about him made a person want to lean on him. Like he could handle anything, and everything would be okay.

"Until we meet again, then." Looking pleased, he held the door open for her and waved before walking away to his squad car.

Hope for a brighter future blossomed in Anna's chest as she watched him go, feeling good about Mystic Valley. If all of the residents were like this, then she'd definitely made the right decision in moving here.

"Anna Wilks, as I live and breathe. You're a bitty thing if ever I've seen one," someone squealed.

Anna whirled around to see a woman in her fifties, with a bright orange beehive of hair and tiny spectacles on a chain, charging toward her as if she'd known Anna her entire life. She was a large woman, and wobbled as she wove her way through the tables, waving and talking to everyone as she made her way to Anna to sweep her into a bear hug.

"Misty Monroe of Monroe Realty, I hope?" Anna said on a wheeze as she awkwardly patted the woman's back, trying not to faint from the overpowering perfume that made her eyes water.

"Oh posh, forgive me. Where are my manners? Of course, I'm Misty." The woman grabbed Anna's arm and pulled her over to a table in the corner with a good view of the entire diner. The tables were mostly full, with sounds of silver clanking and the hum of conversation droning on as the delicious aromas made Anna's stomach growl. "Come with me, doll. We'll fix you up, right as rain. Get some good home cookin' in ya and fatten you up a bit. You'll never last a winter with no flesh on your bones."

"Oh, well, thank you, I guess." Anna hadn't had much of an appetite for quite some time, and couldn't remember the last time she'd eaten a full meal. Just one more thing she intended to rectify now that she was here. "Don't worry. I'm from Syracuse. We get plenty of snow."

"Honey, there's snow, and then there's *snow*. Trust me, you're gonna want some curves." Misty patted Anna's hand and winked. "So will the fellers. I saw you talking to Officer Jones outside. That man is a gift from God. Easy on the eyes and as sweet as pie. He's helped just about everyone in town at one time or another, and is as unattached as the day the doctor cut his umbilical cord from his mama. Why, he's the most eligible bachelor in the entire county. He's just been waitin' for the right woman to come along."

"Drew seems very nice, but I've had my fill of fellers lately," Anna said lightly with a smile she knew didn't quite reach her eyes.

Misty's face softened sympathetically. "You've had a hard time of it, have you? Well, you've come to the right place." She patted Anna's hand. "Mystic Valley is special. It has a way of healing a person. You'll see."

Anna felt her lips tremble, so she pressed them together and nodded in response, then picked up her menu. They ordered lunch, and heeding Misty's words, Anna chose a burger instead of her usual salad. At five-foot-two, gaining five pounds looked more like twenty, or so Erik had told her. She'd always been conscious of keeping up appearances for his sake. Defiantly, she bit into the juicy burger with satisfaction, and had to admit it tasted heavenly. Misty told Anna all about the quaint colonial house she'd bought, with its charming front porch. It was right in town on the main drag, just down the street, so she could sit in her own rocker and people-watch.

"I can't wait to see it," Anna said.

"And we will do just that, but first things first," Misty said with a twinkle in her eye. "You can't live in a small town and not know what's what."

It would take some getting used to, living in a small town, Anna thought. Back in Syracuse, no one knew she existed except for Erik's colleagues. Even before her world fell apart, she'd felt lonely. She just hadn't realized how much. That was probably why she'd been so desperate for a baby. Something told her that in Mystic Valley, she would never lack for companionship.

"I'm all ears." Anna's lips tipped up slightly in amusement.

Misty spent the next thirty minutes filling Anna in on all the latest gossip and then excused herself to go to the ladies' room. Anna noticed a young couple near the window with a small boy, and her heart gave a pang of envy. The boy went to the bathroom as well, and he'd no sooner left than the couple started arguing. Anna frowned. More like the man started lecturing. He kept his voice low, but it was obvious he was displeased with the woman. Her slight shoulders slumped, and she didn't say a word. When the boy returned, they left as though nothing was wrong.

Anna knew all about keeping up the façade for appearances' sake. She felt sorry for the woman. She'd often taken the brunt of Erik's anger when something went wrong, especially at the end of their marriage. It was somehow *her* fault he didn't get a raise, and *her* fault they didn't get into a new restaurant, and *her* fault they couldn't have a baby. Except in the end, it truly had been her fault.

"If you're ready, I'd really like to see my house now," Anna said when Misty returned.

"It's time." Misty nodded and picked up the bill. "I insist," she added at Anna's look of protestation. "We don't get many new people in town. You're a treat." She laughed. "Like I said, you'll see." And then she led the way to the counter to pay their bill.

Moments later they walked through the door with Misty in the lead. When she stepped to the side, Anna bumped into a guy, probably around forty, who had to be at least six-four. Over a foot taller than herself. And here she'd thought Drew was tall. She knocked the giant's aviator sunglasses off by accident. He sported messy black curls, a five-o-clock shadow, and intelligent, stormy gray eyes. He reached out and caught her before she could fall, his huge hands wrapped around her slender arms until he steadied her.

He blinked, looking surprised and curious as he studied her. She stared wide-eyed with her lips parted, and for once, didn't look away. He was big and burly and gruff—as unrefined as her new home, her father would undoubtedly say—but something about this man called to her soul the same way that Mystic Valley did. It didn't make sense. Drew was much more her type than this grizzly bear. Then again, nothing that had happened to her this past year made sense either.

The man seemed to come to his senses first and let go of her to pick up his glasses. Taking a step back, he looked to the side at her Mercedes and then back at her with a frown. "That your car?" His voice came out deep and full of gravel.

She nodded, unable to form coherent words. What was wrong with her?

"You're in my spot. Everyone knows this is my spot. Remember that next time." He nodded at Misty and then walked inside with a noticeable limp.

Anna glanced at his large beat-up truck, then at her small immaculate Mercedes before asking, "Who was that?" She stared after his retreating frame. He wore a brown corduroy sport coat over a wrinkled blue shirt and tie, tucked into a pair of jeans that rested on top of enormous feet encased in work boots.

Misty sighed, shaking her head a little. "That was Editor-in-Chief of the Mystic Valley Times, Mr. Clay Sullivan, in the flesh."

"And what exactly is his problem with me?"

"Sweetie, he doesn't have a problem with you. He has a problem with the world, and I don't have the energy or the time to explain. That, my dear, is a subject for another day."

And that, Anna realized, was the first interesting thing to happen to her in months.

3

"Listen up, everybody," Mayor Earl Wilcox said, sweeping his charcoal gray wool cap off his big bald head. Conversations dwindled, the sounds of staplers and shuffling papers ceased, and a tension-filled, awkward silence ensued. He smiled apprehensively with watery blue eyes as he looked at each and every person in the police station, which wasn't many. "This here's Mystic Valley's new police chief, Tessa Fitzgerald."

"You gotta be kiddin' me," a stocky older woman around five-seven, sporting short brown-and-gray hair and a wrinkled black-and-gold uniform, grumbled. Someone coughed as she nailed Tess with hard, equally brown eyes. She looked to be about the same age as the mayor—just this side of sixty—and obviously not thrilled with Tess's presence.

Not exactly the way Tess wanted to start her first day on the job.

As a former Boston homicide detective, Tess had a habit of sizing people up and assessing a situation upon first glance. Her former life had demanded it if she'd wanted to survive. She had to remember Mystic Valley was a small, old-fashioned Vermont town. Night and day from her former home in Boston.

"Pam, please. It's what the town council wanted," the mayor pleaded beneath his breath with a familiarity that bespoke of more than just friendship between them. Pam glared at him and shook her head, crossing her arms in front of her. He sighed, his shoulders slumping a bit, as his gaze met Tess's. "Chief Fitzgerald, this here's Officer Calloway."

"Everyone calls me Fitz." Tess squared her shoulders as she held out her hand. "It's a pleasure to meet you."

After a moment of hesitation and a grunt, Pam shook her hand harder than necessary, but Tess didn't so much as flinch. She was used to opposition, though usually it came from the men in the field. Having a woman treat her this way was a first, leaving her with the impression that Pam must have wanted the job as chief for herself. Part of Tess could empathize. It was tough for a woman to succeed in this line of work. Back home, she worked hard to prove herself every day, but her buttons could only be pushed so far.

A muscular man, probably in his late thirties, dressed in faded jeans and a flannel shirt, with a sandy-blond buzz cut and at least six-foot, stepped forward with a welcoming smile on his face. He held out his much larger hand and looked at her with warm hazel eyes. "Officer Andrew Jones, but you can call me Drew."

Tess smiled back, liking the man already. A take-charge kind of guy who didn't stand around and wait for things to happen. Efficient and to the point, yet amicable. Kind of like herself. She could already tell he would be an asset to have around, once they rectified his attire, that is. She shook his hand firmly. "Nice to meet you, Drew."

"And lastly, this here's our new dispatcher, Randy Scott. He's a rookie. Graduated from our neighboring military school, but decided he wanted to be a police officer instead of a soldier. He gets a little excited from time to time, but you won't find anyone more dedicated and eager to please," the mayor said with a wink.

"Chief, sir, er-ma'am, Chief. At your service." Randy saluted her, every inch of his wiry five-ten frame stood at attention. His milk-chocolate skin was clean-shaven, his dark hair precisely cut, and his uniform wrinkle-free and crisp. He looked as though he was barely legal to drink, and Tess was beginning to feel like she needed one. This one would be a lot of work.

"At ease, Randy. Chief Fitz will do." She held out her hand, and he finally relaxed, reaching forward and grasping her palm eagerly.

Tess blew out a breath, looking around the small, quiet police station with the simple dispatch counter, chief's office, a couple of desks for the officers, an interrogation room, and a couple of holding cells. White walls, nothing fancy. A far cry from the large, noisy, cluttered precinct she'd come from. This place was a bit messy for her liking, with way too many personal items scattered about, but the food looked better here. Several pies and pastries, instead of stale donuts, lined the side table that held the coffee pot.

So this was it. She took a deep breath, hoping she wouldn't come to regret this life-changing decision. The ever-present pain in her shoulder that the bullet had left behind reminded her of why she'd said yes. She couldn't go back to Homicide, but she didn't know how to be anything other than a cop. She was afraid that if she didn't get back on the horse now, she never would. Becoming a small-town police chief had seemed to be the perfect compromise.

"Okay, then," she said to the room in general, then promptly ushered Earl to the door. "Thank you, Mayor Wilcox. I'll take it from here."

He blinked, opening and closing his mouth several times, before clearing his throat. "Oh, okay. Guess I'll be leavin' then.

I'll be over at City Hall with the town council. Give a holler if you need anything at all."

"Will do." She closed the door after him and then turned to her new four-man crew. Her smile was pleasant enough, but she knew if she didn't firmly establish herself as the person in charge, they would walk all over her.

Smoothing her hair back and fixing the short strands at the base of her neck, Tess said, "First order of business, we need to get a few things straight." She looked them each in the eye. "I like to run a tight, professional ship, with order and rules and people who follow them. There's no room for rule breakers in our line of work. That means as police chief, I give the orders and you follow them. We clear?"

They all nodded slowly, except Pam, who simply narrowed her eyes.

"Everyone wears a uniform—creased, tucked in, shined shoes, polished badge, the works," Tess continued. "What you wear while on duty and how you carry yourself says a lot about you. Have some pride in yourselves as well as this department."

Back in Boston, her department had worn tactical uniforms with cargo-pocket pants; military battle dress uniform or BDU-style shirts that held lots of gear; sturdy, comfortable boots; and a baseball-style cap. No ironing or creases necessary, going for a more practical, ready-for-anything appearance that showed they meant business.

In Mystic Valley, the town council had made it clear they preferred a more traditional uniform that included ironed and creased dress shirts and ties, dress pants with no cargo pockets, and black, laced dress shoes, sporting a round hat with a badge. They were going for a more approachable, community service–based appearance that showed they were here to protect and serve. Either was fine with Tess, so long as they looked professional.

Randy beamed, while Drew arched a brow, and Pam outright scowled.

"Lose the white t-shirt beneath your uniform, Randy. Wear black. The last thing you want to create is the dreaded white triangle of death in low light. When a bad guy's eyes are drawn there, his gun follows his eyes. You're giving them an easy target. Other than the brain, that's one of the worst areas to get hit." She'd found that out the hard way, she thought, but kept her face firm and no-nonsense as she pushed away the memory that threatened to be her undoing on a daily basis.

Randy paled, Drew looked thoughtful, and Pam smirked.

"Everyone shows up on time," Tess continued.

Randy stood straighter, while Drew nodded approvingly, and Pam looked downright pissed-off.

Tess finished with, "And finally, no personal business while on the clock, including phone calls."

Drew stared straight at Randy, and Pam looked smug, while Randy flushed and dropped his gaze to his feet.

"Other than that, I'm not fussy. Let's do our jobs, and we'll all get along just fine." Tess nodded once. End of discussion.

"Tess, isn't it?" Pam said. "I hope you know our job mostly involves writing tickets and breaking up petty squabbles. Everything closes early here, and the people are simple. Their idea of a good time is sitting in lawn chairs out in front of the shops, people-watching and playing checkers. Nothing fancy around here. I would imagine that kind of thing would get boring to a bigwig city girl like you. Why'd you come here, anyway?"

"I came here to protect and serve, Officer Calloway, no matter how small the crime may seem. And it's Chief Fitz to you. Any other questions?" Tess stared the woman down until she blinked first, and then looked questioningly at the other two.

They just shook their heads "no" and averted their gazes.

She didn't enjoy being a hard-ass, but establishing the top

dog was necessary. Now that she had, she could ease up a bit and start to form some bonds. "Officer Scott, if you could order me some business cards and bring Chief Harper's badge to my office, that would be great." She smiled. "I don't need his gun. I like to carry my own."

The department used the Smith and Wesson because of its reliability and accuracy, but it was a bit large and heavy for a concealed-carry. Tess had always preferred her Glock for its slimline design. The short width fit in her hands comfortably and made controlling the recoil very simple. It was easy to use, hard to see, and tough to face—just the way she liked it.

"Jones and Calloway, carry on with whatever cases you were working on. You're both pros. I'm confident you know what you're doing." She tipped her head in their direction as a form of salute. "I will be in my office going over Harper's files if anyone needs me."

"YOU CAN'T GO IN THERE, Sully. Chief Fitz doesn't want to be disturbed," Randy's voice rang out, sounding panicked.

Tess had been going over the former chief's files for the past few hours, but there wasn't a lot to wrap up. Pam had been right. Not much happened in Mystic Valley. Tess had been considering taking a break when she'd heard raised voices coming from the dispatch desk. Standing up, she walked over to her door and opened it. "It's okay, Officer Scott. I said I was free if anyone needed me."

"Trust me, Chief, Clay Sullivan isn't just anyone," Randy said in a hushed voice, adding, "He's a nuisance."

Tess stepped through her door and saw a big bear of a man who looked to be a few years older than herself. A little rough around the edges, but in an interesting sort of way. She'd heard about the infamous Sully. Born and raised here, he'd gone to NYU and worked at a fancy newspaper, covering stories abroad and even a war.

He returned to help his mother after his father had passed away, working his way up to Editor-in-Chief, and then staying on after his mother died a couple of years ago. He'd been the only child of much older parents. As far as she knew, he was all alone, unlike her. She had an overprotective father and three older brothers, all involved in law enforcement, and a mother who was absolutely no help whatsoever. Ever since Tess's accident, she sometimes wished she was alone. She couldn't imagine what would keep a worldly man like Sully here, unless he was harboring a few demons of his own, which was definitely like her.

Unsmiling and no-nonsense, he gave her a two-finger salute. "Chief Fitz, I take it?"

"Sullivan, I'm guessing," she responded with a raised brow. He was handsome in a rakish, rugged sort of way, but completely unpredictable and all about making waves, or so she had heard. The kind of guy she usually avoided. Besides, she was determined not to need anyone anymore. Not after what had happened.

"You're much prettier than I'd expected," he commented bluntly, studying her with an intensity that was unnerving. She had a feeling he didn't hold anything back. If there was something on his mind, you would know it.

"I get that a lot," she said in a neutral voice, not smiling either. "Don't let it fool you. What can I do for you, Sullivan?"

"Call me Sully. Can I call you Tess?"

She knew what he was doing. Trying to become familiar, break down her defenses. People who wanted a favor tended to do that. "Chief Fitz will be fine."

"A stubborn blond with a no-nonsense Boston accent, just

what Mystic Valley needs. I like that. Fitz it is," he said, not fazed in the least.

She would have to watch out for this one. He was a rule breaker if she ever saw one, and she *always* followed the rules.

"I was hoping I could have a word with you," he added.

She glanced at her watch. "I was just thinking of taking a break." She stepped back and held her door open. "Please, come in."

He hesitated, glancing around suspiciously. "How about coffee. My treat." He led the way outside, walking with a slight limp.

Grabbing her regulation, standard-issued, black-and-gold jacket to ward off the chilly spring air, she followed, stepping out into the crystal-clear sunlit afternoon, not a cloud in sight. The morning fog had burned off, thank God. She loved the sun. So full of life and energy and hope. She knew she would make a full physical recovery. It was her mental state of mind that worried her the most. She inhaled a cleansing breath, focusing on the here and now.

"Where's your car?" she asked as she caught up to him, looking around the nearly empty parking lot while she zipped up her coat. The two Dodge Chargers were gone, which meant Calloway and Jones were out on patrol or responding to a call. The Dodge Ram was only used in special situations and remained at the station with the dispatcher. The only other vehicle in the lot was the black-and-blue Dodge Durango meant for the chief.

"I walked." Clay shrugged. "Newspaper office is just down the street." He patted his right thigh. "Gotta exercise the leg or it stiffens up something fierce." At her raised brow, he added, "Old war injury. Walk with me?"

"Sure."

War was something she understood, whether far away in

another country or on hometown city streets. Battles were fought, lives saved and lost every day, but the scars stayed forever, especially the mental ones. She fell into step beside him, yet was still several inches shy of being on equal footing with her five-foot-eleven-inch height. Many men were intimidated by her height and her job. Needless to say, she didn't date much, no matter how pretty they told her she was. Her father and brothers were tall, her mother being the only short one. She'd pretty much disappointed them all when she'd chosen law enforcement, like her father, over modeling, like her mother.

"Where are we going?" She squinted, wishing she'd grabbed her sunglasses from her police SUV.

"No place fancy, but the best coffee you'll ever drink. Sam's Cafe."

"Contrary to popular belief, I don't need fancy. I wouldn't be here if I did." She adjusted her utility belt, feeling every ounce of the ten pounds it added to an officer when fully loaded with gear.

"Touché," he said, and she relaxed a little.

After a while they fell into a comfortable silence, like they'd known each other for some time. Clay Sullivan was a mystery to her. Rugged and attractive and totally not her type, yet tough and honest and easy to talk to. Officer Drew Jones was the kind of man she usually went for, but they worked together, and she wasn't about to go down that road again. He made it hard to concentrate, and she needed to keep a clear head. Stay focused. Stay independent where she would never need anyone again. But she *could* use a distraction to take her mind off her troubles.

Something told her Clay Sullivan was the man for the job.

A HALF HOUR LATER, seated across the table from the mysterious, hard-to-read, yet undeniably attractive Chief Tessa Fitzgerald, Clay Sullivan tried to find the right words to bring up the subject of today's meeting. At first, he wasn't sure what Tess would be like. He had to say he'd been pleasantly surprised. Pale blond hair in a simple chic cut, light blue eyes, and tall enough to make things easy. He liked easy, not complicated. Not like petite Anna Wilks, with her soft auburn hair, mesmerizing green eyes, and curves in all the right places. He'd only met her briefly, yet he hadn't forgotten about her for the rest of the day. Her eyes had been full of surprise and wonder, sucker-punching him with a sadness she couldn't hide that made him want to take her in his arms and comfort her.

Instead, he'd acted like an ass.

He hated complicated, and he sure as hell didn't need to get involved with someone who made him feel anything other than lust. Someone who needed to be taken care of, which was something he was no damn good at. She was too damned fragile to make it in Mystic Valley. She was a city girl, through and through. Country living would be way too rough and dangerous for her, she just didn't know it. Dammit, he didn't want or have time to worry about her. Bad things happened when his heart got involved. History had proven that much.

Focusing back on Tess he decided she was a damn sight for sore eyes in a small town like Mystic Valley. Strong, independent, and fully in control, she didn't look like she needed anyone. Maybe things would finally get interesting around here. His fresh-faced, young and eager assistant was interesting enough, but she didn't count because he worked with her, no matter how many times she told him that didn't matter. He might not be a lot of things, but he *was* a man with principles.

Attractive or not, that didn't matter. He'd brought Chief Fitz here for a reason today. She was tough and fair, he could see it in her eyes. He had plenty of nerve, but not a lot of tact, and his mouth had landed him in trouble more times than not. Pretty much shutting doors in his face all over town. Fitz was new to Mystic Valley. This might be the only shot he had at getting her on his side before the town council placed her firmly in their pocket.

"You may as well just come out with it," she said, after swallowing the last of her coffee and wiping her mouth with a napkin.

He'd already finished his coffee but had been stalling. She studied him with sharp blue eyes that told him she'd been through a lot. Seen a lot. *Knew* a lot. She looked at him through an imaginary magnifying glass, analyzing his every move, every word, as though she could read his mind and see deep into his soul. It was damned unnerving. And she spoke carefully, screening her words through a filter, her body ready to react at a moment's notice. Being a homicide detective could do that to you. He wondered what must have happened to bring her to a town like Mystic Valley.

Nothing good, he was positive of that.

"I can see it's eating you up inside. I'm the chief of police. It's my job to listen and not judge." She sat back and waited patiently after interrupting his thoughts.

"Blunt and to the point." He dropped his napkin, deciding to just get it over with. "You don't beat around the bush. I like that, too." Though smiling felt awkward for him, he smiled at her just the same, striving to win her over. He needed someone on his side because no one else in this town was. He'd burned those bridges long ago. "I've decided I like you." He waited a beat, testing her to see how she would react.

"The jury's still out on my end," she replied to his unasked question, her face not giving anything away.

He fought a grin. She had spunk and resolve, a sense of right and wrong, and a passion for seeking justice—she wasn't the only one who'd done her homework. He'd always been good at seeing the truth. While he had grit, believed in the people's right to know, and was just plain stubborn as a mule. Truth and justice for all... they were going to make a hell of a team. *This* was the woman he needed. Not Anna Wilks. He frowned over thinking of her again, and shook his head to clear it.

"What happened to not judging?" he asked, getting back on track.

"I'm *not* judging," Tess said easily, taking a sip of her iced tea. "That doesn't mean I have to like you."

He did smile fully this time, and damned if it wasn't genuine. "Fair enough." He took a slug of his coffee. "It's about a case I want you to look at."

A crease marred her forehead. "What kind of case, and why didn't you go through dispatch?"

"Because it's a cold case," he said carefully.

"Then why didn't you bring it to the attention of Chief Harper?"

"I did."

"And...?" She arched a sleek blond eyebrow at him.

"He shot me down," Sully said point-blank, earning a moment of silence. He couldn't afford for anything to go wrong today. This case was the first case he'd ever worked on, and one that had left him many a sleepless night but had never left his mind.

For over twenty long years, Cindy Taylor's disappearance had haunted him.

"I see." Tess studied him with a look that said she really didn't. "What makes you think I won't do the same?"

"I don't know that you *won't*. I simply have hope that you will give this file an unbiased, impartial look. I'm confident if you do, you will see the merit in reopening this case."

She sat silent for a long moment, gnawing on the inside of her cheek as though he had piqued her interest, which was exactly what he'd hoped for. That the homicide detective in her wouldn't be able to turn her back on an unsolved mystery.

"Why would Chief Harper dismiss the case if there was just cause to reopen it?" she finally asked.

Sully searched his mind for the right words. He'd followed so many leads on his own, but nothing had ever panned out, and no one would help him keep looking. He just needed to know what had happened to Cindy once and for all. He decided to keep it simple and be honest. Tess seemed to like that sort of thing. Or as honest as he could, anyway. No one could ever know the full truth.

No one could ever know his secret.

"Honestly, I don't know," he finally said. "Maybe there isn't just cause, but that doesn't mean Cindy doesn't deserve justice." Especially after what he'd done to her. "What I *can* tell you is that I'm not going to stop until I find out what happened to her."

"Why is this so important to you?"

"Because I loved her."

4

"Hi, Mom, it's Anna. I just wanted to let you and Dad know I got here safely," Anna said through the ancient phone hanging on her kitchen wall, and couldn't help smile a little at the charm of her house. The charm of Mystic Valley. Her smile faded a little and she wound the cord around her finger as her mother brought her back to the conversation at hand.

"You can't expect us not to worry." Her mother sniffed, sounding sad, but Anna had to stay strong. She couldn't worry about other people right now. It was time she thought of herself for once. "You're all alone in a foreign place," her mother added.

"Mystic Valley is in Vermont. It's not like I moved to another country." Though the thought had crossed Anna's mind initially, when all she could think about was getting as far away from her former life as possible. "I've already met a few really nice people at a quaint diner earlier today." And one not-so-nice man, but she wasn't about to mention him to her mother. She didn't need anything negative put out in the universe for her family to pounce on as a reason why she shouldn't be there.

"Why didn't you call then? If you had time to eat, then surely you had time to talk." Her mother had a way of sounded wounded over the least little thing.

"I couldn't," Anna replied calmly, refusing to let anything get to her. "I was with my realtor."

"Did the movers get there yet?"

"Yes. Right after lunch so I couldn't call then either," she quickly added. "I had to supervise while they spent the afternoon unloading my things. Now I'm getting ready to unpack."

"You probably shouldn't lift anything heavy because... well, you know."

That made no sense, Anna thought. The lump she'd fought so hard to keep out of her throat came back in full force. Leave it to her mother to constantly point out her flaws and remind her of things she was trying to forget. Her mother had never gotten over Anna's closer relationship with her aunt than with her.

"I can't have a baby, Mom. I don't have a disease and I'm not dying. I'll be fine." Anna had checked in to let them know she was okay because it was the right thing to do. Beyond that, she wasn't ready to deal with anything from her past. "I have to go now."

"But your father wants—"

"Goodbye, Mom." Anna gently hung up the phone.

She knew what her father wanted. He wanted her to get over being sad. He wanted her to marry a man of his choice. He wanted her to come home, but that wasn't going to happen. She was thirty-four years old. He didn't get to be in charge of her life anymore. *She* did. And it was about damned time, she thought with a small smile, feeling more like her aunt than she had in a long time.

Mystic Valley was her fresh start. It was a special place, and she could feel her aunt's presence with her every step of the way. Everyone that she'd met had been so nice, except for the editor-in-chief of the newspaper, Clay Sullivan. All she'd done was run into him and knock his glasses off. What on earth gave him the right to have his own parking spot at the diner? There clearly hadn't been a sign posted, so how was she supposed to know? None of those things had warranted the scowl he'd given her, and his tone of voice had been snippy to say the least. He didn't even know her, yet he acted like he thoroughly disliked her.

So why in the world was she still thinking about him?

He was mad at the world. She had enough of her own issues without having to help someone else with theirs. If anything, she should be thinking about Officer Drew Jones. Now there was a man who was thoughtful and nice. He was handsome and helpful and the complete opposite of grizzly, yet her heart didn't race just from looking at him.

Huffing out a breath in disgust with herself, she turned on the lights in the living room and kitchen. Dusk was settling, and there was something spooky about spending the first night alone in a new place. She had always lived at home, and then with Erik. After he left, she had been alone, but that house had been familiar. They had lived in it for thirteen years. That place hadn't been spooky...

Just lonely.

She squared her shoulders and reminded herself she could do this. She didn't need a man to take care of her. That was the whole point of moving here—to be forced to make it on her own. Locking her door and then looking around, she realized her furniture didn't quite fit with the antique colonial home. Erik had chosen their home and their furniture—rich brown leather. She hated leather. It was hot in the summer and cold in the winter and made her feel clammy. But Erik had never asked her what she wanted.

Now that she thought about it, he'd made all their decisions: house, furniture, what to order at restaurants, what shows to see at theatres, right down to where she should shop for clothes and get her hair done. Anna had been so used to her father being the same way with her mother and sisters, she'd never thought twice about it. Until now. Now she had no idea how to arrange her furniture or what to hang on the walls.

How had she gone through life without having an opinion?

She might have run Erik's house and organized his parties, but he'd always told her in detail what he wanted. It wasn't just her new home or being on her own that was scary, *life* was scary. Thinking of her aunt, she decided not to let herself feel overwhelmed. If her aunt could be brave over something so much scarier, then surely Anna could as well. Glancing around once more, she decided if she was going to do this thing, then she was going to do it her way.

First thing in the morning, she would donate all the things Erik had picked out that she didn't really care for to Goodwill. Digging through the box that said "office supplies," she pulled out her laptop and sat at the table in the kitchen. She would start by ordering dinner, slipping into her favorite pajamas, and then she would buy brand-new furniture that *she* liked and that went with her new home.

Maybe then she would finally discover just who exactly Anna Wilks was.

HOURS later after dividing up what she was keeping and what she was getting rid of, she scoured the Internet and created her new life, feeling excited. She was proud of all she'd accomplished once she set her mind to it. It had been really hard making decisions. Who would have thought there would be so many choices? It was difficult enough choosing a style of furniture, but deciding on a pattern and color was impossible. At one point she'd used *eenie meenie miney mo* to decide, but it had still been her finger that had pointed to the winner.

She was the one in charge of her destiny this time.

Closing her laptop and yawning, she cleaned up the mess she'd made on the table. Chinese food takeout. Another thing Erik had never let them order, so of course that's what Anna had chosen for dinner. She had devoured it all, in wonder over how quickly her appetite had returned since moving away to a place with rejuvenating air, a world of possibilities, and plenty of hope for happiness.

Finding her trash bags, she bagged up all the trash from unpacking. Propping her door open with a shoe, she hauled all the bags and boxes out front by the road. Breaking down the boxes, she neatly stacked them beside the bags. Trash cans and recycling bins were next on her list to pick up. Misty had said tomorrow was trash day, and Anna didn't want to miss out because she had a whole bunch of packing supplies that needed to be recycled. The wind whipped up around her and the temperatures had dropped drastically.

She wore a navy-blue satin pajama set with a matching robe and slippers. While her house was on the main drag, it was at the end of the street, backing up to the woods. The houses were spread out as well, instead of on top of each other like back in New York. She felt bold and daring and adventurous, taking the trash out in her pajamas. Yet another thing Erik would have been horrified over.

Dusting off her hands, she marched back to her house, climbed the front steps, walked across her porch, and stopped dead in her tracks. The door had slipped closed. With a sinking feeling, she reached for the door and tried to open it. She was a complete idiot. She tried the knob again. Nothing. She'd locked herself out. Scrambling to her front windows, she tried both but they were locked as well. The wind howled and whistled now,

sounding like a pack of wolves. Anna's gaze darted about frantically. It was almost midnight. Wild creatures came out at night.
She shivered, tightening her robe around her. She was being
silly. This was a small Vermont town, not a wild jungle full of
deadly beasts.

She glanced down the street, relieved to see most people's
lights were off. People retired early in Mystic Valley. Well, at least
most people, she thought, as she heard a vehicle turning onto
her road from a side street. It was a truck. Squinting, she looked
closer.

"Speaking of beasts," she muttered to herself.

Of all the people to witness her foolishness, it had to be him.
Grizzly Bear Sullivan. She flattened herself against her house
and stood still, trying to blend in with the woodwork, a
chameleon, praying he wouldn't notice. Her house was blue, her
pajamas were blue... it could work. He drove right by her, and
she sighed in relief. But then his brake lights came on, followed
by the squeak of a stopping vehicle. He slowly backed up until
he reached her house and then pulled into her driveway. Rolling
down his window, he raised a brow as he eyed her position
against the house, pajamas and all.

"Anything wrong?"

Coming to her senses, she quickly moved forward and stood
casually. "Nope, nothing at all. Thought I saw a snake." She
laughed nervously. "Nice night, isn't it?" She looked up as
though she'd been star gazing. Frowning over the dark cloudy
sky without a star in sight, she looked back at him as though
standing outside in her pajamas at midnight was perfectly
normal in her world.

"No," he said simply. "It's not a nice night. It's damned cold
and about to rain." He grunted. "You're gonna catch pneumonia
dressed like that."

Desperate not to look any more ridiculous or incompetent,

she pointed to the curb. "Trash day tomorrow. That's why I was out here. I remembered last minute and was already in my pajamas, so I didn't bother changing. I certainly didn't expect to see anyone at this time of night. I'm just finishing up, then I'll head back inside."

"You do that." He shook his head, eying her clothes as though he still thought she was the most foolish person on the planet.

"I will." She eyed him suspiciously, crossing her arms in front of her and resisting the urge to tap her foot. "And what are *you* doing out at midnight, Mr. Sullivan? Don't you have work tomorrow?"

"Last I checked, I didn't have a curfew."

"Well, neither do I. By the way," she raised her chin a notch, "you're in my spot. Remember that next time."

He grunted again, rolled up his window, and backed out of her driveway. Putting his truck into drive, he gave her a parting look full of mischief and a single salute, then tooted the horn loudly as he drove away.

Anna yelped, actually jumping off the ground, and then ducked behind a tree as her neighbor's light came on. The curtains moved, but after a few moments they turned the light off. Anna finally relaxed. What was with that man? He was determined to get a rise out of her, probably hoping she would pack up and leave. Well, he didn't have a clue how determined she was to stay. She needed this, even if it meant standing up to the beast. But first she still had to find a way inside her own house before she froze to death.

There was a shed in her back yard. Hiking through the soggy grass, knowing her slippers were ruined, she reached the shed, which she was surprised to discover wasn't locked. That would never happen in New York. The previous owner had left some old garden tools, an axe, an old rusty lawn mower, and... bingo!

A sledge hammer. She could barely lift the thing it was so heavy. Half lifting, half dragging, she managed to haul it out of the shed and through the yard, her pajamas as muddy as her slippers now.

Falling three times will do that to a person.

She wouldn't begin to know how to break and enter a locked house, but the hammer was heavy enough to break something, that was for sure. Using both hands and all her strength, she lifted it high and whacked it on the doorknob. It took five more whacks before the knob finally broke off, and the door swung open. Thrown off balance, Anna tumbled inside still holding the sledge hammer. Stubbing her toe, she dropped the hammer, which cracked the floor, and she fell through to her knees with a squeal.

What next, she thought, and looked up asking, "Why does life have to be so hard?" Some strange premonition told her things were about to get a whole lot harder.

5

"Why didn't you tell me you were a person of interest in the disappearance of Cindy Taylor?" Tess asked Clay Sullivan as she barged into his office the next morning at The Mystic Valley Times and slapped Cindy Taylor's case file down in front of him.

He stood slowly, the scent of his earthy cologne wafting through the air as he crossed the room and closed his door like he was gathering his thoughts. The sounds of clicking keyboards, ringing phones, and mumbled conversations ceased, leaving him standing with his back to her for a moment. The man had an obvious habit of carefully choosing his words. One of these days she would ruffle him enough to find out what was really on his mind.

"I was afraid if you knew that, you wouldn't agree to take a look at the file. Am I right?" he asked calmly as he sat back down behind his desk, which was just as messy as he was. In fact, the entire newspaper reflected his habits.

Set up the same as the police station, with an office for him, a front dispatch desk to take incoming news tips and assign them to the journalists, as well as a couple of desks for his assistant editors and a room to question their sources. Instead of holding cells, they had printing presses and photo labs. And of course, the ever-present table loaded with the area's local treats and a never-empty pot of coffee. The biggest difference between their departments was that she was organized, where he clearly was not.

"Don't judge," he said, as though reading her mind in his uncanny way of being able to see right through a person to the truth hiding beneath. "I have a system; it works for me. Quit getting distracted and answer the question."

She schooled her features and recapped her emotions to make it harder to read her. "Your involvement might have made me hesitate, but how can you blame me?" She remained standing, facing him with her arms crossed in irritation. She felt duped. "I can't help but be suspicious that you might simply want to clear your name. Is that what this is all about?"

"If you read the file, then you know that it isn't. Cindy didn't just run away. She wouldn't do that. Something has been off from day one, and I have the clues to prove it."

"The same clues that cast suspicion on you, I might add. An overheard argument between the two of you. The last person to see her. A necklace you gave her found at the edge of the woods."

"Yes, we argued. Yes, I was the last person to see her. And yes, they found the damned necklace I gave her after prom. But she was never seen again, and I clearly didn't leave town. That means I didn't abduct her or run away with her, though I sometimes wish that we had. Then maybe nothing bad would have happened to her."

"How do you know something bad did happen to her? Maybe she just ran away on her own."

"I repeat," he said a bit more sternly through his teeth, "she wouldn't do that."

"How can you be so sure?"

He didn't hesitate at all as he said with confidence, "Because she loved me, too."

"Then why did you argue?"

"Because she didn't get into the college I was going to. She wanted me to stay here, and I wanted out. I was an idiot and said some things I shouldn't have," he growled. "That's why we argued." His voice softened, and his gray eyes looked both sad and frustrated, making Tess want to help him even though he really didn't have enough evidence that anything at all had happened to the girl. Certainly not enough to reopen a case. "We were stupid kids. We had plans, dammit." His face hardened. "Was I angry? Hell yes! It pissed me off. We were a team. She ruined that."

Tess kept her tone neutral, and her voice quiet. "Why?"

Clay stared off into space, deep in thought for a moment before answering. "I've had a lot of years to think about that. I think she was afraid. She didn't come out and say so, but that had to be it. She was afraid of change. Afraid to leave and be on her own."

His intense gaze locked with Tess's, and for a moment he let down his guard. She could see how haunted he was and feel his pain. Her gut told her he was telling the truth, and over the years, she'd come to live by her gut.

"If only I'd tried a little harder, I might have been able to stop her before it was too late," he added.

"You were just a kid yourself," Tess said gently.

"A kid who grew up in a hurry that summer." He grunted.

"And then left town first chance he got." She watched his face closely.

His eyebrows formed a deep V. "Wouldn't you?"

"I don't know," she said honestly, pondering his words, unsure of what she would have done. They were two very different people. He wanted the truth, she wanted justice, but they went about seeking that in two very different ways. She followed the book, while he ripped every blessed page out.

"Maybe Chief Harper dismissed the case because you're too close to it to be impartial. Your judgment might be clouded."

Sully stilled, staring hard at her as though trying to see inside her brain. Damn, he was good. "So what are you saying?" he finally said. "That you're going to keep the case closed?"

She didn't hesitate this time. "No. I'm not saying that at all."

He blinked, studying her curiously. "Why?"

"Because I read the damn file." She sighed and sat down across from him, and because she needed something—anything—to focus on so the nightmares would stop. "Got any coffee?"

A look of surprise mixed with that of relief, followed quickly by pure satisfaction with a hint of determination settled over his rugged face. He pressed a button on the intercom in front of him and spoke. "Can you bring in two cups of coffee, Lynn?"

"Sure thing, Chief," came a soft feminine voice that fairly purred.

"Thanks, doll."

Tess leveled him with a look that said, "Seriously?" and struggled against the impulse to roll her eyes.

He just shrugged as he fought a grin.

A moment later a tall, leggy, darker blonde than her—much younger, in her early twenties, with deeper blue eyes—came strolling into the office with a serving tray of coffee, cream, and sugar. There were three cups on the tray. No big surprise there.

"Anything I can do to help, Chief?" she asked, eying Tess with blatant interest and a hint of territorialism.

"Chief Fitz, this is one of my assistant editors, Lynn Anderson."

Tess nodded once.

"Thanks, Lynn. If you could follow up on my other calls, that would be great."

"Sure thing, boss. I'm on it." Lynn picked up her mug, shot Tess one last look, and then sashayed out of the office with unmistakable energy and drive. Great. Just what Tess needed: a young go-getter out to make a name for herself, who wasn't above screwing the boss along the way. Well, Tess had wanted a distraction, she thought.

She'd gotten one in spades.

LATER THAT AFTERNOON, Sully watched Chief Fitz in fascination as she stepped out of her police-issued, black Dodge Durango with blue writing on the side and lights on top. She checked her neatly trimmed blond hair at the base of her head and adjusted her round hat. Next, she smoothed her hands down her pressed and crisply creased black-and-gold uniform, stopping at her fully equipped duty belt. One by one she checked each piece of gear with precision, like a well-oiled machine.

Now here was a competent woman. A woman who knew enough not to go out in the cold in ritzy, flimsy PJ's in the dead of night. He resisted the urge to snort over the mental image forming in his mind's eye, and focused back on the rational, sane woman standing before him.

Touching her taser and fingering her pepper spray, she moved on to her baton hanging through another ring, and then secured her handcuffs and firearm in its holster.

"We're not going into battle, Chief," he said teasingly. "I'm just showing you what happened."

"You never can be too careful," she replied in a telling, somber way as she rubbed her shoulder, then added, "I just wish the department provided body armor." She shrugged. "Oh well. I'm as ready as I'll ever be, I guess."

"How about you, Perez? You ready?" Sully looked at his right-hand man.

Diego Perez might only be five-seven, but he packed a hell of a punch. He was a seasoned editor in his forties, who had worked on the same New York newspaper that Sully had. Covering plenty of intense assignments together, Diego had welcomed the chance to come work for Sully after he'd become editor-in-chief of the Mystic Valley Times. His salt-and-pepper hair had a lot more salt these days, and he'd grown a bit soft in the middle from consuming one too many apple and blueberry pies and maple cookies, but his dark eyes were as keen and sharp as ever.

"I was born ready," he said, "and things have been way too quiet around here lately." He rubbed his slight pot belly. "I need some action," he declared, making Tess chuckle.

Sully found himself grinning a little. He liked her laugh. Hell, he liked her. The fact that he kept thinking about Anna disturbed him greatly. He had to remain focused and see this case through to the end. He owed Cindy that much.

"So why are we hiking through the woods?" Tess asked, leveling him with a pointed stare.

"This is where Cindy's necklace was found, and the last place I saw her. I've searched these woods a ton of times, but never found a thing."

"What makes you think this time will be different?"

"You're fresh eyes. I want to retrace her steps. See what she saw along the way. See if I missed anything."

"You do know there was a minor earthquake the other day," Diego chimed in. "We don't usually get them, but sometimes minor ones occur. Things might have shifted a bit."

"That's what I'm counting on," Sully said. "Maybe it will uncover a clue."

"Only one way to find out," Tess pointed out. She grabbed the long and heavy Maglite from the charger in the SUV and slipped it through the flashlight ring hanging on her belt. Checking another pouch, she tested a smaller tactical flashlight, making sure its bright LED bulb worked. "Onward, Sullivan. We're burnin' daylight, and you're not gettin' any younger."

"Neither are you," he added. "I'm guessing we're about the same age."

"I'm guessing you're older, and I'm a whole lot prettier." She winked, surprising him into a laugh. "Let's roll. I need more than speculation and theories if you want me to reopen this case. I need some hard evidence."

"She got you there, boss." Diego chuckled.

Sully knew she was right. He had plenty of theories and a few clues. The chief might have agreed to hear him out and had even said yes to accompany him on a run through of Cindy's last known whereabouts—which was more than he'd expected. But if he were truly ever going to get some answers, he needed some hard evidence.

They started their trek through the woods, with him in the lead. The wind picked up, bringing with it the threat of rain. The hot and steamy dog-days of summer would be upon them soon, but for now it was chilly, especially under the canopy of the woods. Ignoring the pain in his leg and tightening his corduroy jacket, he retraced the steps he knew by heart, looking closely at everything in hopes of finding something, anything. Too much time had gone by. The odds of them finding any hard evidence were slim. He had hoped Chief Fitz would be fresh eyes, but neither she nor Diego saw anything useful either.

About to give up hope, they ended up at the quarry. Where granite and marble had once been excavated, the gaping hole had now started to fill with water. They still had several working quarries in the area, but this one had recently been abandoned. Even the excavation of sand, gravel, and crushed rock used for construction sites had ceased operation here.

Sully had heard the earthquake had shaken things up a bit, so the public was told to keep out until the site was inspected and reinforced. Back in the day, the rocks here were some of the oldest worldwide, and the granite and marble harvested had been some of the best in the country. Other sites still brought in a lot of revenue for the area, but this one had been the largest. Most of the resources had long been exhausted.

"I wouldn't go down there if I were you," Diego said, leaning over the edge and peering down in trepidation.

"No worries, I'll be careful." Clay climbed down a ladder that probably hadn't been used in far too long.

He carefully looked around but didn't see anything out of the ordinary. Nothing except memories in his mind's eye. He couldn't believe what Cindy had done to him that day. They'd had plans, dammit, but she'd ruined them. And then he'd pushed her away. She'd run into the woods because of him, but he didn't believe she'd left for good and never told anyone. If she were still alive, someone would know. He didn't care about clearing his name. To be honest, he just wanted closure. He'd never felt free to truly let her go without knowing for sure if maybe she hadn't loved him enough.

He inhaled deeply, pushing his doubts away. He'd always believed she left the necklace in the last spot he'd seen her as a clue to where she was. That she was sorry and had forgiven him. Or maybe if she'd been abducted, she had wanted him to follow into the woods and find her. He'd had to live with his failure for far too long. The earthquake had been a sign that someone upstairs thought he had suffered long enough. It was time.

So where the hell were his answers?

"I hate to be the voice of reason," Tess called down from the top of the quarry a while later, "but it's getting dark. I don't think we're going to find anything."

Sully cursed softly. He'd been so sure this time they would find something, but Tess was right. If they didn't leave soon, they'd be stuck in the hills after dark. He let out a long sigh and nodded, not trusting himself to speak. Climbing back up the ladder, he led the way once more. They started back towards the woods just as the rain began. They hadn't traveled more than fifty feet when Chief Fitz said, "Wait!" She shined her bright Maglite off to the side of a small hill in the distance that was covered in dirt and crushed rock. It looked like the earthquake had caused a landslide.

"It's just a pile of rocks, Chief," Diego said.

Tess looked them both in the eye. "I know they say the hills are alive, and I'm no expert, but since when do rocks wear clothes?"

A sharp pain pierced Sully's chest. Could Cindy really have been right under his nose all these years? He'd been looking in the woods, never thinking to check the quarry until after hearing about the earthquake. The area had been searched years ago, but no one had rechecked it since. He didn't say a word, just followed the flashlight beam to the pile of rubble. Staring down, he studied what appeared to be an article of clothing. How the hell had Tess seen that? He didn't hesitate, just started digging.

"Wait," she said again. "You don't want to compromise the scene."

"I won't touch anything with my hands, I just need to see something," he said, digging around the article of clothing with a stick to expose more. When the purple hood of a jacket appeared, he sucked in a breath and stifled a sob. "It's hers. It's Cindy's," he said in barely more than a whisper.

"How can you be sure?"

"She loved this jacket. It's what she had on the last time I saw her." He took a moment to compose himself until he could speak without his voice wobbling and looked up at Tess with anger in his eyes. "I knew it. I knew something was wrong all along, but no one would listen to me."

"I'm listening now," she said with a serious tone.

"What does that mean?" He hated the vulnerability he heard in his own voice.

"That you've found enough hard evidence to reopen the case."

6

"**M**y name is Chief Fitz, for those of you who haven't met me yet," Tess said later that night at City Hall after calling an emergency town meeting for the council and all citizens to attend.

Their department didn't have a special CSI team or coroner here in Mystic Valley, so she had to make do with what she had. It was pretty much up to her four-man crew to investigate, take pictures, and use Doc Burns—who mostly dealt with family practice issues and would probably freak out if they ever needed him to examine a dead body. He'd helped them dig up the jacket, but no body had been found. Sully had looked disappointed yet relieved.

Leaving Randy to man the desk and Pam to handle any other calls, Tess had put Drew on the missing person case of Cindy Taylor. He was taking pictures of her jacket at this moment. The council probably wouldn't be happy with using their manpower and tax dollars by looking into a cold case, but Cindy wasn't just anyone. She was one of their own. Not to mention something about this case was pushing Tess to look into it further. She had a feeling they were close to cracking the case, and she always trusted her gut.

She stood behind a podium in front of rows of folding chairs in an ancient building. The council members sat at a side table with the mayor, while the school board and principal, the town historian/librarian, business owners, and residents alike filled the seats. It seemed the entire town had come out in droves, even their newest resident, Miss Anna Wilks. Probably because this was Tess's first public speaking event as the Mystic Valley police chief.

They wanted to assess her every move. They were either going to be with her or against her after this. She wished the topic could have been a more positive one, but she couldn't worry about public opinion at a time like this. They had hired her to do a job, with or without their support. And that's exactly what she planned to do.

"I think it's great you called this meeting to introduce yourself to the town," Mayor Wilcox said proudly. "I knew we made the right decision in hiring a fine new chief, gents." He winked at the council members who nodded approvingly.

"Unfortunately, I didn't just call this meeting to introduce myself, though I am happy to meet you all," she corrected carefully. "You can rest assured I take my job very seriously and plan to do everything in my power to uphold the law and keep the peace."

"Just what we want to hear," someone said.

"The kind of chief our town needs," another chimed in.

"The perfect replacement for Harper," someone else added.

"You gettin' this down, Sullivan?" another resident said, as people clapped and cheered. "You should do a nice spread for tomorrow's paper about our fine new police chief."

"Oh, don't you worry, I've got it covered," Clay Sullivan

replied, surveying the room at large. "I have a feeling the best is yet to come."

"I'm glad you all approve." Tess gave Sully a warning look that said, *Let me handle this.* "It's very important for a town to come together and lend their support at a time like this," she said to the crowd, and the room fell quiet.

"A time like what?" the mayor asked, eying her suspiciously.

She hesitated a moment, dreading the inevitable. "A time when a person goes missing."

A few gasps rang out among muttered questions and a general sense of confusion.

"What does that mean?" a member of the council asked. "No one that we know of has gone missing. Are you saying it's an outsider? People do come from different parts for our dairy festival."

"No, I'm not saying that at all. The person definitely was a resident of Mystic Valley," Tess responded slowly, trying to find a delicate way to say what needed to be said. "I've examined the facts, and I think this case is worthy of our department's attention."

"Facts? What facts?" the mayor asked, with obvious growing concern.

She blew out a breath and then said, "The facts in Chief Harper's file of the missing person."

"The Spring through Fall festivals and shows are important," someone said.

"Those are a huge source of revenue for this town," someone else added.

"The last thing we need is a scandal putting a damper on everything," another resident chimed in. "Can't this investigation wait until Winter, when not much is going on except the carnival?"

"Calm down everyone." The mayor stood and raised his

hands, then looked at Tess with disapproval. "What do you mean you want the department to look into some missing person case? I haven't heard anything about this, and as the mayor, I would expect to hear first before a town meeting." He narrowed his eyes suspiciously. "How long has this file been around?"

"My guess is over twenty years," Sully said with satisfaction, earning several scowls.

A couple in front had to be Cindy Taylor's parents, based on their reactions. The mother covered her mouth and sobbed quietly, while the father comforted her as he stared down at his feet.

"That case is cold. No one wants to reopen old wounds when we all know the leads are a dead end. We're never going to find Cindy. Do you really want to put her parents through that again, Chief Fitz?" a member of the council asked with undisguised displeasure.

"We found the jacket Cindy Taylor was wearing when she disappeared at the abandoned quarry today. That's hardly a dead end. I want to give her parents closure. I would think you all would as well. I am reopening Cindy Taylor's case, and that's final," Tess said with resolve, knowing her approval rating had just plummeted, but also knowing her desire for justice outweighed her need to be popular.

Several protests rang out.

"You might want to rethink that, Chief," the mayor said. "It's been a long time since the incident. A missing persons investigation at the present time might not be in the best interest of the town."

Mystic Valley itself was a wonderful place. Special, even mystical almost, where people come to heal. The town folk banded together and took care of their own, but the town council liked things done their way. They didn't like outsiders who made waves, that much was clear. They put the town's stellar reputation and source of revenue above the desire to find out what had happened to one of their own. Obviously, the former Chief Harper had gone along with whatever they'd wanted when it came to the law. Tess shook her head and looked upon them disapprovingly, but something told her they were beyond being shamed.

"A missing persons investigation is never a good thing, Mr. Mayor, no matter what time of year," she finally responded. "But getting some answers and giving Cindy Taylor's family some closure is the right thing to do. And I always do the right thing."

"Yeah, well, your father assured me you were also good at following orders," the mayor grumbled, glancing apprehensively at the members of the council who looked angry, to say the least.

His words finally registered, and Tess ground her teeth. Things finally made sense. This job hadn't fallen into her lap at the precise moment she'd needed it. Her father had pulled some strings and gotten it for her, getting her out of the city like he wanted to a place he'd probably thought was boring and safe. Now more than ever she had to prove she was worthy. But one thing was for certain...

She was furious!

She gripped the sides of the podium and spoke directly into the microphone to be sure everyone would hear her every word. "Let me be clear, people. I believe in the system, and I believe in justice. While I took an oath to protect and serve this community—which I'll happily uphold—make no mistake. I'll be the one giving the orders from here on out. I *will* solve this case, and I'm here to stay, folks. I suggest you get used to it."

Clay Sullivan was the only one who clapped.

Ignoring him, she looked into the eyes of the mayor and every member of the town council, one by one, before adding, "This meeting is adjourned."

ANDREW JONES PULLED out of his parents' dairy farm on the outskirts of town on his first day off in over a week. Chief Fitz worked them all as if every call was a life-or-death situation. She didn't tolerate unprofessionalism or slackers, which Drew had no problem with, but if she could just lighten up a bit, things would be a lot less tense around the office. Just because the town council wasn't happy with her reopening Cindy Taylor's case didn't mean the rest of the citizens felt that way, especially not her own team. Well, maybe Pam. She hadn't quite gotten over losing out on the promotion to Chief to a younger outsider, but she would in time. Pam was a good person, but as stubborn as his grandfather's mule, Tilly.

Drew had tried a couple of times to help Tess, but she was having none of that. Beautiful but tough as nails, she didn't need anyone... or so she'd like everyone to think. She wasn't the only one who was good at reading people. He could see she was hurting, and not just every time she rubbed her shoulder, but she wasn't about to let anyone in. She'd made that clear as the water in a Green Mountain stream. So when Anna Wilks called Drew this morning, asking for his help on this gorgeous Spring day, he'd jumped at the chance to be around someone who appreciated him. The tulips were in full bloom as he drove to Anna's house.

It was a sign.

Drew was the oldest, with two younger sisters who'd already married and had children. His parents were in their sixties, his grandparents in their eighties, and they all lived on the farm. They never spoke of retiring because ranching wasn't just something you did, it was a way of life, and it took as many hands as they could find. Someday they would be gone, and someone would need to step in and fill their shoes. Drew knew his father had been upset when his only son became a cop instead of taking over the farm, but his father had an easier time accepting it when Drew didn't leave home. He would probably always be a part of the farm. But with dreams of his own, he didn't want to run the place.

Helping people was in his blood, but so was family. Moving out hadn't really been an option, though it didn't exactly go over well with the ladies—especially independent ones like Tessa Fitzgerald—but he'd had no choice. He couldn't leave his family high and dry in these tough times, so he did what he could around his hours at the station. And when he wasn't on duty or farming, he was helping out around town.

His biggest downfall was that he'd never been able to say no to anyone. It wasn't in his nature. In truth, he didn't mind. He enjoyed helping people, and for the most part, he was happy. But recently he'd longed for something more. Someone to share his life with. Children of his own. His other half. Maybe because both of his sisters already had children, and he was about to turn forty. Maybe he just hadn't found the right person yet.

Maybe that was about to change starting today.

At the other end of the main drag, Anna's house sat back from the road, but within walking distance to everything. She'd bought a charming, blue New England colonial house. It had never been sided, the wood painted a deep blue instead. It was two stories high, with a steep roof and a large chimney in the center. Long, narrow windows covered the upper level as well as the lower level on both sides of the door. A front porch with a roof and pillars had been added after one of the many renovations, but the house was in serious need of a fresh coat of paint. Several boards on the front porch needed replacing as well.

The place was definitely a fixer-upper, but word around town was she had plenty of money to do just that, which made him wonder yet again what her story was. Mystic Valley was beautiful and had a lot to offer, but it wasn't easy acclimating to living here. What had brought such a delicate flower to a place where the landscape was rough and the winters harsh? Her eyes had shown a world of hurt, and something told him she was the kind of woman who not only needed help, but welcomed it. The kind of woman who made a man feel like a man and wouldn't bite his head off for trying to take care of her.

The kind of woman he was looking for.

She stepped out of the front door, wearing tan slacks, a pale green blouse, a white cardigan sweater, and a smile that didn't quite reach her eyes. She waved as he climbed out of his car and joined her on the porch.

"Thank you so much. I'm glad you came," she said, biting her bottom lip and glancing back at her house apprehensively, reinforcing his suspicions that she was in over her head.

He smiled tenderly, his heart melting. It felt great to be needed. "I'm glad you asked, and you're very welcome," he responded sincerely. "Any time you need anything at all, I'm just a phone call away. Let me get my toolbox." Grabbing his tools from the trunk of his car, he followed her. "What happened to your door?" he asked.

"It had a date with a sledgehammer after I locked myself out. The sledgehammer won." She held up her hand after his lips parted. "Don't ask."

"I was just going to say most people don't lock their doors around here." He held up his hand before she could reply. "Not asking. Just sayin'."

She shook her head at him, but couldn't quite hide her smile as she led the way inside. Standing in the foyer on worn out wood floors, she pointed to a huge hole. "I like old buildings," she started off by saying. "My house in Syracuse was an old building, but it was brick, not wood. And it had been fully restored. I have no idea how to fix this. I don't know what happened. One minute it was solid beneath my feet. The next thing I knew, I'd fallen through to my knees."

"You're not hurt, are you?" He looked her over carefully.

"Oh no, I'm fine," she said, looking pleased that he'd asked.

"Let me guess. The sledgehammer two-timed the door with the floor."

She laughed out loud at that. "I have to confess, I'm afraid so. The sledgehammer won again. I'm so embarrassed." She cupped her rosy cheeks. "It took me forever to unpack and order new furniture and take the trash out. Just when I thought I was finally getting things right, things started to go wrong."

"That's the hazard of being a homeowner. Nothing is ever really *right*. There's always something that could be better. There's also things that could be worse."

"True. You're a glass-half-full kind of guy. I am, too."

"A guy or a glass half full?" he teased.

"You have a sense of humor as well. Who would have thought we'd have so much in common," she teased back, then sobered. "On a serious note, I never had to worry about any of these things before my divorce. My husband owned the home; I ran it. I'm good at planning menus, laundry lists, parties, and to-do lists for the cook and maid and staff, but pulling off the tasks myself is another matter entirely." Her cheeks turned full pink this time, and she looked surprised she had said that out loud.

"Don't be so hard on yourself. You'll get the hang of it. I have faith in you."

"Sorry, that was probably more information than you cared to know. There's something about you that is so easy to talk to. I find myself running away at the mouth, which I tend to do when I'm nervous anyway. Sorry, there I go again." She looked away and smoothed a hand over the fancy up-do thing she had going on at the back of her head.

"Hey." He tilted her chin his way so she would look at him.

A warm feeling swept through him as her eyes met his. So big and hopeful, yet scared as hell, and sad. When he got married, he planned to do so only once. That was how he was raised, but he didn't care if she had been divorced. He only cared about her. It explained a lot, in fact. He just wanted to be the one to erase the pain and doubt smothering her joy. She deserved to be carefree and happy, and he planned to spend every day proving to her that good men still existed.

"I'm happy to listen," he finally replied.

"And I'm so out of my element. Maybe moving here was a mistake. Nothing has gone right since I moved in." She crossed her arms in front of herself. "I feel so alone."

"Moving here wasn't a mistake, and you're *not* alone. That's what's great about Mystic Valley." He winked. "We take care of our own. You'll see."

"You're a lifesaver." She looked so relieved, he wanted to take her into his arms and keep her safe for the rest of his life. But past experience told him to slow down. He tended to come on a bit strong, and the last thing he wanted to do was blow this. Whatever *this* was.

"Can I get you some lemonade?" she asked, looking happier. "It's not fresh squeezed, but it tastes pretty good."

"No need for fresh squeezed. We're pretty simple in Mystic Valley." He smiled and meant it.

She headed for the kitchen with a noticeable spring in her step.

"Miss Wilks?" he called out.

She paused and looked over her shoulder at him. "Please, call me Anna."

"No worries, Anna." He stared hard into her eyes, trying to convey everything he wanted to say but didn't dare just yet. "I'm here now, and I'll fix everything. You'll see."

7

A nna did see.

After Drew fixed the hole in her floor and put on a new doorknob, he'd spread the word. The next thing she knew the entire town had come to help her. Her gutters were cleaned, her yard raked and aerated, the outside of her house painted, the porch secured... she hadn't even needed to ask for a thing. They were all so helpful, and Drew was right. They took care of their own. Anna smiled a genuine smile that was coming easier by the day. She was one of their own, and it felt wonderful. Surprisingly much easier than she'd thought it would be to adapt to country living.

The phone rang, and Anna glanced at the caller ID. Her mother. She wasn't ready to talk to her mother or father again. They were still angry with her for changing her name and moving to a remote small town they knew nothing about, all on her own. And quite frankly, she was still angry with them for how they'd raised her. They knew she was alive and okay, and that was all they would get for now. If they could only see her now, they would realize for sure that she was doing just fine on her own.

Are you really? whispered the voice in her head that had been there since she'd read her aunt's diary. Had been there most of her life, if she were being honest.

Anna frowned, ignoring the whisper and ignoring the phone. Grabbing her purse, she headed out the door to The Country Store. So far, she had gone to the main grocery store, Deb's Diner, Sam's Café, the bank, and City Hall. That was pretty much it. The Country Store had odds and ends for pretty much whatever else you needed besides food. And right now, Anna needed something to do.

She still didn't know what she was good at or what she wanted to do with her life. All she knew was that something about Mystic Valley had called to her, and she had followed. There wasn't exactly a need to plan a big party right now, she didn't have a staff to give a list to, and she didn't have a husband or children to tend to, so that pretty much left *her*.

Yet something was still missing.

Pulling into the parking lot of The Country Store, Anna cut the engine and walked inside, defiantly not bothering to lock her car. No one else here did. If she wanted to become one of them, then maybe it was time she started acting like one of them. She walked inside and was struck with the small-town, charming atmosphere. The place looked like something from an old TV show, like *Little House on the Prairie*. With rows of every item someone might need—a one-stop shop, so to speak—and jars of candy at the check-out counter, no less.

Anna loved it all.

She headed to the back where the paint was kept and browsed the selections. She'd decided her first project was going to be painting the inside of her house, but she had no clue where to start. She'd never painted a thing in her life. Working at the winery had involved running the cash register up front when she was underage, to running the wine tastings when she was finally old enough. Other than that, she literally had no skills. With all the money she had, she really didn't need any skills, but that wasn't living.

Not like her aunt, anyway.

So, painting the inside of her house it was going to be. She spotted Clay Sullivan and didn't hesitate to approach him. After all, from what she had seen, everyone in this town had come around, being friendly and more than willing to help her. She'd become accustomed to that kind of behavior. Maybe he had come to his senses and decided to play nice in the sandbox. Lord knew she would love a chance to start over and forget both times they'd run into each other. She was willing to let bygones be bygones and start fresh, if he was.

"Mr. Sullivan, we've never officially been introduced. I'm Anna Wilks." She held out her hand, staring up at his impressive height. He was so big and masculine, with shoulders wider than any she'd ever seen. He wasn't exactly handsome, but there was something so ruggedly appealing about him, making it hard to concentrate. She cleared her throat. "I know we exchanged a few words not long ago, but I don't believe you really know who I am."

He ignored her hand, looked her up and down with disdain, and simply grunted. "Oh, I know who you are. You're a fraud."

She dropped her hand, her spine stiffening. "I beg your pardon." His man-appeal was waning quickly.

"You can beg all you want, honey, but I'm not about to help you." He crossed his muscular arms arrogantly in front of his firm chest.

"I wasn't going to ask you for help," she lied. "I was simply going to introduce myself properly."

"First of all, Mystic Valley is anything but proper. And secondly, here's a tip. Never play poker. Everything you're thinking is written plain as day across your face." He pointed to the racks behind him. "Paint. Tools. Book on painting." Then he jabbed his finger in her direction. "Able-bodied person. Have at it, princess."

She gasped. "You are a piece of work."

He leaned into her intimidatingly, hovering over a foot above her. "You'd better become one if you plan on surviving in this place." And then he was gone.

She ground her teeth, furious with him for calling her out. A nagging tingling throbbed in the back of her mind, and she sighed. Her shoulders slumped as she realized he was right. She should have known adapting to country life wouldn't be that easy. What *had* been easy was falling back into old habits and letting everyone take care of everything for her. She was such a fool. Her aunt never would have allowed that. Anna was supposed to be following in her aunt's footsteps by doing something adventurous every day, but she hadn't done even one adventurous thing since she moved here.

Taking a deep breath, she vowed that was about to change.

Starting today, she would tackle every obstacle that came her way on her own. Sully was right, no matter how much it irritated her to admit that. But it was true. And liberating, if she really thought about it. Maybe even exciting. There were books and there was the Internet. If she didn't know how to do something or fix something, she could learn. She had plenty of money and not much to do. Becoming independent might just be the answer she'd been looking for.

If only to show Mr. High-and-Mighty Clay Sullivan she was a winner.

She grabbed a basket, repeating *I'm not a loser*, then picked up a book on painting and thumbed through the pages. After filling her basket with all of the supplies she would need, she headed to the counter to pay for her purchases.

The clerk rang up her purchases, and Anna made eye

contact for the first time. She blinked and smiled wide. "Hey, you're her," Anna said.

The woman tucked her shoulder-length brown bob behind her ears, her face looking wary. "Her who? I swear I didn't do anything."

Anna raised her brows. "I didn't say you did anything. I just meant I remember seeing you at the diner the first day I drove into town. He's precious, by the way. You're so lucky."

"Who's precious?" the woman asked, still looking nervous, her amber eyes even a bit frightened.

"I'm sorry. I'm not doing a good job of explaining. I saw you with your husband, I'm assuming, and your son. Your son is adorable. How old is he?"

The woman relaxed for the first time, and her face glowed. "I'm the one who's sorry. Where are my manners?" She held out her hand. "My name is Sarah Shaw and my son's name is Bobby. He's four."

"And your husband?" Anna asked tentatively.

"Oh, Jud." Sarah's face dimmed. "He's fine. He works hard at the lumber mill to provide for us. It takes a toll on him sometimes, but he's a good man most of the time."

"Those are some nasty bruises on your arm," Anna replied, thinking Jud was something, all right, and it didn't have anything to do with *good*, she suspected.

Sarah pulled down her sleeve. "I'm so clumsy. Can you believe I fell down the stairs?" She laughed, but it sounded forced.

"My goodness, something tells me you'd better be more careful," Anna said with an innocent enough smile. "I would hate to see anything worse happen to you. Do you want to come to my house for coffee sometime? And bring Bobby. It's lonely being the new girl in town, and I could sure use a friend."

"Really?" Sarah said in wonder. "Everyone's great here, but

most people have jobs. I really don't have any friends. People don't have a lot of extra time on their hands these days."

"Well, lucky for you, I have too much on mine." Anna smiled at Sarah reassuringly, thinking she just might have found someone who needed more help than she did.

THINGS DIDN'T GO WELL with Henry today. We've been close our entire lives. I mean, all we ever had was each other, but he's ten years older than I am. My big brother, yet my biggest pain in the ass. He's so protective of me, it's smothering at times, but he can't help it. It was the way he was raised. The way we both were. Family first, but always conscious of society and how others might perceive us. He doesn't get why I changed my name, and I can't tell him. It has nothing to do with defying Father, and everything to do with needing a new identity. Needing to start becoming the person I was meant to be.

Needing to start living the first days of the last year of my life.

ANNA CLOSED her aunt's journal and set it on her coffee table, empathizing with her. Her father didn't understand why she'd changed her name either. And just like her aunt, it had nothing to do with defying him. While Anna might not be literally dying, she was dying on the inside, and had been for a long time. She was desperate to become the person she was meant to be and start living, she just didn't know how. Taking a deep breath, she decided baby steps were the way to go.

And she would begin by painting her living room all by herself.

She'd waited until the next day to start her painting, having spent the evening reading the how-to book that she'd bought yesterday. Staring at the book, she thought of Sully, as everyone seemed to call him. Misty had said he was angry at the world, but for some reason, he seemed even angrier at Anna. She didn't get it. What had she ever done to him? She hadn't even asked for help, even though the thought had crossed her mind. She'd simply tried to be nice. He had said her face showed everything. Maybe he could see more of her than she'd hoped. She'd never been good at hiding her feelings. Then again, she'd never had to play that game. She didn't like games. Never had.

Sully found her weak and helpless and lacking. She could see it written all over *his* face. Obviously, he had no use for people like that in his life, which really told her she had no use for someone like him in hers. Yet she couldn't stop thinking about him. No matter how hard he tried to hide it, she could see he was hurting too. A part of her longed to help him, but she'd never helped anyone in her life. And she was pretty sure he'd never allow it, especially coming from someone like her. So, she would start by helping herself.

How hard could it be?

An hour later, she found out as she stood back and surveyed her handiwork. She'd chosen a pretty mauve shade. Erik would have hated the color, but he didn't have a say in anything she did anymore. Paint was everywhere. In her hair, on her clothes, on the ceiling and floor. It didn't matter that she'd laid a drop cloth or taped the walls. She was horrible at using a roller, and she was pretty sure she'd used the wrong kind, judging by the bizarre streaks and pattern it had left in its wake. Feeling defeated, she kicked the book across the room, and then burst into tears. For someone who hadn't cried in so many months, she'd turned into a blubbering fool ever since reading her aunt's journal and learning her secret in the fort they'd built so long ago.

Anna wiped her tears and headed to her kitchen to take a

break. She opened the window wide. It was late May now, and flowers were in bloom. Inhaling a deep breath, she stared out at her back yard. Her lot was at the end of the main drag and backed up to the woods. She loved the woods, so filled with all of nature's wonders just waiting to be discovered. Everything had been wet and soggy. She hadn't really found the courage to venture out yet, but she would soon. One failure did not mean she was a loser, she reminded herself, resisting the urge to call someone to help her.

A hummingbird buzzed around her feeder outside, and she stared transfixed, brought back to another place and time.

"Look, Erik," Anna had said excitedly, staring out the window of her brick home in Syracuse at the city streets, sidewalk, and people buzzing about. But she wasn't looking at the people. She was mesmerized by the wonder before her. "There's a hummingbird just outside our window."

"Hmmm," he'd replied, not looking up from the stack of college papers he was grading. "That's nice, darling."

"It reminds me of home at the vineyard. I put a feeder right outside my window, and every year the hummingbirds would come. I find it fascinating that one would come here in the city when I didn't put anything out to attract it. Maybe it's a sign of good things to come."

"Your home isn't the vineyard. Your home is here." He'd chuckled softly, if a bit condescendingly, but of course she hadn't noticed that at the time. "You and your signs," he'd said, but his tone had implied, *you're such a gullible, naïve, innocent woman*.

Ignoring anything negative, as she always had, she'd replied, "Do you think this month will be the month we get lucky?"

"I hope so," he'd said with less amusement, still not looking up. "Because if it isn't, then we're doing something wrong. I'm not used to failing, darling. I always get what I want. Something has to change."

And something did. *He* did.

She'd changed the subject, replying, "Maybe I should paint the living room red. Then they will come every day for good luck."

That got him to look up, finally, but what she'd seen in his eyes should have been her final clue to the man he really was. It certainly wasn't her first clue. No, those had been all the little sarcastic, belittling remarks she'd ignored for so many years. Her father had treated her like a princess, meant to be cherished and loved, never letting her lift a finger. Smothering, yes, but done with nothing but the best misguided good intensions. Whereas her husband had treated her like an inferior species, only meant to look nice on his arm and fulfill a need he couldn't do by himself—create a child to carry on his family name. She wasn't sure he even really *wanted* a child as much as he wanted his legacy to continue.

He'd laughed at her and told her that her idea was preposterous. "Darling, there are no such things as signs, and you of all people couldn't handle painting anything. Stick to what you do best—running my house and having my baby. Focus on what's important, and let me make the decisions. This is no time to get sidetracked." And then he'd gone back to work.

She remembered thinking he was right. He'd been so good to her, taken such great care of her, while she'd often caught herself daydreaming of silly, fanciful things. She'd stifled the urge for something more and had done what he'd asked. Following his orders and running his house she had down to a science, but having his baby, she needed to seriously work on. In the end, it hadn't mattered because of her abnormal ovulations and hormone issues.

No matter how hard she'd worked, that dream would never come true.

It suddenly hit Anna. Erik had never really loved her. He'd

simply loved the *idea* of her—wife and mother of his children. When she couldn't fulfill that role, she'd been replaced. Plain and simple. End of discussion. The only part of her that he had ever really cared about had been her womb. When he'd discovered her womb was dead, then she became insignificant. No matter how much her misguided father had worshiped her, he'd had no idea that he had played a significant role in her utter failure as a human being. By instilling in her a belief that a woman's primary role was that of wife and mother, he had added to her belief that she was nothing now.

A divorced woman who couldn't have children was unlovable.

Anna loved her father, but at this moment, she hated him as well. She hated her ex, hated her father, and if she were being honest, she hated herself. All the feelings she had suppressed for so long came surging to the surface these days. A delayed reaction, so to speak. She'd never had a friend when she lived with Erik. There had been no time for anyone or anything except for him. She was lucky he'd even let her see her family. Now she felt cheated for all she had missed.

A knock at her door made her jump back to the present. Wiping the last of her tears away, she went to answer it, hoping her eyes weren't puffy.

"Hi," Sarah Shaw said, looking terrified yet as desperate to feel wanted as Anna felt. She frowned. "Are you okay?"

Anna pushed her door open wide. "Hi yourself, and no, I'm not okay. You have no idea how happy I am to see you right now." She'd just met Sarah and would probably push her away with how needy she sounded, but the poor girl had caught her at a vulnerable moment. A moment where she had decided she was done with biting her lip and holding anything back.

"Really?" Sarah blinked in awe, not appearing scared off in the least. In fact, she seemed relieved that Anna wasn't as put together as she must have first appeared to her when she'd met her at the store. "I don't know anyone who's ever been really happy to see me, except my son, of course. And for the record," she said shyly, "I'm not okay either."

Anna nodded once, in affirmation of their shared pain, and then peeked around her. "Speaking of your son, where is he?"

"Preschool," Sarah said proudly. "He's a smart cookie. A lot smarter than me." She wilted a bit. "It's my lunch break at the store, and well, you said you'd love to have company. I thought maybe you'd want to have that coffee break now, but I can totally leave if you don't. It was probably a stupid idea." She started to back away.

"It was *not* a stupid idea," Anna blurted, wanting her to stay, "and I would *love* the coffee break. You are a lifesaver, Sarah Shaw."

"I am?" She looked wide-eyed and innocent and shocked and heartbreakingly wounded.

"Yes, you are. I am in dire need of a friend right now. Think you can handle it?"

Sarah closed her mouth, squared her shoulders, and lifted her chin. "Absolutely. Lead the way, Miss Wilks, and I'll follow."

"It's Anna, and I don't need you to follow me, Sarah. I need you to be right by my side. If that's okay with you. I don't know about you, but I am so unbelievably tired of following people, following what they want, following what I'm told to do. Sometimes I just want to scream."

"Me too." Sarah smiled a smile so full of compassion and understanding, Anna felt a connection as though they were kindred spirits. And then Sarah said the most remarkable thing. "Maybe we can scream together, because I am ridiculously tired of screaming on the inside alone."

8

S ully went home for lunch for the first time in ages. He stood outside the low, broad-framed, one-and-a-half story, ancient, white wooden Cape Cod house he'd grown up in. It had a steep pitched roof with end gables and a large central chimney, with two multi-paned windows on each side of a central front door. He really needed to paint the outside again, but unlike Miss Anna Wilks, he would do it himself. His lips turned down as he took in his mother's flower beds, thinking she would turn over in her grave if she saw the state he'd left them in. That was one area he knew he needed help in. No book or Internet could cure his lack of a green thumb.

Unlocking the door, he stepped inside and tossed his keys on the antique secretary by the coat tree. The house was smaller than a traditional colonial, with the upstairs half-floor containing small bedrooms because the roof was so steep, making the ceilings slanted instead of square. But he had been an only child, so the layout had suited him just fine. His parents' bedroom had been on the first floor, leaving the upstairs to him, with a guest bedroom to spare.

Now that he was an adult, he had moved into the downstairs

master bedroom, and the upstairs had pretty much remained empty. He literally had to be the only person in Mystic Valley who locked his doors. After living in the city and abroad, old habits were hard to break. The rest of the world wasn't like Mystic Valley. It was filled with danger and cynicism and disrespect and criminals. People had tried to get him to believe for years that this town was his, and these were his people. This place was different. But he knew better.

Cindy Taylor's disappearance had taught him that much.

He wandered into the kitchen and looked in the fridge, realizing he needed groceries. Other than coffee, he didn't keep much food in the place. He normally ate out, but after running into Anna at Deb's Diner and at her house and then at The Country Store, he didn't want to take the chance of seeing her again anytime soon. In a town this size, that meant going to work and staying home as much as possible. The woman was small and quiet and incompetent and so not his type, yet she'd occupied far too much of his mind lately.

Why?

No woman since Cindy had been on his mind this much. Sure, he'd had lovers. He was a healthy male with needs, but he wasn't a masochist. He didn't enjoy inflicting himself with pain and avoided it at all costs. Why was he letting Anna Wilks torment him? She was *way* the hell too needy, yet those goddamn eyes had burned a path straight to his heart.

"Christ!" He punched a pillow as he walked by the couch.

He did *not* need this shit right now. For the first time in forever he was making progress on solving Cindy's missing persons case. Chief Tess Fitz had been amazing so far. She'd jumped into this case with such passion, she almost seemed more obsessed than he was to finally gain some answers. Something more than justice was driving her, but Sully didn't really care what her reasons were. He was grateful to have someone, anyone, on his side after all this time.

Of course, they still hadn't found Cindy. They'd scoured the woods again, and searched every area of the rock quarry and beyond, but still hadn't found any further leads beyond the jacket she'd had on the day she'd gone missing. Tess had even broadened the search into nearby towns, while Sully kept using his media contacts, hoping someone somewhere would know something.

Cindy's parents weren't the only ones who needed closure; therefore, Tess was the only woman Sully should be thinking about these days. Yet one auburn-haired, green-eyed petite woman, with curves he longed to run his hands over, refused to leave his brain. No matter how harsh he was toward her, she stared at him with compassion and wonder and understanding, as though she could see straight through his façade into his goddamned soul.

This couldn't be happening. Not now. Not after so long of searching for answers. Why would the universe throw this temptation in his path when finding the truth about his past had been his only obsession for so many years? He didn't have time for this distraction, and he certainly didn't have time to *feel*, no matter how much he wanted to scoop the little imp up in his big strong arms and make her believe everything was going to be okay. That's why he was eating lunch at home today. He couldn't risk seeing her again.

He stared at the kitchen table, his mother's favorite place in the house. She'd always said the kitchen table should be a place for families to connect and talk about their day. Talk about their hopes and dreams. Just talk. Sully had many talks with his mother at this table over the years, while his father had always been at work. He'd come home late, and his mother would heat up the dinner plate she'd prepared for him, but even then he hadn't talked. Said he was too tired. He would eat and go to bed, leaving her to clean up his mess. She'd spent her life cleaning up his mess. Sully couldn't stop the memories from flooding back.

"Clay, sweetie, I am so glad to have you home," his mother had said. "I worried so much about you when you were off covering the war and so many parts of the world that were, well, just plain scary."

"I'm here now, Mom," he'd said.

"I know. I just missed you, is all," she'd replied while making him lunch.

He'd pitched in to help, thinking she looked smaller than he remembered. Frail, even, as though the world had beaten her down. He felt bad about leaving her, but he'd been so desperate to get away back then. Had needed to find himself, was what he'd said. In reality he'd needed to escape. Run away from his father. Run away from the condemning town. Run away from his guilt. But that didn't mean he couldn't have come back sooner for her. Like a stubborn coward, he'd waited until his father had died and his mother had needed him before he'd returned.

"Your father wasn't all bad, you know," she'd added quietly.

Clay had grunted. That was all his father had deserved in his book.

"He really didn't know how to handle you," she went on. "You were a free spirit. He was practical. You wanted to conquer the world. He wanted to survive it. He didn't mean to ignore you. He just didn't know how to be anything else other than what he was, which was a worker. Put on this earth to provide for his family. He was a worker bee, while you were a seeker. Venturing out into the world, looking for something sweeter. Some excitement. You were a real trailblazer. That doesn't mean he didn't love you, or me, for that matter. I think he never learned how to show it. He worked to pay the bills, while you worked to change the world."

Clay remembered her touching his arm back then until he'd looked at her. Really looked at her so he would see the sincerity in eyes so like his own. He was big like his father, but he had his mother's soul, and she'd wanted him to know it as she'd said, "I was so happy when you got out and left. I'm only sorry you had to come back for me. Don't let this place suck the life out of you."

"Don't be silly, Mom," Clay had said, shrugging off her acceptance. He didn't want her to make everything okay. He needed his guilt so it would remind him he was no good. He might have her soul, but his was destined to go straight to Hell. She was the good one. "I would do anything for you. You're my angel. Always have been."

That was one of the last conversations he'd had with his mother. His father had died of a massive heart attack, gone in an instant. Lucky bastard didn't deserve to go that quickly. Meanwhile his kind-hearted, sweetest-person-he'd-ever-met of a mother had to suffer a long, slow death from breast cancer. She'd said she preferred it that way. That it had given her more time with her son to say goodbye. She'd never given up on him. She had made him promise before she'd died that when this was all over, he would either sell the house and leave, or find some peace and find something or someone who made him truly happy.

The problem was, Sully didn't know how to be happy.

All he knew was that he couldn't go on the way he was. The first step to peace was in finding out what had happened to Cindy Taylor. Maybe then he would be able to move on and live. No matter the cost to his heart, he had to remain focused and stick to his destiny. That meant sticking close to Chief Fitz.

These days she was the only woman who should count in his book. The only woman who should matter at all.

So why the hell was he still thinking about Anna Wilks?

"Do you have a problem with me re-opening the Cindy Taylor case?" Chief Fitz asked Officer Jones, standing less than a foot in front of his clean-shaven, chiseled face.

She'd called Drew into her office, shutting the door behind him, and then squaring off against him. She'd learned a long time ago to stand tall and strong in the face of opposition. She'd just never imagined that opposition would come from her Drew. Of course, she couldn't think of him as *her* anything because they worked together, and she'd been down that dangerous road before. They stood nearly the same height, yet he still made her feel petite and feminine, and that was half the problem. She needed to feel strong. She bit back a groan. Why did he have to smell amazing, like fresh mountain air, soap, and a hint of chocolate chip cookies.

There had been tension between them ever since she'd made the announcement about reopening Cindy's case at City Hall. He was a good cop. He had great instincts, wasn't opposed to hard work, hadn't balked at wearing a uniform instead of street clothes, and kept his hair cut to precision. She'd really thought he would be her ally, her right-hand man. Especially since Pam made a point of letting everyone know she had it out for Tess, and Randy was... well... *Randy*. Wet behind the ears and as green as they came.

Being a cop and having all brothers, Tess was used to not having many girlfriends. But she'd kind of hoped Drew would fill that role. Letting him fill any other role was out of the question, no matter how many nights she lay awake thinking about him. He was manly and gorgeous and just plain good. That's why it killed her that he was acting so standoffish around her. It wasn't that she needed for everyone to like her. She just needed for *him* to, especially when she didn't understand what had gone wrong.

"No, ma'am," he said through clenched teeth, standing at attention and looking over her shoulder straight at the wall. "Opening Cindy's case was the right thing to do, ma'am."

"Ma'am? Seriously?" She clenched her own teeth now, and resisted the urge to ball her fists. "Would you stop being so formal?"

"Sure, *Chief*," he said, still not looking at her, but a muscle in his jaw pulsed.

"Goddammit, Drew, I need you to be on my side! What the hell is your problem?" She did clench her fist this time and pounded it on her desk, then stiffened her arm and winced as she grabbed her shoulder. *Shit*! Dammit all to hell, he was the only one who made her act unprofessional and lose control.

He automatically reached for her, his large hand covering hers and his face softening instantly as he looked her in the eye for the first time in days. Really looked at her, like there was so much he wanted to say, but he didn't know where to start. She sucked in a breath and quickly stepped back from all she saw shining within his compassionate hazel gaze, until his hand fell away.

"*That* is my problem," he ground out with uncharacteristic anger, frustration evident in his expression, posture, and tone of voice.

"What, my injury? It doesn't make me less of a cop," she said defensively, hating that she felt the urge to explain herself to anyone.

He took a moment to compose himself and breathe deeply before responding in a quieter, less antagonistic tone. "No, it

doesn't. You're a fantastic cop. Smart, tough, fearless... beautiful."
His eyes met hers and held her captive this time. He wasn't like
most men she knew. He tended to wear his heart on his sleeve,
leaving no doubt to what he was thinking or feeling, unlike
Sully who hid behind a brooding wall, making it hard as hell to
read him. "I would stand proud by your side anytime,
anywhere," Drew went on. "My problem isn't with your injury.
My problem is with *you*."

"Me?" She gasped. "Why?"

"You're trying so hard to prove you're worthy of being our
chief. We all know that, believe me. What you fail to realize is
that we are a *team*. This is *not* the city. This is a small town. You
are our chief. We would follow you anywhere. Even Pam. You
just have to start letting us in, instead of ordering everyone
around and riding us so hard. I don't know what happened to
you, but you can't keep pushing us away." He leaned into her
meaningfully. "You can't keep pushing *me* away."

"I don't do that," she said defensively. "I'm just establishing
boundaries. Making sure you realize I'm your boss." She didn't
say the words, but she knew he heard her silent *nothing more*.

He shook his head almost sadly. "Oh, don't worry," he said
with a scoff. "You've made that perfectly clear." His tone gentled
as he continued with, "What you don't realize is that we're here
for you anyway. *Especially* me!"

He stared at her long and hard with such passion and
emotion, she almost fell into his arms and let him push every
worry she'd ever had away. But she couldn't do that. She *wouldn't*
do that. She had to stay focused. Stop thinking of herself and
what she really wanted, because all that got anyone was a world
of pain. No, it was better this way. She had to think of the job
and the department and her career.

"Let me help you. Is that so hard?" He finished with such raw
emotion she almost caved.

"Yes," she said without hesitation, swallowing the lump in her throat. Damn him for seeing through to the real her. The vulnerable her. The her she didn't want anyone to notice.

"Well, that's a start, then," he said and looked at her with such beautiful, understanding eyes, she wanted to cry. She wanted to fall into his big strong arms and let him take care of her.

But she didn't.

That would show weakness, and that was something she just couldn't allow. Weakness would be her undoing. She knew from experience she couldn't rely on anyone but herself, and she would never *ever* put anyone she cared about in harm's way again. Drew had no idea how much she'd come to care about him already.

Enough to know when to back the fuck away and run.

"It's not a start," she said matter-of-factly, squaring her shoulders. "It's not anything. We have work to do."

"Agreed." He sighed and let it go for now. Something told her he wouldn't forever. "We also have an obligation to this town. The dairy festival is this weekend. The revenue it brings in is just as important as keeping the citizens of Mystic Valley safe. I think we can take a little break, don't you? Show our support as members of this town and not simply officers of the law. Connect with the people. Cindy and Mr. Sullivan aren't the only ones who deserve our time and attention. After all, my family's livelihood depends on this festival."

"Fine." Tess nodded, keeping things all business. "Good call."

"Great." He grinned. "Pick you up at noon?"

She blinked. Oh, he was a sneaky one. She'd almost said yes without even thinking. "Um, I'll meet you there. I have a few things to wrap up with Mr. Sullivan before taking a weekend off."

"I'm sure you do." Drew's grin dimmed a little.

"I said I would be there, and I will. Then first thing Monday morning I expect you all to clock in on time, no excuses. Are we understood?"

"Oh yeah," he said dryly. "I got the message loud and clear."

9

"You ready to do this?" Drew asked Anna Saturday afternoon at the dairy festival, after Tess had made it clear they were just friends.

The sky was overcast, the threat of rain imminent. At least they had a few barns to work with if the weather turned nasty. Yet for some reason, Anna seemed happy that the sun wasn't shining. That was a first for Drew. Most women he knew loved the sun. Tess, for one. Every time the sun came out, she turned her face toward the warmth of the rays. He frowned. There he went again thinking about Tessa Fitzgerald, aka his boss and *only* his boss. She'd made that abundantly clear. She hadn't shown up yet today, and he began to wonder if she would. Anna was a much better fit for him than Tess, he kept telling himself. He just had to get his heart to listen to his head.

"Oh my, I um, well... it looks hard." Anna looked up at him with nervous yet trust-filled eyes while biting her bottom lip. He liked that. He liked her.

At least she wasn't pushing him away.

She'd left her hair hanging down past her shoulders instead of in her fancy up-do, and she wore jeans with a peach-colored t-shirt and sneakers, looking far more casual than the last time he'd seen her. Okay, so her jeans were designer and her t-shirt silk and her sneakers some crazy brand he'd never even heard of, but still, it was progress in his book. He was glad she'd said yes to help him today.

The festival was held at his parents' place, since they had the biggest dairy farm in the area. It ran all weekend long, with a parade through town yesterday, followed by the 5k milk run, and a scholarship pageant. Today consisted of a dairy baking contest, a milking demonstration, and an animal barn tour. The festival would end tomorrow with the antique tractor and engine displays, and the horse pull contest, as well as music and food from all the locals. There would be cowboys with fiddles and banjos and guitars, ready to make even the most non-rhythmic person tap his foot and head to the dance floor. Old man Ike Jeffries, who ran The Country Store, would play his kazoo. Heck, even realtor Misty Monroe would take part, playing a mean set of spoons.

Drew's parents and grandparents and sisters were all running different stations filled with samples of milk, cheese, and baked goods, as well as giving tours of the barn, while he was in charge of the cow-milking station, and Anna was his assistant. He couldn't very well have her assist him if she didn't have a clue about the process of milking a cow herself. Their farm was a modern farm where machines did the milking, but for the interest of the dairy festival, they always demonstrated the process the old-fashioned way.

"It's not hard," he said to Anna to ease her fears. "It's just different than what you're used to. Martha has been around for a long time. She's gentle and used to the festival. You'll see."

He walked over to the enormous cow and set a stool beside her, gesturing for Anna to sit on it. She hesitated, but then lifted her chin and complied. He squatted down on his haunches and wrapped his arms around her to take her hands in his own. She smelled of some expensive perfume, reminding him of yachts and champagne and caviar. The fact that she was here, willing to step out of her comfort zone, spoke volumes about her character. She might come from money, but she was hardly stuffy.

"Wh-what are you doing?" she sputtered, looking over her shoulder at him, wide-eyed and terrified.

"Showing you how it's done," he said softly. "You didn't think I would leave you alone, did you?"

She gave a nervous laugh and shrugged. "Some people think I need to do things for myself. You know, on my own."

"I know no such thing," he said easily. "Some people are fools, if you ask me. There's no shame in asking for help, Anna."

"Except when you do it all the time." he thought he heard her mutter.

"What's that?" he asked.

"Nothing," she quickly said. "Demonstrate away."

He placed his hands on top of hers, leaning into her back to push them both closer to Martha, until they had to turn their heads to the side to reach beneath the cow. She fit so nicely in the circle of his arms, his chest pressed against her back. Drew's cheek brushed Anna's as he guided their hands over Martha's teats, and he wondered if she could feel his heartbeat.

"You want to grab on up top, where they are the fullest," he said by her ear, "and then squeeze and force the milk in a downward direction so it squirts out into the milk bucket."

"Oh, okay," she said, sounding embarrassed. He peeked around her, and sure enough, her face had flushed cotton candy pink. He bit back a chuckle. She really was a breath of fresh air, so naïve and innocent, and not just when it came to country living. It was almost as if she'd been sheltered her whole life. "Like this?" she asked, as she yanked down on Martha's teat.

Martha let out a loud *moo*, and kicked the bucket.

Anna yelped and jerked back into Drew's waiting arms. That's how Tess and Sully found them: Drew knocked on his ass with Anna in his lap, cradled snugly against him. It felt good, holding her. He needed a woman like her in his life. His smile came slow and sweet as he said next to her ear, "Word to the wise, less is more. Be gentle. Cows have feelings too." He winked, and she laughed.

Tess scoffed and Sully grunted. A rumble of thunder sounded.

"Apparently so," Anna responded to his comment as she scrambled to her feet and righted the stool the cow had knocked over, ignoring their new spectators. Her pale skin had flushed with a pink hue, but like the trooper that she was she sat back down and tried again. This time her touch was much gentler. A weak stream of milk shot out, but missed the bucket completely. Martha moaned, sounding pained, and Anna huffed out a frustrated breath.

"You'll get it, just keep trying." Drew rubbed her shoulders. "Try to relax. She can sense when you're tense."

"Thank you. You're a wonderful teacher, Officer Jones." She shot him a grateful smile. "Unfortunately, I'm not the best student."

"Nonsense. You have a positive attitude, and that's half the battle," he replied, and couldn't stop his gaze from slipping to Clay Sullivan.

"I see you're asking for help again." Sully had eyes only for Anna. Even Drew could see that. His brow puckered and a knot of worry settled in his gut, despite the fact that she was there with him.

"I know there's probably a book on how to milk a cow, but I wasn't the one who asked for help." Anna hoisted her chin at Sully, seeming stronger and more sure of herself than when he'd first met her. "Drew asked me to help him and his family with the dairy festival today. I wasn't about to refuse after all the nice people of Mystic Valley have done for me. The dairy festival is important to this town, and this town is important to me. I am simply trying to help in any way that I can. Give back, if you will."

"Is that what you call what you're doing?" Sully responded dryly. "Wonder what Martha would say if she could talk. Her moan didn't exactly sound grateful. In fact, I think she might burst if you don't figure it out soon."

Anna glanced beneath Martha and then turned a worried look up at Drew. "Can that really happen?"

"Martha's not going to burst. Mr. Sullivan is just messing with you. He can't resist the challenge of ruffling someone's feathers. If you haven't figured it out yet, he likes to cause trouble." Drew smiled reassuringly at her, frowned disapprovingly at a bored-looking Sully, and then let his gaze settle pensively on Tess. "Hey, *Chief*, so good of you to make an appearance."

Even out of uniform she looked tough. Sturdy jeans and boots, a sensible light blue cotton t-shirt that matched her eyes, minimal no-nonsense makeup, and an easy-to-maintain practical short haircut. Without her hat on, he couldn't help noticing how the style complimented her face. Short on the sides and back, with a long top that she'd swept into a wave off to one side. The strands were so pale and silky-looking, he had the strongest urge to run his fingertips over them. Soft, feminine, and delicate came to mind. He bit back a grin. She would be pissed if she could read his thoughts right now. He sighed. What was he doing, and why did he always feel the most for the wrong women?

"I told you I would be here," she said, staring at him oddly as she took a step closer to Sully. "Mr. Sullivan and I had a few things to wrap up before we could take any time off. It only made sense to ride here with him."

"I see." Drew knew his face expressed his irritation. He had no claim on either woman, yet they both seemed to be drawn to Clay Sullivan. For the life of Drew, he couldn't figure out why.

The man was about as rough as they came, and had made it clear he didn't give a shit about much of anything other than himself. He had a sad past, but who didn't? No one got to be their age without going through heartache and disappointment and loss. Some got hit with it worse than others, but character was formed in how you handled yourself after. The problem was, Sully hadn't *handled* anything, and he wasn't about to let anyone help him. He and Tess made a perfect pair.

Maybe that was Drew's problem. He cared too much. When he was younger, they'd lost everything in a fire. The house, the barn, and nearly their livelihood. The entire town had come to help, and Drew had been changed that day. That's when he knew he was meant to give back and help others in return. He'd never been any good at hiding his feelings, and frankly wouldn't want to if he could. Life was too short to play games, even when most of the time people didn't want to know what you really thought.

He took a breath and relaxed his features into a pleasant expression. He'd always been the bigger person and let things go. No sense changing his ways now. "I'm just glad you're here, Chief," he finally added. It was the truth, yet it was a safe enough comment.

"Yes, well, carry on, then." Tess nodded once, sharply, just short of saluting him. "We have to make the rounds, show our support. Isn't that right, Sullivan?" She kept her emotions in check, always professional, never letting anyone know how she felt or get to her.

Drew smiled on the inside, suddenly realizing that wasn't always the case. It certainly wasn't the case with him. He seemed to be the only one she lost her temper with. She still wasn't the right woman for him and would undoubtedly break his heart, but a small seed of hope blossomed deep in his chest anyway. He decided right then that one way or another he *would* break down her walls.

Something told him only then would he meet the real Tessa Fitzgerald.

A COUPLE OF HOURS LATER, a streak of lightning lit up the sky, followed shortly by a boom of thunder. It wasn't quite Summer just yet, but still warm enough to have a storm. Sully didn't like how close that sounded. The forecast hadn't called for anything like what they saw in the heart of summertime with some of the intense thunderstorms that blew through. Still, he didn't like storms of any kind, but especially thunderstorms. He glanced around at the crowd of people milling about. The dairy festival had always been a popular one among the locals, but the people who traveled from miles away amazed him. They came from all over, fascinated with Mystic Valley. Vermont itself was a great state, offering all four seasons and plenty to do, but there was something special about Mystic Valley.

He had to admit the town was charming and the people overly nice, but the land was the real draw. At least for him, anyway. He'd traveled the world, yet nothing called to him like his home. The green mountains with the pristine lakes and rugged rock quarries were majestic, sweeping past rich forests that opened into meadows filled with wildflowers, down past the plush green pastures belonging to dairy farms. The apple orchards and sugar shacks were pure bonus. Not to mention the town itself with its covered bridges, antiques, and crafts. There was something mystical about the place. Something peaceful and tranquil and healing, almost. But the weather could be a son-of-a-bitch.

When it took a turn for the worse, people got hurt.

Diego snapped a picture of the darkening sky and checked the image on the camera. "Damn, I missed it." He scrubbed a hand over his salt-and-pepper hair and looked up at him, his dark eyes filled with apology. "Wish I was a better picture taker. Lynn usually handles that."

"Don't worry about it, man. The pictures aren't half as important as the story. You know that." Sully clapped him on the shoulder. "Lynn's inside interviewing people about the rest of the festival. I need you for the big stories, and she needs experience, so you're on picture duty today. Don't worry about the weather. Make sure you get all the events. And the people. Try to capture what it is about the festival that draws them here."

"Already did. Gotta say that Miss Wilks sure is cute trying to milk Martha." Diego chuckled. "I got a great picture of her face all screwed up in concentration. She bites her bottom lip and tries so hard, but she ain't exactly made of a sturdy breed, if you know what I mean. I've never seen anyone mess up so many simple tasks. There's something about her that makes a man want to step in and help her, but last I heard she's been trying to do everything herself now. I still don't get what a woman like her is doing in a place like Mystic Valley. She doesn't really fit in, but she sure is something to watch."

"She's somethin' alright," was all Sully said, but his tone must have given him away.

"Well, I'll be damned," Diego said in wonder. "Never thought I would see the day."

"You're damned, all right, straight to Hell." Sully shoved him with a scowl, and Diego laughed. "You're not seeing anything, you blind fool."

"I might wear glasses, but that doesn't mean I can't see she's getting to you," Diego said with a more serious tone. "It's okay to feel something for a woman again, buddy. You haven't in a long time."

"Please, just the other day you were telling me to go for it with Chief Fitz. Make up your mind, already." Sully tried to make light of the conversation.

"Okay, I get that you feel something for the Chief. Hell, with a woman who looks like that, who wouldn't? But I'm not talking about lust, and you know it." Diego patted his chest and his voice gentled, keeping the conversation exactly where he wanted it. Damn good journalist. He didn't stop until he got to the truth. "I'm talking about your heart, man."

"You're crazy," Sully grumbled. "That crazy woman has no business in Mystic Valley or anywhere near me." His mouth said one thing yet his gaze couldn't help but wander in Anna's direction, and damned if it didn't soften. He cursed silently. "You of all people know why I can't feel with my heart, Diego. Dangerous territory, my brother."

Diego was the only person Sully had ever told what had really happened. The only living soul who knew his secret. And the only reason he'd told him was because they'd been lying in a bunker, covering the war, positive they weren't going to make it out alive. Sully had wanted to die having confessed to someone. Who better than his best friend? But damned if they hadn't survived. He really didn't understand why he kept surviving when everyone he cared about had never been that lucky. He wasn't special. He didn't deserve to survive.

"Caring about someone doesn't have to be dangerous." Diego squeezed his shoulder. "Talk to her, my friend. Tell her how you feel. Don't you think you've punished yourself long enough?" He looked him in the eyes. "Tell her what happened."

Another streak of lightning lit up the sky, followed by an even louder clap of thunder. A sign of impending doom, which is what would happen if Sully opened up. He didn't deserve to be happy. No, he would take his secret to the grave and die alone. That would be the only way justice would be served. The lightning and thunder were closer together this time.

Not good.

"You might want to give Chief Fitz a heads-up on moving the festivities inside. I'm sure Officer Jones is prepared for that, but no one seems to be doing anything and that storm's getting closer."

"I'm on it." Diego saluted with a wink, dropping their heavy conversation in the blink of an eye, with no judgmental looks or sound effects. That's what Sully loved about the guy. Diego knew when to push and he knew when to back off, and he loved Sully like a brother anyway. No matter what, he always had his back. That was rare, and about the only thing Sully treasured these days.

Diego headed toward Tess while Sully made his way over to Drew.

Drew held up his hand. "I'm way ahead of you, Sullivan."

"There's a first time for everything, Jones," Sully couldn't resist adding.

He didn't have anything against Drew in particular. Sully was pretty much brash and sarcastic with everyone around town. If he were being honest, he would admit he was afraid they all still blamed him for Cindy's disappearance. Or pitied him. Or forgave him, which would be even worse. It was easier acting like a son-of-a-bitch than it was getting close to any of them. Keeping them at arm's length and acting ornery stopped them from saying anything he might not want to hear. Being lonely was a small price to pay, because it hurt a hell of a lot less than facing the truth.

"Funny," Drew responded, not looking irritated in the least. The man really was way too damn nice. "Do me a favor and help

Anna move Martha to the animal barn." Sully nodded his consent. "Clay Sullivan helping. I guess you're right. There really is a first time for everything." Drew didn't wait for Sully to respond; he made a beeline for the chief with a walkie-talkie in his hand and a let's-get-down-to-business look on his face.

Chief Fitz made an announcement moments later through a megaphone with Drew by her side, instructing her on where to put everyone. There were several barns. This festival had gone on for so long, everything pretty much ran like a well-oiled machine. Sully looked in Anna's direction. Everything except for the milking station.

What in the hell is that woman doing now?

She had her hands on Martha's hindquarter, pushing hard. If Anna wasn't careful, she was going to get kicked in the gut. She really didn't have any idea what she was doing or how to last in a place like Mystic Valley. He marched over to her, feeling his anger well up. He was harder on her than anyone else, he admitted, but only because she made him worry. He was angrier at himself than at her, really. She brought out a protective feeling in him that he didn't like one bit. He didn't want to worry about her or protect her or care about her. Damn Diego for bringing his feelings to the surface. The truth of the matter was that Sully didn't deserve to feel anything.

"Do you not see the lightning?" he barked, as he came to a stop beside her, his feet spread wide apart and his hands on his hips.

She startled, whipping around and staring at him all wide-eyed, in her fancy excuse for casual with her hair all loose and wavy around her slim shoulders. She had curves, in *all* the right places, in fact, but she was still way too petite and delicate. "Yes, I saw the lightning," she said carefully, with her hand over her chest as though she were afraid her heart would pop right out.

"Then why aren't you headed to the barn?" He drew his

eyebrows together and hardened his features into the most serious expression he could muster to help drive his point home. "Are you trying to get yourself and Martha killed?" She needed to realize this territory wasn't all fun and games, and the weather was nothing to mess around with.

Anna squared her shoulders, looking like she was trying to stand taller. As it was, she had to tilt her head way back to meet his eyes, which were over a foot above her own. He could have leaned down a bit to make things easier, but he didn't want things easy for her. He wanted her to realize she was in over her head. Maybe then she would leave before things turned ugly. Not to mention he didn't dare get any closer. There was just something too damn powerful about her, magnetic almost, and it scared the hell out of him.

She scared the hell out of him.

"I'm trying to get to the barn," she finally said in a calm but firm voice, "but Martha has a mind of her own."

Sully had to give Anna credit. He knew he could be intimidating, but she was growing stronger. Bolder. Hell, she might even raise her voice at him someday. He almost smiled, but then another flash of lightning zipped way too close for comfort.

"Try harder," he growled, sounding a bit harsh, desperate even, as he leaned down over her until their faces were only six inches apart. He couldn't help it. He truly did *hate* storms. Breathing slowly, he added with a more reasonable tone, "Your milk bucket is metal. Not very smart, princess."

The loudest boom of thunder they'd heard yet shook the ground, and that was all it took. Martha bolted in the wrong direction. Anna let out a soft curse under her breath, which actually did make Sully's lips tip up ever so slightly this time. But then she gave chase right out in the open, headed for the woods. The heavens opened up and rain came down in sheets now.

Forget under his breath. Sully cursed loudly and ran for the nearest horse. Drew beat him to the punch, having witnessed the whole thing. He vaulted onto the back of a saddled horse, shot Sully a parting look that was anything but nice, and took off after Anna in true hero form. Damn the man.

"What happened," Tess asked as she reached Sully's side, holding an umbrella over them both.

"I fucked up," he said honestly. "I had one simple job to do, and I couldn't handle it." He punched his fist into his other hand and stepped out from beneath the umbrella to pace. "Dammit!"

"I ran over here as soon as I saw," Tess said. "I'm sure it's not as bad as you think."

Sully ground his teeth. Here he chastised Anna for not being able to handle a place like Mystic Valley with all of its untamed surroundings and wild country ways. Yet he'd stood there getting in his zingers instead of assessing the situation. He should have seen that she'd already untied Martha when she had been trying to shove her toward the barn. Martha was huge and heavy, making Anna no match. Hell, the cow was almost as stubborn as Tilly the mule. Sully made his living on being observant. How had he missed that? Just one more reason to stay far away from Anna Wilks. She was *distracting*, to say the least.

"Thunder scared the cow, and she bolted. Miss Wilks ran after her." He threw his hands up in the air helplessly. "Don't know what she thought she could do on foot."

Tess shook her head on a snort. "City folk."

He smirked at her, his lips twisting wryly. "Aren't you city?"

"Honey, there's city and then there's *city*." She winked at him.

"Ain't that the truth?" He chuckled, relaxing a little and enjoying Tess. She was tough, yet she knew how to be sexy. His lips tipped down into a hard, flat line. More importantly, she knew how to take care of herself.

"Look, there's Drew." Tess pointed to the man on horseback, sitting tall and capable in the saddle, with Anna behind him, her arms holding on with a death grip. She looked like a drowned rat, terrified and chilled to the bone. The rain had dropped the warm late spring temps by ten degrees. Martha trotted along behind them, her rope tied expertly to the saddle. "Always the hero," Tess added, with a look Sully recognized because it was hauntingly similar to the one he wore every time he looked at Anna. One of longing mixed with a healthy dose of fear.

"Amen." Sully grunted softly. "Now what?"

"Now we take shelter and wait out the storm before we both get pneumonia or struck dead by lightning." She headed for the barn after Drew and Anna.

Sully stood there for a moment, briefly wondering if getting struck by lightning would be such a bad thing. With his luck, it would never happen. He always survived. Only the good died young, and all that crap. Nope, he was destined to live a long life, and deep in his heart he knew he didn't have a death wish. Besides, he couldn't stop the thought that kept repeating itself in his brain like a broken record.

If he died... who would save Anna Wilks?

10

Dammit, Henry is pissing me off! He didn't understand why I changed my name, and now he doesn't understand why I keep switching things up. He keeps telling me if I'm not going to become a wife and mother like God intended, then I need to find something I'm good at. The truth of the matter is that it doesn't matter what I'm good at. I won't live long enough to make a career of it anyway, so why not try it all? I can't tell him that. He is my brother, my hero. I would rather see anger and frustration in his eyes than pity. He thinks I'm wasting my life. I laugh at him, and he gets mad, of course. He just has no clue I'm not wasting my life.

I'm finally living it...

"HE'S RIGHT, YOU KNOW," Anna said to Sarah in The Country Store on a warm June afternoon, while fiddling with the pieces of hard candy in the hand-painted bowls on the check-out counter.

Anna had opted for tan cotton capri pants with a mint green, short-sleeve blouse, while Sarah wore faded jeans and a red long-sleeve cotton shirt, which didn't exactly seem appropriate for the weather. The shop wasn't too warm. The windows were open and a lovely southwesterly breeze was blowing through, bringing with it the smell of flowers and fresh-cut grass. Anna looked away from Sarah's clothes and focused on why she was troubled. She had read her aunt's journal just that morning, and Clay Sullivan had come to mind.

He truly thought she wasn't good at anything and was wasting everyone's time. Wasting her life. Like her aunt, she would rather see his anger and frustration than to see him pity her, which he would surely do if he knew the truth. They all would. If anyone found out that she was broken, she would be humiliated. Mystic Valley was supposed to be her escape from all that. Her fresh start.

"Who's right?" Sarah blinked her amber eyes up at Anna in curiosity.

Anna was a good ten years older than Sarah, but that didn't matter. They had become fast friends in a short amount of time, and had been meeting every day for lunch, either at Anna's house or at Deb's Diner. On the days that they ate at the diner, Anna met Sarah at The Country Store just before her lunch hour. They could only meet on working days, because Sarah's husband Jud would never allow it on her days off. He was the possessive sort, and wanted her to himself every chance he got. Anna had tried to tell her she should stand up for herself and tell him what she wanted, but Sarah always made excuses for Jud, defending him.

"Mr. Sullivan." Anna sighed in response, thinking Sarah wasn't the only one who needed to stand up for herself. Anna didn't quite understand why she let the newspaper chief get under her skin. She might be drawn to him, but that didn't mean he was good for her. Then again, neither was Drew, with his constantly trying to take care of her. She'd decided she didn't need a man in her life right now. Not until she figured out who she was and what she wanted.

What she was *good* at.

Sully didn't come right out and say it, but his expression and tone had said it all. She wasn't good at anything and didn't belong in this town. He was just waiting for her to fail and high-tail it back to where she came from. He thought she was all fluff and no substance, but he had no clue she was made of stronger starch than that. She had her aunt's blood running through her veins, inspiring her every step of the way. Not to mention she had nothing to go back to. No husband, no child, no life. When she thought about that, those were the moments when her insecurities surfaced, and her doubts crept in.

Sarah shook her head and waved her hand in the air. "I wouldn't take anything that man has to say seriously. Can't you tell by now he's all bark and no bite?"

Anna's hands stopped fiddling with the items on the counter. "What do you mean?"

"Let's just say I can spot a wounded soul better than anyone." Sarah discreetly pulled her sleeves down lower.

Anna suspected she knew why Sarah had chosen long sleeves on a warm day. She hadn't seen any bruises since the first time she'd met Sarah, but that didn't mean anything other than her husband was getting smarter. He knew where to abuse her so the scars wouldn't show. Anna couldn't prove it yet, but she wouldn't stop trying. Sarah had said she'd fallen. The minute Anna found out otherwise, the man was toast. She had five sisters she would fight to the death for. Sarah was no different.

"What makes you think Mr. Sullivan is wounded?" Anna asked, honestly interested.

Sully fascinated her. He was so big and scary, and yet there was something about him that drew her in. She turned into an idiot in his presence, and couldn't seem to look away from his stormy gray eyes, yet he was so standoffish and looked at her like she didn't have a clue. He would leave her dumbfounded, standing there like a fool, unable to process all that he'd said to her until he left. And then indignation would set in. At him, but mostly at herself. Why did she keep letting him do that to her? Sometimes she suspected she was no better than Sarah.

"The lines of pain in his face," Sarah finally responded, as she stared off into the distance. Lines Anna had never noticed etched Sarah's forehead and the corners of her mouth as she spoke. "Even when he's not scowling at someone or acting like he doesn't care, the lines are still there. Those aren't lines of anger. Those are lines of pain. Lines you can't erase with makeup or Botox or facelifts. They come from a pain that lives somewhere so deep in your soul, it sucks the life right out of you, little by little. He can't help the way he is. It's the only way he knows how to survive."

Anna had heard the story of his ex-girlfriend from high school who had gone missing after graduation. She'd heard how the whole town had suspected him of foul play. She'd also heard how Cindy Taylor's body was never found, and that people had reached out and tried to help him, forgive him, but he would have none of that. She didn't really know much else about him, other than he was an only child with older parents who were now deceased, and he had covered the kind of stories that could change a man forever. But if Mystic Valley had forgiven him, then why couldn't he forgive himself? Unless he was guilty. What had he done to Cindy Taylor to make him hate the world and everyone in it, including himself?

"Still," Anna replied with a heavy sigh. "He does have a point. I need to figure out what I am good at. What I want to do with my life. I went from my parents taking care of me to my husband sheltering me from the world. I feel like I've wasted so much time. Now that I'm on my own, I really don't have a clue what to do."

"Maybe you don't have to do anything," Sarah said. "I would love for someone to take care of me for a change. I've worked my entire life just to barely get by." Anna noticed Sarah didn't mention Jud. She'd said he worked hard at the mill, but Anna had heard he spent most of his wages at the local bar, with not much left over. She was afraid Sarah's thin shoulders couldn't handle her heavy load forever. She was bound to break at some point.

"Trust me, being taken care of is not all it's cracked up to be." Anna stared down at the counter. "I need to feel worthy. Like I'm useful or needed on this earth. You're a mother. Your son needs you every day. I have nothing but money. That can be cold and lonely. I need something else." She had her family, but she was still angry with them. Her mother and sisters called weekly, but Anna had made it clear she wasn't ready to talk to them. That she was okay, she just needed some space. Her father was too stubborn to call or apologize. She knew he loved her, and she would forgive them in time, but not right now.

"Have you ever thought of having a child?" Sarah asked innocently. "You don't need a husband for that, and you certainly have enough money for artificial insemination."

A dagger of pain pierced through Anna's heart, and she was taken back to that day in the doctor's office that had changed her life forever. Agony exploded and the wind got sucked right out of her like the balloons that deflated after her last birthday party. Another childless year gone by. She hadn't anticipated the question, and it had taken her by surprise. She would have to get used to that. The people here didn't know her story. They only knew she was divorced. It took a moment for her to catch her breath.

"Oh my goodness, are you okay?" Sarah rushed around the

counter and grabbed her arm. "You look like you're about to faint. I'm so sorry if I upset you in any way."

"I'm fine, just a little dizzy. My ex and I tried artificial insemination once, but it didn't work," Anna finally responded, unable to say the words that were true. She was sterile. No amount of insemination or money would ever change that.

"I really am so terribly sorry. Maybe it would work the second time. I've heard of it taking a few times before it works," Sarah added desperately, looking at a loss for how to make things better. "Or there's always adoption." She looked ready to cry over the thought of upsetting Anna.

"It's okay, Sarah." Anna patted her arm, and realized it really was going to be okay. "I think what I need is to figure out who I am first. I spent so long pleasing my family and then my husband, that I truly haven't really met Anna Wilks. I want to discover who I am as a person first, and then I will definitely think about adoption." That much was the truth, at least. Anna had decided from the moment Erik had bought her off, she would use his money to make her dream of becoming a mother true. To hell with him.

To hell with all men!

"That sounds like a plan, Anna Wilks," Sarah said, "and I think I just might have a way to help."

~

"ALL RIGHT, TESS," Sully said into his office phone at the newspaper a couple of weeks later. "Thanks for the update."

He hung up and tried not to get discouraged. Even branching out into other towns hadn't helped find Cindy. He knew trying to solve this case would be a long shot, but it was hard to give up hope. Chief Fitz and her crew were doing all they could. Hell, his own team was as well. There just wasn't much to find after all these years. Cindy's jacket had been their only ray of hope so far. He wasn't giving up, but in the meantime, he still had a job to do. The town was already pissed off at him enough for spending too much time on the case. He'd heard grumbles at the diner that the paper was too thin. People complained that there was more news to cover than rehashing old sorrows.

Today he was proofing Lynn's piece on the wildflower festival. It wasn't bad. A bit too much fluff for his taste, but she'd covered the essentials. Wildflowers of all sorts of colors, shapes, and scents grew throughout Mystic Valley in the open meadows. Many bouquets had been carefully cut, arranged, and displayed throughout the tents in the park where the festival was held. Local artisans used the flowers to make essential oils, soaps, fragrances, medicines, teas, and more. They each had a booth, demonstrating the process they used, as well as selling their goods. Like the dairy festival, the wildflower festival lasted all weekend with food, music, and events.

Lynn had interviewed the artisans, the spectators, the musicians, and pretty much everyone else. There was only one area she needed improvement on. Her photography. Like Diego, she needed a how-to course. The photos showed what was happening well enough, but they didn't capture the people or the essence of what the festival was all about. This piece in the newspaper would bring in more people for next year's event if they did it justice. He closed the folder and tossed it on his desk, running his hands through his thick curly hair. He'd have to pay a visit to Nick's barber shop soon. Not that he cared much about how he looked. It was just getting hard to manage.

A knock sounded on his office door.

"Come in," he said in a loud voice.

The door opened and he dropped his hand to his desk as he stared in surprise. He'd never expected to see *her* in his office.

"Have a seat, Miss Wilks," he said, eying her curiously.

She wore a casual denim skirt, a pretty pink flowy shirt, and strappy sandals. She still looked perfectly put together, but there was something decidedly more relaxed about her these days, with her hair hanging loose and wavy. He liked when she wore it down, but then his gaze met hers. She still had a layer of sadness shining in her hypnotic green eyes, but it was hidden behind an interesting top layer of excitement. She didn't look as wary, either. Like maybe she was finding her groove and settling in. Of course, she still hadn't lived through one of their winters yet.

"What can I do for you?" he asked, after she sat down across from him and placed a folder in front of her on his desk.

"Well..." She cleared her throat. "I was hoping I might be able to do something for *you*."

He sat back and folded his arms across his chest. "I'm listening."

"I know you think I can't do anything for myself. That I don't belong here. That I'm not good at anything—"

"I never said that last part," he interrupted, refusing to deny her first two points.

She sat a little straighter. "You didn't have to. It was quite clear, really. But you were right."

He raised an eyebrow. "Can I get that in writing?" He tried not to let his lips twitch.

Ignoring his jab, she continued. "I admit I was used to people doing everything for me. First my family, and then my ex-husband, but I've learned a lot already since coming to Mystic Valley."

He'd heard she was divorced, but something told him there was more to her sadness than a failed marriage. "Why did you come? This town doesn't exactly seem up your alley."

"You don't know anything about my alley, so how would you know what's up it?" she said dryly, arching a shapely auburn brow.

He bowed his head, giving her a *touché* grin.

"The funny thing is I didn't know anything about my alley, either, apparently," she admitted. "But then I saw a brochure for Mystic Valley. It's hard to explain, but it called to me. It somehow seemed like a great place to start over, so here I am." She shrugged.

"Here you are. In my office. With a folder in front of you. I admit my curiosity is piqued."

"Back to that, yes." She took a breath as though striving for courage. "Anyway, I realized I had no idea what I wanted to do with my life. But then Sarah Shaw down at The Country Store showed me a book on photography. She said I always talk about nature and point out the most beautiful things, that I make her wish she could remember them forever. That's when she thought of photography. I've done a ton of reading-up on the subject, and even purchased the best equipment, and, well, the wildflower festival was my first photo shoot."

"Okay, I'm glad you're finding something that makes you happy, Miss Wilks, but—"

"Please, call me Anna," she interrupted him this time.

Calling her by her first name would be way too dangerous for him. Way too intimate. Ignoring her request, he asked carefully, "What exactly does this have to do with me?"

"Well, I remember reading the paper after the dairy festival. The article was good, but the photos seemed a little bland. That's what gave me the idea for shooting the wildflower festival. I thought that if I caught you in time before you published the piece on this festival, that you might want to buy some of my shots for the paper." She tried so hard to look all business and professional, but she really wasn't good at hiding her feelings. She looked on the edge of her seat, ready to jump for joy or burst into tears, unable to hide the hope simmering in her eyes.

He paused a moment, trying to think about what he wanted

to do. But then he caught a whiff of her expensive perfume mixed with something simply Anna, and his body stirred. Sitting up straight, he cleared his throat gruffly. "What makes you think you're any better than my editors? They've been at this a whole lot longer than you have."

She lifted her chin a hair, as though determined to brave and refusing to be intimidated. "True, but as you said, they are editors. Their passion stems from the written word, where mine lies in the stories that are told through a camera lens. You know what they say—a picture is worth a thousand words."

He stared at her for a long moment, grudgingly admitting he was impressed. She had more gumption than he'd thought. He pulled her file in front of him. "I can't promise anything more than taking a look."

And look he did.

Damn, she was good. She'd captured everything he'd been searching for. Everything Lynn's photos had been missing. The vibrant colors of the flowers. Crazy techniques that made the images leap off the page as if they were alive. But what he loved the most were the people. They weren't posed. In fact they probably had no idea she'd even photographed them. They were each in their element. Artisans at work. Spectators looking on in fascination. Locals talking and smiling with sheer joy. Reactions to a certain color of a flower, emotions over the scent or taste of something made from a flower, true pleasure as people danced to the music and sampled the food.

Sully looked up at Anna and studied her in wonder. He'd been hard on her. Harder than was necessary, yet she'd persevered and proven him wrong. Not many people had the balls to even try, but she had, and succeeded. Hell, she'd done more than succeed, she'd thrived. This was the easiest thing he'd said to her yet. "You have a gift."

Her face blossomed with pleasure, and she gave him the first genuine smile he'd ever seen from her. Not forced like her other ones, but easy and real. "You think so?"

"I know so. You're a bit raw still, but these show so much potential. They're full of realism and emotion. I'll buy all of them." He looked her in the eye. "And if you cover the other festivals, I want those as well. We'll need to get release forms from the people in the photos, but I'm sure everyone will love how you've captured them. You should really think about branching out and exploring the landscape and animals. I'm sure you could sell your pictures to some magazines, too."

"Wow. I don't know how far I'll take this. I mean, I don't really need the money. I'm mostly doing this for me, and Mystic Valley of course."

"You might not need the money, but you deserve the fame."

"I'll keep that in mind."

"You do that. In the meantime, I'll be in touch with a contract and payment."

She stood and held out her hand. "Thank you, Mr. Sullivan. You won't be sorry."

He took her small hand in his much larger one and held on longer than was necessary. "I'm not sorry. You did me a huge favor. I never thought I'd say this, but I look forward to working with you."

"Me too," she responded softly, and bit her bottom lip as she walked out the door.

What the hell had he just gotten himself into?

11

"Hey, Anna, how are ya?" Old man Ike Jeffries said, standing in front of an oscillating fan as she walked up to the check-out counter of The Country Store just after the Fourth of July picnic. Ike was an older gentleman of indiscernible age, with a pot belly and a full gray beard.

It was another dark and gloomy day out. Not stormy like it had been at the wildflower festival, but not sunny either. A light steady rain fell down, giving the parched earth a life-sustaining drink. Summer had surged in on a wave of heat, and it wouldn't take much for all those beautiful flowers to wither away. Anna didn't mind the rain. It made everything seem clean and fresh. Kind of like how she felt now that she had found something she was truly good at. And even better, something she loved to do.

"I'm fantastic, Ike," Anna said and meant it. "I have a brand-new batch of pictures I need developed for Clay Sullivan."

"Those the ones from the picnic?" His face brightened eagerly.

"They sure are." She almost laughed. He'd made certain he was in at least half of them.

"You done a great job with the wildflower festival. The article was good, but those pictures spoke to so many people. You really have a way of telling a story with that there camera of yours."

Her face warmed with pleasure. "Thank you, Ike. That means more than you know." Anna looked around the store. "Is Sarah in yet? I told Mr. Sullivan I would have these ready for him today, and Sarah is the best at developing them. One of these days I'm going to buy my own machine and have her teach me what to do."

His forehead puckered. "She was supposed to be in an hour ago. I called her place, but there was no answer. She doesn't have one of those fancy cell phones, and her car has a habit of breaking down. She's probably walking here as we speak."

"Did you try Bobby's preschool? I know school is out, but they have year-round daycare."

"Well, now, I didn't even think to do that. In fact, I don't think I even have the number, but I'm sure I could look it up. Mystic Valley isn't exactly big. We only have one daycare around these parts. See how smart you are?"

"Don't worry about it, Ike. I'll take care of it." Anna winked at him and walked away, pulling out her cell phone. She dialed information and got the number for St. Rose Church, which held the only preschool in town. Anna called the preschool, but the director said Bobby wasn't there, and Sarah had never called him in sick.

"I'm going to drive by Sarah's place. I'm sure she's just running late. Maybe I can give her a lift," Anna said to Ike, who was waiting on a customer. She waved as she walked out the door, acting as if there was nothing wrong. But a knot had formed inside her stomach that said something was very wrong. It wasn't like Sarah to miss work, and Bobby was the center of her world. She wanted him to grow up with opportunities so he could live a better life than she had. If he wasn't in school, it had to be serious.

Taking the most direct route to Sarah's trailer on the outskirts of town near the lumber mill where Jud worked, Anna searched both sides of the road along the way. No sign of Sarah. When Anna got to the trailer, Sarah's car was there. Maybe it wouldn't start. Jud's car wasn't there, thank goodness. Anna had never met him in person. Only saw him from a distance, which was fine by her. He was handsome enough, and he wasn't very big, but his dark eyes were hard and scary. His shoulders were always a little hunched and tense, like he walked around in a fighting stance, ready to pounce at any moment. Anna didn't care to be on the receiving end any time soon. Cutting the engine, she walked up to Sarah's door and knocked.

No one answered.

"Sarah, it's Anna. Are you in there?"

Still no answer.

Sarah was an hour late for work and Bobby wasn't in school. If she'd walked, Anna would have passed them. They had to be inside. Most people in Mystic Valley didn't lock their front doors. Anna had a hard time getting used to that, but she had to admit it made her feel safe that they trusted their neighbors in Mystic Valley. Not to mention that after her getting-locked-out fiasco, she hadn't locked them since. When she thought of Sarah, she realized what she had to fear wasn't on the outside of her house. It was the monster within.

Anna tried her door, and sure enough it was unlocked. "Sarah, I'm coming in." She walked through the door.

The place was small, like a typical trailer, but it was immaculate. Sarah had put her own special touch all over the place, making the most out of what she had. Anna looked into the kitchen and living room but didn't see anyone. Walking down the hall toward the bedrooms, she called out, "Bobby? Are you here? It's me, Anna. It's okay, honey. I'm here to help you."

She heard a whimper from his bedroom on the right. Slowly

stepping through his door, she stopped in the middle of the room but didn't see him. The whimper sounded again, and she squatted down. Her heart squeezed tight over the small form huddled into a tight ball under the bed. His eyes were shut, and his arms wrapped around his knees as tears slipped slowly down his cheeks in silent cries of agony.

"Come here, baby," she said with a soft voice, careful to control her sobs. "Auntie Anna has you now."

His little pink lips parted. He sucked in a small breath of air as he blinked open his amber eyes exactly like his mother's and stared at Anna in hope and wonder.

"That's right. See, it's only me. You can come out now." She held her arms open wide.

That was all it took. He scrambled out from beneath his bed and threw himself into her arms, sobbing out loud now.

"D-Daddy's gone? You sure? You have to be sure," he said repeatedly.

Anna sat on the floor, cradling him in her lap with her arms wrapped tightly around him, stroking his back over and over. This is what it would have been like to be a mother. To love your child and hold your child and comfort your child. To soothe your child's fears and let him know you would make everything all right.

"Yes, he's gone. I'm not going to let him hurt you any more, okay?"

"H-He don't hurt me," Bobby said, way too wise for a child his age. "He hurts Mommy."

Anna squeezed her eyes tight for a moment as a sharp pain of fear seized her, then she took a fortifying breath for courage as she sat back and looked Bobby in the eye. "It's going to be okay. Do you believe me?"

He looked at her with such longing and yet such fear, it broke her heart.

"I promise," she added, running a hand over his soft brown curls.

He nodded. "You're like my mama, and she don't break her promises."

"Good boy. Now, I need you to be brave and tell me where she is. Do you think you can do that?"

He sat up, still looking afraid, but trying really hard to be the man of the house. "If Daddy's gone, I can do anything." He wiped his eyes with the sleeves of his long-sleeve shirt and looked out his bedroom door toward his parents' room. "Mommy always has me hide when Daddy's sick."

"Your father's sick?"

"Yeah, when he walks funny and slurs his words and stuff."

"Ah, yes. I see. Then what happens?"

"He yells a lot, and she cries. Then when Daddy leaves to get more medicine, Mommy comes and finds me and makes it all better."

"Then why are you still under the bed?"

"Because she didn't find me this time."

Anna nearly fell over, terrified of what that could mean. She took a minute to catch her breath, and then made up her mind. "Do you like adventures?"

His whole face lit up. "My teacher showed me all kinds of books, and the ones I liked best she called adventures."

"Well, how would you like to go on a grand adventure?"

His smile spread across his flushed chubby cheeks, and he nodded so hard his bangs flopped in front of his eyes.

"Good boy. I want you to pack a bag, while I go help your mother pack a bag. Can you do that for me?"

His smile dimed a bit. "Does Daddy have to come too?"

"No, your father is much too sick for that. I think we should stay far away from him until he gets better. We don't want to catch what he has, now do we?"

Bobby shook his head so hard, he looked like he might break his neck. Anna vowed right then and there that if Jud ever touched another hair on either of their heads, she would gladly break *his* and never look back.

~

THAT EVENING SULLY headed to Anna's house to pick up the pictures she had promised him for the Fourth of July piece. Lynn's story covering the wildflower festival with Anna's pictures had been a huge success. His instincts had been right in hiring her on spec as a photographer for all the upcoming festivals. Lord knew she didn't need the money, but she *did* have a gift. And she seemed to love the attention, blossoming as she discovered who she really was. It was a sight to behold.

Dangerous territory for him, but a sight to behold nonetheless.

He'd called her earlier, but she hadn't called back. The piece was scheduled to come out in two days, so he wanted the pictures ASAP. Maybe something had happened in developing them. Growing tired of waiting to hear from her, he'd decided to drive to her place. The deadline was the excuse he gave himself, not wanting to admit that he longed to see her. Ever since they'd called a truce of sorts after she'd proven him wrong, insisting she did belong in this town and had something worthwhile to offer, things had shifted between them. He still didn't see her lasting through the winter, but he had to admit she had gumption.

He pulled into her driveway and saw her car. Next to that was Jud Shaw's car. An irrational anger surged through Sully. Jud was a married man, yet his wife's car wasn't there. What the hell was he doing at Anna's house alone? Is that why Anna hadn't answered Sully's calls? Because she was having an affair?

The normal him wouldn't bother with caring, as long as the pictures were good. He stayed out of other people's business. But nothing about his relationship with Anna was normal. She tore him up inside like no other woman had, turning him into someone he didn't recognize.

A madman who was mad as hell right now.

Then suddenly Sully remembered Jud had a drinking problem. Fear mixed with anger as he stormed up to the front door through the rain and didn't bother with knocking. With Anna determined to fit in at any cost, he was sure she didn't lock her door either. He was right. He barged in, ready to lay into her, but he froze in his tracks.

"What the hell?" he said, staring at the scene before him.

Sarah Shaw sat on the living room couch, looking frail and scared as hell as she held her young son Bobby on her lap protectively. And the petite dynamo Anna Wilks stood before them, holding the mean end of a broom before her like she didn't have a clue what she was doing, but she was damn sure gonna do something.

"What's going on?" Sully asked, looking at Anna.

"None of your business, Sullivan," Jud snarled. It was clear he'd been drinking. "I've come for my family, but this outsider is holding them prisoner." He glared at Anna, then gave Sarah an intimidating look. "Isn't that right, honey? You want to come home with your man, don't you? You wouldn't keep a son from his old man, would you, now?"

Sarah trembled harder but didn't say a word, and Bobby buried his head in her shoulder. Sully didn't miss her wince. He ground his teeth. "Miss Wilks?" Sully asked, thinking this scene had better not be about what he suspected it was. He could ignore a lot of things that weren't okay, but not that. Women and children weren't meant to be manhandled by anyone.

Ignoring him, Anna snarled back at Jud, "Why don't you tell

Mr. Sullivan why I won't let them leave even if they want to." Anna surprised him. She was normally so calm and proper, even a bit mousy, but now she was standing up like a fierce mama bear, ready to do whatever the hell she had to in order to protect her kind. He hadn't known she had that streak in her, but then again, it was hard to see past the still lingering sadness in her beautiful green eyes.

"I don't have to tell him shit," Jud spat. "My wife fell, just like she told the hospital."

"She only said that because she's afraid of you and has never had anyone to turn to. Well, she has *me* now, and I'm not afraid of you. You're nothing but a pathetic bully."

"You bitch!" Jud lunged at Anna.

Even with a bum leg, Sully moved lightning fast, grabbing Jud by the throat and slamming him against the wall as he growled, "Watch your mouth, dirt bag."

Jud blinked in shock, then the kind of cold anger that ate at a man's soul settled into his eyes like that of a dog that had been tortured for too long, and snapped back the only way he knew how. He glared at Sully and said defiantly, "Make me."

Sully let his own eyes grow hooded as he stared at Jud with all of his own pent-up anger and frustration. "I can make you disappear forever, you piece of crap." Sully never had been completely cleared of any involvement in Cindy Taylor's disappearance, so the dangerous aura surrounding him remained. On top of that, he knew he was a scary-looking giant no average man would want to mess with, period. But Jud wasn't average, he was crazy, and that made *him* dangerous.

"Butt out, Sullivan," Jud said harshly, but a flash of wariness cleared his drunken haze. Smart man. "This has nothing to do with you," he finished in a desperate plea.

"Technically, it does." Sully squeezed Jud's neck tighter. "You're threatening Miss Wilks, and she works for me now. Your wife develops the pictures Anna takes, which makes her an important part of my staff as well. You hurting them is hurting me." Sully thrust his face about an inch in front of Jud's as he growled, "I don't like to get hurt... do you?"

"I didn't do anything," Jud whined pathetically.

"Right, so that's why I just got home from the emergency room with your *wife*." Anna swept her hand toward Sarah who sat on the couch without a mark that Sully could see on her yet somehow looking broken. "I guess punching her in the stomach so many times until she spit blood doesn't count. Just because you're smart enough to hide the bruises doesn't mean you won't ever get caught, you coward. Not to mention you traumatized an innocent boy. Your own *son*. You're a monster."

Sully saw red. He didn't hesitate as he drew back his fist and punched Jud square in the face, breaking his nose. Jud cried out in agony, but Sully didn't let up. He hauled him to his feet and punched him in the stomach for good measure. Sully's mother had always taught him that violence was never the answer, but over the years he'd learned some people just needed to have some sense knocked into them. He was done now. Sully had seen his fair share of injustice and violence, enough to last a lifetime. Acid churned in his stomach. He'd had enough of giving it, of seeing it, of being anywhere near it.

Shoving his face close to Jud's, he hissed, "My father ignored me, and my best friend's old man beat the piss out of him. Neither one of us could do anything about it at the time, but I'm back now. I'm bigger, I'm stronger, and I'm meaner. You so much as lay a finger of any of them, I will find you, and I *will* kill you. Are we clear?" He hoped like hell Jud heeded his warning because he was pretty damn certain he would follow through on his threat if it came right down to it.

Jud nodded once and then the second Sully released him, he scrambled free and ran. Sully slammed the door behind him.

Dammit, he'd been afraid to believe Sarah had been abused. The signs were there, but he hadn't wanted to believe so he wouldn't have to get involved. He didn't do complicated. She'd always looked skittish and had been quiet, but she'd acted fine when she was in the presence of her husband. They hadn't exactly appeared like a happy little family, but they had at least seemed like a normal married couple.

Something touched Sully's back. He whirled around in a ready position, but it was only Anna. She didn't so much as flinch, just looked at him like he was a hero. *Well, hell.* Relaxing, he dropped his hands. She picked up his fist, and electricity hummed in the very air around them. She stroked her thumb across the bruised knuckles he'd hit Jud with, before looking up and meeting his eyes.

"Thank you," she said softly, but her eyes said so much more.

"You're welcome," he responded, clearing the gravel from his voice and trying to act casual. He was uncomfortable with the role of hero or anything else, but even he couldn't deny something powerful had just happened between them.

12

"Simon, what are you doing? You're supposed to be on the North end of the harbor, covering Bonnie, while I keep an eye out for Clyde," I whispered to my partner, Detective Baker.

We were Boston Homicide detectives, and we'd been searching for the modern-day Bonnie and Clyde bank robber cop killers for months now, with no luck until tonight. One of our informants had called with a tip that Bonnie and Clyde were going to make a run for it and slip away on one of the cargo ships in the harbor this very night. If that happened, we would lose them for good. I couldn't let that happen. We had worked too long and hard on this case.

"I was worried about you, Tess," Simon responded in a hushed voice from beside me, as we hid behind a dumpster next to a warehouse by the docks.

"See, I knew getting romantically involved with each other was a bad idea," I hissed. "You have to think of me as a cop and not your girlfriend when we work a case. You're going to get us both killed. Besides, Bonnie is the more dangerous one, I'm told."

"Partners have each other's backs." He touched my cheek as he added softly, "It has nothing to do with you being my girlfriend."

"Liar," I said with less venom, softening against my will. "You're just trying to protect me."

"That too, baby." He winked. "But I can see you're just fine. I'll radio you when I get back to my post."

"You'd better." I punched him lightly on the shoulder. "You're not the only one who worries."

He stood and gave me one of his adorable lop-sided smiles as he got ready to turn around and walk away... but he never made it that far. I would never forget the look on his face for as long as I lived. One of love and happiness, followed by stunned surprise and then horror. His gaze locked onto mine and a myriad of emotions blazed back at me: fear, regret, sadness... and then nothing at all. He fell forward, face down on top of me, knocking me flat on my back. The wind whooshed out of me, and I couldn't breathe, couldn't move, couldn't do anything. I lay there helplessly as I listened to the lapping of the water as it slapped against the cement wall. The smell of fish floated through the air. The sound of a foghorn wailed in the harbor as a ship pulled away from the docks. The sound of...

Footsteps.

Finally, my breath came back in a surge of relief seconds before I would have passed out. I struggled with all my might, but Simon was a big guy. His beautiful brown eyes remained open, his lifeless gaze staring blankly back at me, the warmth of his body quickly slipping away as his life's blood soaked into my uniform. I breathed in his scent for what would be the last time, trying to memorize his musky Old Spice smell, and I kissed him softly knowing I would never again taste the sweetness of his coffee-flavored lips. Tears welled up in my eyes, but the footsteps grew closer. This was no time to cry. I would relive this day for the rest of my life and grieve forevermore.

Right now, I wanted revenge.

Simon's muscular body weighed on mine like an anchor, but I managed to wiggle just enough to slip out from beneath him, partway at least. I propped myself up on my elbow with Simon still covering all *of my body except for my head and my right arm. My right hand. My gun. Bonnie and Clyde came to a stop before me, and I didn't hesitate. They must have thought they'd killed us both, because they hadn't seen me yet. I had the advantage, but I didn't say 'freeze' or read them their rights or any of that. I simply reacted, screaming to the top of my lungs as I pushed Simon off me and sat up, catching them by surprise. I opened fire, killing them both for shooting Simon in the back. Their looks of shock before they died would never be enough. I hadn't even realized they'd gotten off a shot and I was hit in the shoulder until the paramedics arrived. I'd told them that it was self-defense, and no one had ever questioned it. No one knew I was a fraud.*

No one would ever know I was the one to shoot first.

"No!" Tess surged to a sitting position at the desk in her office. It took a minute to realize where she was. Mystic Valley police station, and she was the new police chief. She must have fallen asleep at her desk from all the hours of overtime she'd been putting in lately and not sleeping well at night.

Drew came running in, his eyes wide and hand hovering over his weapon, so big and strong just like Simon had been. And just like Simon, he was always ready to protect her and save the day. "What's wrong, Chief? You okay?"

She wanted to say no, she wasn't okay. That she'd been lying to everyone, including herself, in thinking she could just jump back into work like nothing had ever happened. She'd lost her partner, her best friend, her lover. And she'd killed two people. They sure as hell weren't innocent, but it hadn't been for her to decide whether they lived or died for their crimes. Part of her wondered what she would do if faced with another situation like that. Would she shoot first again? She took a deep breath and vowed she would never *be* in another situation like that, because she would never allow herself to fall in love again.

Especially not with someone she worked with.

"I'm okay, Officer Jones. Just a bad dream." She rubbed her shoulder.

His gaze flicked to her hand. "Anything I can help you with?"

Her fingers stilled, and she casually dropped her arm. "No, I'm fine on my own."

"So you've said." He crossed his arms over his wide chest in an I'm-listening-and-not-going-anywhere stance. "Ever think it might help to talk about it?"

She had talked to plenty of people: her family, her captain, her colleagues, her therapist. She'd just never shared her secret, and that was the part she was having a hard time living with. But she couldn't change the past. She'd done what she did for Simon, and that was that. No looking back, just moving forward. The problem was she didn't seem to be getting anywhere. She hadn't even taken Misty Monroe up on her offer of helping her find a new house yet, choosing to stay at the bed-and-breakfast on the lake for now. Or at least until she got her head screwed on right. It was hard to get settled when she still felt so unsettled on the inside.

"The only thing I want to talk about right now is the Cindy Taylor case," Tess finally responded. "Pam and Randy are picking up the slack on our other cases, but Mayor Evans and the town council aren't happy that I'm tying you up in all this."

"Mayor Evans isn't my boss. I only answer to you. Besides, I happen to believe Cindy Taylor deserves justice, and her family certainly does. I was friends with Cindy back in the day. In fact, I was just thinking about her the other day, which made me realize things have changed a lot since she went missing. We have a lot more tools at our disposal now, and so does Sullivan. He just hasn't broadened his reach far enough."

Tess eyed him curiously. "What do you mean?"

"Every person who goes missing doesn't draw nationwide

attention to begin with, but they especially didn't back then. Now we have the Internet and social media, and hell, Sully has a ton of newspaper and television connections. If someone kidnapped Cindy, or even if she ran away, she wouldn't have seen the news coverage about her disappearance if she traveled far enough away from Vermont. If we broaden our search and post her picture now, we just might get somewhere. Unless she was murdered or died by accident, which is something I don't care to think about right now."

"No, death is not something I want to think about anymore either." Tess shuddered, and Drew gave her another concerned look, so she smiled reassuringly. "Officer Jones, you're a genius. I'm putting you in charge of that assignment while I take care of some other business."

"I'm on it, partner. I won't let you down." He saluted her playfully, but all she could think about was the word "partner."

She masked her face and looked him in the eye. "'Chief' will be fine. I don't have a partner anymore, and frankly, I don't plan to have one ever again."

"It's just a word, Chief, meaning we work together. Help each other out." His smile faded a bit to one of sympathy and a tinge of sadness as he added, "You gotta let someone in someday, Tess."

She watched him leave her office, his broad back and muscular shoulders willing to carry her burden if she would give in and let him, he just didn't realize she couldn't afford to. She couldn't take the chance of anything bad happening to anyone else she cared about because of her. Sighing with weariness, she said quietly, "Not today, Drew. And definitely not you."

～

ANNA ADJUSTED the shutter speed setting on the DSLR camera she bought. It was larger, bulkier and sturdier than a compact point-and-shoot camera, but the quality of the pictures was better because of the larger image sensor. She also liked the freedom of the removable and interchangeable lenses, as well as being able to shoot in full manual. She'd purchased a starter camera, but she was growing and developing quickly as a photographer since Sully had agreed to let her shoot the festivals for the stories he covered.

It was mid-July already. She had been here for just over two whole months. It didn't seem possible, yet she really felt like she was starting to belong. Today they were at the American Legion where the blueberry festival was being held. There were tables with food inside the Legion, as well as a band with music. And outside there were all sorts of tents set up where everything blueberry existed. Once again, the local artisans had surprised Anna with their creative wares. Blueberry oils and candles and teas and medicines and food occupied the tables in the various booths scattered about. And of course, there was the baked goods contest, as well as the always popular pie-eating competition.

Walking throughout the tents, Anna stayed back a ways and did what she did best. Took pictures of people in their element, rather than being posed. Those were always the best shots and the town favorites. She had just walked out of the last tent when she spotted Sully squatting down beside young Bobby. He was showing him the branch of a shrub with indigo-colored berries clumped together in bunches, and explaining how the plant first produced bell-shaped, pale pink-and-white flowers and leaves before the berries come. He explained that blueberry bushes were a perennial plant that bloomed halfway through the growing season.

Bobby looked on in awe, his gaze worshipping as it stayed

locked onto Sully, eagerly soaking up all the male attention he was getting. Sully had been incredible. He might act like he didn't care about anyone, yet ever since the day he'd scared Jud off, he'd been hanging around Anna's house, checking up on all of them. As much as he said he wouldn't help, she kept catching him tending to little things that needed fixing.

"Bobby idolizes that man. Mr. Sullivan isn't at all what he seems," Sarah said a little sadly as she joined Anna just outside the tent. She looked better, stronger, and a lot less afraid. "If only my son's father were half the man Mr. Sullivan is, Bobby might just stand a chance of turning out okay.

Anna patted Sarah's shoulder. "I'm beginning to think you're right. There's a lot more to Sully than even he realizes. He's a good role model for Bobby. Your son will be fine, you'll see. I'm more worried about you. I know you're healing on the outside, but what about on the inside. Are you okay?"

"I'm okay, I promise. With Sully hanging around, Jud hasn't dared to try anything. He called a couple times, begging me to take him back. When I refused, he threatened to seek custody of Bobby. He's never hit him, but with me out of the way, I wouldn't trust him not to turn on Bobby. I'm just terrified he would win in court. He makes the main money, and I never did report him for abusing me." Sarah crossed her arms over her mid-section. "I don't know what I would do, but I do know he'd have to kill me before I would let him take my son away."

"It would never come to that," Anna didn't hesitate to state firmly. "I have money and plenty of connections. Bobby's not going anywhere. Not to mention you're a great mother. No court around would separate a child from his loving mother. And you have a support system now." She looked Sarah in the eye and nodded once. "Me."

"I don't know what I would do without you," Sarah responded in a shaky voice, looking on the verge of tears.

"Well, you'll never have to find out because I don't know what I would do without you either." Anna swallowed past the lump in her throat and then picked up her camera, snapping the perfect shot of Bobby and Sully.

Sully's sharp gaze sliced to Anna with a look she couldn't read.

"He likes you," Sarah said matter-of-factly. "I can tell."

Anna blinked. "How can you tell?" She was almost afraid to ask.

"How can you *not*?" Sarah laughed softly.

Anna tore her gaze away from the magnetic pull of his. "It doesn't matter anyway. He's in no shape to date anyone, and frankly, neither am I." She busied her hands, checking the settings on her camera.

"I know your divorce was hard to go through, and you're just getting to know yourself, but you have to go on living." Sarah squeezed Anna's hand. "You deserve to be happy. I'm not saying you have to marry the guy, for crying out loud. I'm just saying talk to him, go out with him, have a little fun. I'll bet your aunt wouldn't have sat back and missed out on anything that caught her eye. She sounded like the type of person who would go after what she wanted with no regrets."

Anna had talked about her divorce and even her aunt to Sarah, but she still hadn't revealed her secret. She'd said fertility treatments hadn't worked, but she'd never actually said the words that a doctor had declared her sterile. It was hard enough to even think about, but was just too painful to say out loud— except Sarah was right. This thing between Sully and herself didn't have to be anything heavy. Just a little harmless fun between two consenting adults. Anna's aunt would have seized the day and taken what she wanted; consequences be damned.

And right now, Anna wanted Clay Sullivan.

"Can you develop these for me later?" Anna asked Sarah as she handed her the camera.

"Sure, where are you going?" Sarah asked to her retreating back.

"To take your advice," Anna called over her shoulder.

"Well, it's about time." Sarah clapped with joy.

Anna didn't stop walking until she reached Sully. She crouched down to Bobby's level. "Hey, squirt. Having another adventure?" She ruffled his brown curls.

Bobby nodded with a huge grin. "Sully has the best kind."

"I'll be he does. He *is* a great storyteller, after all."

"I know," Bobby said breathlessly. "I wanna be just like him when I grow up."

Anna looked up at Clay and smiled, but his lips dipped down into a frown.

"Trust me, kid," his voice was grittier than usual, "you don't want to be anything like me. Why don't you run along and take care of your mom. You're the man of the house now, remember?"

Bobby stood straight and saluted Sully before running off after his mother like a fierce little warrior.

"You've done wonders for his confidence," Anna said, as she stood once more.

Sully shoved his large hands in the pockets of his jeans, his arms bulging beneath his snug t-shirt. "I haven't done anything."

"You might have most people fooled, but I've seen you in action. You care about him."

"No kid deserves to live like he was. No mother does either. I'm just making sure his old man stays away from them. That's all." He shrugged. "You're reading too much into things."

"Am I?" Anna took a step closer to him and studied his eyes. "I don't think so. You care more about people than you let on."

He held her gaze and didn't say anything for a long moment,

then he shook his head slightly. "You're too naïve and innocent to see the truth. I'm damaged goods."

"Aren't we all," she responded with a soft voice, thinking he had no idea. "Let me make you dinner."

"I don't think that's such a good idea."

"It's not a date. It's a thank-you meal for all you've done for Sarah and Bobby and even me."

He raised a brow.

"Did you think I wouldn't notice the work you've done around my place?"

"You've proven you can take care of yourself, and I was there anyway. I didn't see the harm in helping out a bit. That's all."

"And I don't see the harm in thanking you with a meal. *That's* all. So what do you say, Mr. Sullivan?"

"I say you've got yourself a deal, Miss Wilks."

Sully held out his hand as though this were a simple business transaction. Anna slid her palm into his and shook, feeling sparks of electricity hum between them. Neither let go. The look on his face said that he'd felt the connection too, and there was nothing simple about any of this. For a moment, she hesitated, but then a voice whispered through her mind...

No regrets.

13

I did it. I finally did it. I faced my biggest fear and went scuba diving. I'm terrified of the water, but facing my biggest fear was on my bucket list, so scuba diving it was. Of course I spent a fortune going to New Guinea. Papua has everything from deep drops to shallow reefs, atolls, and private lagoons. I even got to see several shipwrecks originally from World War II. Hey, if I was going to be scared shitless, then I was going to damn well make it worth my while. Henry is baffled, to say the least. He can't understand why I am spending all of my inheritance instead of saving for retirement, and I don't have the heart to tell him this is my retirement, and I'm loving every minute of it.

ANNA SMILED as she set her aunt's journal down and wiped a tear away from her cheek. It helped knowing her aunt had been happy. She didn't hold back, even when she was afraid. Anna took a breath. Face her biggest fears. She nodded once. She could do this.

Now that the festivals were over with until Fall, and Jud had pretty much stayed away from Sarah and Bobby, Sully was coming around less and less. Ever since Anna had invited him to dinner as a thank-you for all he'd done, he had backed off. They had connected, and he had freaked out. Plain and simple. Sarah had said to go after what she wanted, but it wasn't that easy with one stubborn Clay Sullivan. He was hardheaded and way too cautious.

Anna had had enough.

She decided to focus all her time and energy into taking her craft to the next level. She was going to photograph some scenic shots and pictures of Vermont wildlife in hopes of selling them to a few magazines. Maybe she would even see a bald eagle. Today was a beautiful day. May as well make the most of it, even if it involved facing one of *her* biggest fears. The woods. She loved nature, but there was something about the deep dark woods that scared her.

She'd always been afraid of getting lost, never finding her way out, and dying alone. She'd always been afraid of *being* alone, which was crazy since she'd grown up in a big family and went straight from living with her parents to moving in with her husband. Maybe because she'd grown up *lonely*. Even after her wedding, she'd still been lonely. Maybe if she faced her fear, she wouldn't be so afraid to stand on her own.

If her aunt could do it, then so could Anna.

Packing a backpack with her photo equipment, a bottle of water, and a couple of granola bars, she donned hiking boots, shorts, and a t-shirt. It was August, and hot as the dickens. Sweeping her hair up on top of her head, she grabbed her sunglasses and headed for the door. She'd wandered into the woods right behind her house, but she had never ventured deep into the forest by the big hills and the rock quarries, with the Green Mountains just beyond that.

Sully was right. There was a book on everything, with the Internet to fall back on. Typically, you would follow a trail map, but she wasn't taking any chances. She'd read up on hiking and had even bought a compass. *It wasn't possible to get lost with a compass, right*? she kept telling herself. This was something she wanted to do on her own, so she could finally prove to everyone —including herself—that she belonged here.

Sarah was working and Bobby was at daycare. Anna left a note and then headed out to her Mercedes, which she planned to sell and buy an SUV before winter. Total transformation from the inside out was her plan. It didn't take her long to drive to a parking spot by a common hiking trail. Stepping out of the car, she donned her gear and walked into the woods with a feeling of terrified excitement.

It was dark and cooler beneath the canopy of leaves from the tall trees, but it wasn't so scary. Needles, cones, leaves covered the forest floor instead of grass, filling the air with the smells of pine and dirt. Looking up, she watched the branches sway in the breeze, and rays of sunlight stream down to the ground below like flashlights from heaven, to guide the woodland creatures. It was comforting to realize she still really wasn't alone. A twig snapped and something scurried about. Anna jumped. Searching the area, she saw a chipmunk scramble into a bush and a squirrel dart up a tree, making her laugh.

This was nature, and nature wasn't evil.

Pulling out her compass, she pointed it west. The Vermont Piedmont ran north to south through the entire state of Vermont. Mystic Valley was located right in the middle of the piedmont, with hills on both sides of the valley. She wanted to head west toward the old abandoned rock quarry she'd heard so much about. It was off the marked trail, but that was why she had a compass. Beyond that were the Green Mountains, home of the bald eagle.

Searching her brain for the information she'd read on how to operate a compass, she was pleased to see the well-worn path headed in the direction she wanted to go. A good sign in her book. So she stuffed the compass away and started hiking. The air might be cooler in the forest, but it was still an oppressive day. She took breaks along the way to sip her water and recheck her compass, and then kept walking, enjoying being alone. It wasn't so scary, and she didn't feel as lonely here. There was something truly magical about nature. Peaceful.

The quarry was farther than she first thought and more tiring than she ever imagined, but she felt good about her journey. She stopped a few times to photograph a raven and a Canada jay. She really wanted to see a saw-whet owl, but they only came out at dawn and dusk. Soon after, she came upon a stream, and a white-tailed deer with her baby popped their heads up and looked right at her, taking her breath away. Beautiful. She managed to get the shot before they darted off. She even saw a snowshoe hare and a red fox, but hadn't seen a coyote yet, which was fine by her. She came to a clearing with a stunning view of a pristine mountain lake surrounded by wildflowers, and a green meadow with sugar maple, butternut, white pine, and yellow birch trees beyond. This was going to be gorgeous in the Fall.

She took several pictures when a movement high in one of the trees caught her eye. She couldn't believe what she was seeing and held her breath, afraid she would scare it away. The most beautiful bald eagle sat majestically on a branch at the top of a tree, looking out proudly over his kingdom below. Lifting her camera up, she tried to snap a shot, but the eagle spread his graceful wings and flew to another tree. Without thinking twice, Anna followed, even though there was no longer a path. This was her moment. She wasn't sure why this was so important, but something deep inside her compelled her to follow, no matter what. Something about her future was riding on her capturing this shot.

Trailing the eagle for some time, she finally came to another clearing much higher up on the edge of a cliff. Stopping short over how high she was, she carefully lifted her camera. The eagle looked right at her, spread his impressive wings to their fullest span, and she snapped the perfect shot seconds before he soared off into the sky and disappeared for good. It took her a moment to catch her breath, and a feeling of accomplishment like no other filled her being. Photography had become her lifeblood, so rewarding and fulfilling. She told herself this life she'd chosen would be enough to fill the void in the pit of her stomach. Her pictures would be her babies.

She took a few photos of the valley down below and a couple of the mountain peaks off in the distance. A tranquil feeling settled over her. She felt like she was the only person on earth at that moment, closer to God than she would probably ever be, and her aunt's presence was all around her. Anna finally understood why her aunt had gone on so many adventures. That need for excitement and freedom. It was like being on top of the world. If only she hadn't died in a tragic accident, she could have experienced more before the angel of death told her it was time for her to go.

Suddenly Anna heard thunder.

Nearly jumping out of her skin, she looked at the sky and gasped. When had it gotten cloudy? Actually, it wasn't just cloudy, it was downright stormy. The sky looked angry, swelling with various shades of gray and enough moisture to rain down its wrath and flood the hills. The electricity in the air snapped and popped, reminding Anna that nature might be beautiful, but she was a temperamental beast. She'd heard about the intense thunderstorms they could get, especially when the heat and humidity were this high. It was probably time to head back home. She bit her bottom lip, realizing she didn't have a clue where she was now.

Anna moved away from the ledge and went to pull out her compass to figure out what direction to head next. Her hand stilled, and her heart leapt to her throat. It wasn't there. How could it not be there? She wouldn't panic. Maybe she put it in a different pocket. Taking off her pack, she carefully searched every pouch with no luck. It must have fallen out when she'd scrambled after the eagle. The wind picked up with a vengeance now, and the first wave of hysteria hit her. Her eyes darted about frantically. The days were longer, but she had spent all afternoon in the woods. It wouldn't take long before evening settled over the hills and the night creatures emerged.

Oh, God. She forced herself to breathe slowly and deeply and to think.

Another idea came to her. She pulled out her cell phone, hoping that maybe she would have at least one bar since she was in a clearing. She stood in several places and held her phone high. Nothing. Sighing, she put her phone away. Maybe if she retraced her steps, she would find her way back. Or at the very least, find her compass. A raven crowed ominously overhead, and a chill trickled down Anna's spine. It was a sign.

She'd faced her fear, and now her worst nightmare was about to come true.

❧

"SULLIVAN HERE," Clay barked into his phone while driving home after work, struggling to see through the rapid swish of his windshield wipers. It had started to rain hard, but that was nothing according to the weather channel. They were in for a doozy of a thunderstorm, the likes of which they hadn't seen in years. Everyone had been warned to stay inside.

"Oh thank God," Sarah said, sounding panicked.

He swerved sharply and pulled off the road, stopping just

shy of the ditch. "What's wrong?" If Jud had dared to come anywhere near them, he would rip his throat out and not think twice.

"It's Anna," Sarah said on a sob.

Sully's chest tightened to where he could barely breathe, the thump-thump-thump of the wipers matching the beat of his heart. He swallowed past the dryness of his throat. "What about her?"

"When Bobby and I got home, Anna wasn't here. She left a note saying it was a beautiful day so she was spending the afternoon in the woods. She was hoping to photograph the abandoned quarry, but it's getting late and she hasn't returned. I tried her cell, but it goes straight to her voicemail. You don't think she's lost, do you?" Sarah's voice cracked.

Sully cursed. Beautiful day, his ass. Crazy fool didn't know enough to check the weather forecast before heading out on a hike. "Sit tight, Sarah. Don't go anywhere tonight and keep your phone on in case she gets a signal and calls. I'm going after her."

"But the storm..."

"She won't survive on her own. I've been hiking, hunting, and tracking these woods since I was a boy. I'll get her and find a safe place to ride out the storm. We'll be back when it's over. I'll let Chief Fitz know in case we don't—"

"You will," Sarah blurted with a desperate tone. "You just have to."

Sully hung up and turned his truck around. He always kept his pack with supplies in the back, ready to go in case a story broke. Or in case he needed to get away from the town. The woods had always been his special place to shut the world out, to think, to dream. He'd just never imagined he would need his pack for a search and rescue mission. Several streaks of lightning lit up the sky like the strobe light parties of his youth, followed by the loudest crack of thunder he'd ever heard. The rain came down in a waterfall now.

What the hell had Anna been thinking?

He spotted her car right by the trail that led to the quarry. Pulling off to the side, he grabbed his rain slicker from the back as well as his pack, his climbing stick, and his gun. Woods at night were no place to be unarmed. He made a quick call to Tess, but she didn't answer, so he left a message. Locking his truck, he headed into the woods, his bum leg aching already. He made quick work of picking up Anna's trail. The rain hadn't washed it away yet, but it would soon. He couldn't bear the thought of any sign of her existence being washed away forever.

Like Cindy Taylor's had.

Traveling as quickly as he could, he followed Anna's trail for a long way, noting all the places she'd stopped to rest or take pictures. His leg throbbed like a son-of-a-bitch now, but he couldn't take a break. The storm was growing worse and the daylight fading quickly. The sky had darkened considerably with raging gray storm clouds, the trees taking a beating from Mother Nature's fury. When Sully found Anna—he refused to consider any other alternative—he would wring her pretty little neck.

He was taken back to the last time he had seen Cindy. It was a day just like today. They had planned to hike but had changed their minds when the storm clouds had rolled in. Sitting on the back of his truck to talk before going home was when she had told him her news.

"Sorry our day is ruined," Sully said.

"It's okay, it could never be ruined when I'm with you," Cindy said. "I only wanted to hike because I had something important to tell you." She tucked her long, golden-blond locks behind her ear and looked at him with trusting and hopeful baby-blue eyes. So young, so innocent, so full of life... and all his.

"You can tell me anything, babe. You know that," Sully said. "It's you and me against the world. We're a team. I can't wait to get the hell out of Mystic Valley and start fresh at NYU."

"I'm glad you think we're a team. I do too. I love you, Sully," she said.

"Me too, babe." He kissed her, feeling the softness of her skin and smelling her apple blossom shampoo. "This is going to be great, going away together. Only a couple more weeks."

She took his hand in her own. "About that." She wouldn't look at him, and the first wave of doubt washed over him. He was terrified of what she might say. Nothing good ever worked out for him. Just once he had thought he might catch a break, but the next words she spoke sealed his fate. "I didn't get in."

He felt the first punch to his gut, worse than what it would have felt like if his father had actually hit him. "What do you mean?" He knew damn well what she meant. He was just afraid of what it might mean for their future.

"I mean, I'm not as smart as you." She stared down at her lap, looking ashamed. "I didn't get into the college."

"That's okay, Cin." He lifted her chin until she looked at him. "There are other schools around there. I'm sure it's not too late to apply. Or we can get an apartment together, and you can waitress or something until you do get in. The point is, we're out of here. Off to conquer the world together like we said, right?" He hated that he sounded desperate.

She hesitated a bit too long, and a stronger wave of doubt slammed into him. "Or maybe we stay in Mystic Valley and go here to the community college. It's much cheaper, and we can still get a place together. As long as we have each other, everything will be okay, right?"

He clenched his jaw. What was she doing? She knew how he felt. All this talk about changing their plans was blindsiding him. "I can't stay here. You know that," he finally said, trying to keep calm. "I need to be away from him." He didn't need to say his father's name anymore. She knew who he meant. She knew everything about him. She was the only person who had always been there for him, and he loved her.

"And I can't leave." She started to cry.

"Why?" He shook his head.

"Because I'm pregnant," she said, on barely more than a whisper.

Her words cut him deep, like a sharp knife thrust straight through the heart, and he felt the searing pain through every nerve ending in his body. When he finally caught his breath, he said, "What did you just say?"

"I said I'm pregnant, and you're the father," she said louder, almost defiantly.

"No, this isn't happening," he growled, looking at her like he no longer recognized her. He could have handled anything but this. "You know how I feel about my father. You know that I never want kids, *ever*. We were always so careful. How could this happen?"

She didn't need to say a word. He read it in her eyes. She'd sabotaged his efforts and had gotten pregnant on purpose to trap him.

"I'm sorry," she finally said almost desperately. "I love you and thought a baby would keep you here with me. I just didn't want to lose you, babe." She reached out to him, but he jerked away from her.

"And now you have." A cold like he'd never felt seeped through his bones and hardened his heart. The only woman he had ever loved had betrayed him. He couldn't forgive what she had done to him on purpose, knowing how he felt. She'd ruined everything. "I don't love you anymore," he said coldly, "and I'm leaving anyway. You're dead to me." His gaze dropped to her stomach. "You both are."

She gasped in shock and then covered her mouth with the realization that her plan had backfired. The thunderstorm started raging at that moment, as though it felt his pain and was doling out its wrath at the injustice of it all. With one final look, he saw the regret and sorrow in her eyes for what she'd done and for all she had lost because of it. She leapt off the back of his truck and took off into the woods, taking all his hopes and dreams with her.

Anger consumed him. Life was so fucking unfair. Young and angry and stupid, he climbed into his truck and drove away, damning her and leaving her on her own. He didn't get far before his guilt had him turning around and going after her, cursing every step of the way. He searched high and low, but he couldn't find her. That's when panic and shame and regret set in. His only hope was that Cindy had been a child of the woods for as long as he had. If anyone knew how to hide from him and survive, it was her. At the time, he'd been pissed and heartbroken. He'd cried like a baby for all that he had lost, he'd just had no idea he would never see her again.

A loud crack of thunder had him snapping back to the present. Here he was searching for another woman who had tied him up in knots. Anna Wilks and her goddamned thank-you dinner. She'd been so sweet and kind and alluring, she was tempting him beyond reason. She acted like she was some worldly woman who could have a simple affair with no strings attached, but he suspected otherwise. She just didn't seem like an affair sort of woman. She would want more than he could give. He could tell. So he'd done what he always did.

Ran away.

He'd stayed away as much as possible the last couple of weeks, yet here she was sucking him back in. He tripped over something on the ground, then bent down to pick it up. Cindy had known how to survive in the woods, yet she'd gone missing never to be found. Anna didn't have a goddamned clue. He held her compass in his hands and cursed. Anger and panic set in once more, propelling him forward.

Where the hell was she?

A while later, he spotted her tracks as they veered off the path. He followed them toward the cliff and held his breath as he looked over the edge. Relief flooded him when he didn't see her down below. A noise sounded above him, and he looked up. What in the world?

"Miss Wilks?" he barked.

She looked down and gave a little cry. "Sully, is that you?"

"Yes, it's me, dammit!" He couldn't help yelling at her. She'd scared him half to death, and he was pissed off. "What the hell are you doing up in that tree?"

"I-I got lost, and m-my phone died, and I-I couldn't find my compass, and I." Sniff, sniff, sob. "I heard a noise and thought I saw a bear. I was always good at climbing trees when I was little." More sniffs and sobs.

He couldn't help but soften. "Apparently, you still are," he said with less bite to his words. He was still angry at her, but he was just so damned relieved to find her alive that he chuckled softly. "There's no bear around here, honey. You're okay." *Honey?* He snapped to attention and cleared his throat on a frown. "You're more in danger of getting struck by lightning or falling down and breaking your neck from the rain than getting attacked by a bear. Come on down and we'll find some shelter. It's too dark and stormy to head back home now." He tried to keep his tone logical, and his emotions in check.

"But Sarah will be worried sick."

Anna talked as she climbed down the tree. She slipped toward the bottom, but Sully caught her. She held on tight to him, shivering as she stared up at him like a drowned rat, rivets of water streaming down her cheeks. The shivers were probably more from shock and fear than anything else. It wasn't exactly cold, but the rain had cut through the heat and humidity, not to mention the temperatures dropped significantly in the hills at night. He held her in his arms while he talked, not quite ready to let her go, needing to touch her to believe she was truly safe.

"I already talked to Sarah. Chief Fitz too. They all know I'm a good tracker. They won't start worrying until tomorrow, and by then we'll be home."

He finally set Anna on her feet, pulled off his rain slicker, and then slid it over her head. She pulled up the hood and wiped her face, looking so small with his jacket engulfing her as it hung to her knees.

"Thank you, for everything." She pulled herself together and stopped crying, standing brave like she was ready for a good scolding. Like she knew she deserved one.

It only took seconds before he was as soaked as she had been. He didn't have the time or energy, or maybe he was getting soft in his old age. Whatever the reason, he just grabbed her hand and let the matter drop for now.

"Come on," he said. "There's an old hunting cabin nearby."

She blinked in surprise, but took his hand and followed beside him without a word. He held on tight, not about to let go, and a feeling he was too scared to identify did the same to his heart. He was falling for her just like he had for Cindy, and there wasn't a damn thing he could do about it, he thought. Then another thought kept running through his mind like a skip in a record...

At least this time he hadn't failed.

14

Anna slipped her wet clothes off, took a hot shower, and dried her shivering body with a towel. There were a few sets of sheets and blankets in the linen closet as well. The cabin belonged to a couple of guys from town whom Sully knew. He said they wouldn't mind them using it. Besides, the men only used it during hunting season, which wouldn't be until the Fall. That was the one thing about the folks in Mystic Valley.

They took care of their own.

The cabin consisted of one bedroom with several cots, one bathroom with a linen closet, and one big main room with a couch, some chairs, a kitchen table, a cooking area, a refrigerator, and a fireplace. No television or cable, but they did have electricity and hot water. The place was warm, dry, and clean. A surprisingly nice smell of maple cedar filled the room. She didn't imagine the cupboards would be stocked with food yet, but she had noticed a bit of wood by the fireplace.

Anna couldn't exactly put her wet clothes back on, so she wrapped a sheet around her body, toga style, with nothing but her birthday suit on beneath, her wet hair falling in soft waves beyond her shoulders, and her face without make-up and natural. She had to admit she felt a little thrill and a bit daring at being so free. Carrying her wet burden, she walked into the main room and was relieved to see Sully had built a fire, the smell of burning oak filling the air. He looked up as she neared him, and he stopped moving, staring at her with hooded eyes and his lips slightly parted.

"Shower's all yours," she said, feeling totally exposed under his scrutiny. "If you bring me your wet clothes when you're done, I will hang them to dry by the fire.

He nodded once as though realizing he was staring, then quickly left the room. Moments later the shower turned on, and Anna smiled. He was such a big burly bear, yet there were times when he was so gentle, doing nice things for people instinctively and not even realizing it. Like with the fire, and earlier when he gave her his jacket. She had felt safe in his clothes with him holding her. She had thought he would holler at her when he first saw her, but he hadn't. He'd been calm and rational and strong when she'd needed it most.

She had expected Drew to come after her, or one of the other officers, or even a firefighter. She'd been surprised to see Sully, yet so relieved and pleased that she couldn't help but cry. He was the only person she had been thinking about the whole time she'd been up in that tree. She didn't really understand what was happening between them. Why him? He was so wrong for her on so many levels, but her heart didn't care. There was something about him that made her want to hold him in her arms and kiss his pain away. She had tried, but he wouldn't let her, and she didn't have a clue where to go from here. For now, she felt the need to do her part. Do at least something to pay him back.

Bringing two chairs from the kitchen closer to the fire, she draped her shorts, t-shirt, bra, and underwear over one. Heading back to the kitchen, she dug through her pack and pulled out the two granola bars she'd brought with her. She didn't have any water left. Rummaging through the cupboard doors, she didn't see any more food, but she did find a bottle of bourbon. There wasn't any ice, but she located some glasses. She brought the granola bars, the bottle of bourbon, and the glasses over to the couch and set them on the coffee table in front of it.

Sully joined her a few minutes later, wearing just a towel wrapped tightly around his waist. Now *she* was the one to stare. She'd known he was well over six feet tall and that he had a muscular frame, but she'd had no idea he looked so manly. His shoulders were wide, his arms corded with muscle, and his stomach flat, but his chest was what held her attention. The perfect amount of dark hair covered his pectoral muscles, thinning as it tapered to a fine line down his abs, only to disappear beneath his towel. His legs were thick and long below the towel, but then she saw a jagged scar that ran from mid-thigh down to mid-calf and her heart melted. The pain that must have caused looked unbearable

Her gaze lifted to his slightly amused one. "Did I miss a spot?" he asked.

"A-a spot of what?" She cleared her suddenly dry throat.

"With the way you were inspecting me, I thought I must have missed a spot of dirt."

"Oh, no. Everything looks perfect." Her cheeks heated. "I mean, you look clean." She stood and grabbed his clothes from him, turning her back. "I'll just hang these up to dry." She draped his jeans over one side of the chair and his t-shirt over the other side, her face coloring even more when she realized he hadn't worn any underwear. It seemed way too intimate a detail to know he preferred commando.

She inhaled slowly, hoping her cheeks had cooled a little as she turned around to face him. He'd moved over to the couch already. Keeping her eyes up above his collarbone, she sat down beside him. It was too early to go to bed. She swallowed hard, not really having thought of where they would sleep until now.

He seemed to be at a loss for words as well. Finally, he blurted with his gravel voice, "Want a drink?"

"God, yes," she said so forcefully, they both laughed.

Just like that the ice was broken. He opened the bourbon and poured them each a healthy amount. He handed her a glass, and she handed him a granola bar.

"Dinner is served." She grinned.

"My favorite," he said. "You shouldn't have."

"The infamous Mr. Sullivan has a sense of humor. Will wonders never cease?" she teased.

"When I'm too exhausted to be angry, I use humor to ease my tension," he said on a more serious note, as he hoisted his foot with a wince and rested it on top of the coffee table. He rubbed his knee.

"I like the lighter side of you." Her voice turned serious as well. "Does your leg hurt much?"

"Sometimes. Especially when the weather turns." He swirled the brown liquid in his glass, staring deep into its depths as though remembering.

"How did it happen?" She took a sip of her drink and waited patiently.

"In a bunker in Afghanistan." His face turned dark with memories that must haunt him. "I was allowed to cover the fighting, but I got a little too close to the action. Lost a lot of good men that day, press and soldiers alike. Diego and I almost didn't make it out. I don't talk about it much."

Taking his cue, she changed the subject. "Thank you for saving my life today."

"You're welcome." He frowned, and some of his initial anger pinched his features. "Don't you ever check the weather?" he snapped a little harshly.

"And he's back," she said on a soft chuckle.

He seemed to deflate at her words, as though all the anger he carried around on a daily basis exhausted him. He took a big swallow of his drink this time, and relaxed. "Sorry, but you scared the shit out of me."

"Don't be sorry." She nodded, taking a healthy drink of her own. "I deserved that. It was a gorgeous day. Now that the festivals are done until the Fall, I was getting antsy. I thought about what you had said in regard to expanding my brand to include wildlife and scenic shots. I didn't even think to check the weather. I thought I was so smart. I was going to face my fear of the woods and prove to everyone that I could take care of myself. All I proved was how green I really am." She fought back the tears that threatened to fall. "Maybe you were right. Maybe I don't belong here. I was so terrified. I don't know what I would have done if you hadn't found me."

He poured both of them more bourbon, the warm haze of alcohol loosening their tongues as he said something she never expected. "Cindy Taylor disappeared on a day just like this."

"Wow," Anna digested his words before adding, "so that's why you volunteered to come after me. You were hoping for a little retribution." His being here suddenly made sense. She felt a little disappointed that he hadn't really come for her after all.

He looked pensive and then finally said, "I couldn't let history repeat itself."

"I'm grateful you didn't." That much was true.

"That's not the only reason I came. You had a big part in my being here." His gaze met hers, making her pause and giving her hope. "I've gotten to know you. Care about you," he admitted, and added on a mumble, "At least you're not pregnant."

Anna choked on her bourbon. "Excuse me? Pregnant?" The ever-present pain sliced through her, and she added with bitter sadness, "No, no chance of that." There would be no retribution for her, she thought, then she studied him as realization dawned. "Does that mean that Cindy Taylor was pregnant when she went missing?" Anna stared at him in shock, wondering how come she had never heard about that.

Sully sighed deeply, still staring into his drink. "That's what we fought about. She knew I didn't want kids. I've yet to see a man who was worth a damn as a father. No way was I taking the chance of being like my old man. Yet she tricked me by getting pregnant on purpose to try to keep me here. It didn't matter that she didn't get into the same college. She could have gone with me anyway. I would have taken care of her. But she had to go and ruin everything. So I told her I was leaving town anyway, and she took off. I let her. I wasted precious seconds by driving away. When I returned, I couldn't find her anywhere, and the storm was raging by then. I made it home, but no one ever saw Cindy again. I never told anyone she was pregnant. That's my dirty little secret." He took a drink. "Guess I'm not so clean after all."

Anna took a minute to let his words sink in. He'd been given such a gift. One she would have given anything for, and yet he'd walked away from that. She didn't understand how he could do that, but then the rest of his words registered. He'd been so young and had gone through so much with his own father. She remembered him saying his best friend's father had abused him, so he'd never witnessed a good role model. He'd vowed never to have children, and Cindy knew that, yet she'd gotten pregnant on purpose anyway.

She'd tried to trap him, and that wasn't right. And he did say he went back and tried to find her. Anna's heart went out to him, for the young, confused boy who had made a mistake but was too late to do anything about it. He'd had to live with that mistake for so many years since, and it was obvious the toll it had taken on him. Who was Anna to judge? There was nothing to do other than forgive him.

The question was, could he ever forgive himself?

"You're not alone in keeping secrets, you know," she finally said.

"I doubt a woman like you has any dirty little secrets." He grunted, finishing his drink in one swallow of self-pity.

"Maybe not dirty, but there is something I haven't told anyone in town." She finished her own drink.

That piqued his curiosity. He studied her before asking, "Yeah, what's that?"

"That I'm broken."

His brow puckered. "You look fine to me."

"I might act like I'm okay, but trust me. I'm anything but fine." She took a deep breath and let it out slowly. "My husband didn't just divorce me. He found out I was infertile, got another woman pregnant, and then left me. She was whole and young and perfect. While I was old, used up, and broken. I don't blame him really. We both wanted a baby more than anything in the world. More than we wanted each other, I now realize. If I were him, I wouldn't want me anymore either."

"I'm sorry for what you went through," Sully said softly, reaching out and threading his fingers through hers as if it were the most natural thing in the world. It somehow felt so right, like two broken pieces of a puzzle that made a perfect whole when put together.

She stared at their joined hands for a moment and then lifted her eyes to his. "I'm sorry for you, too. You shouldn't be so hard on yourself."

"Neither should you. No one is perfect. We're all a little broken in some way." He rubbed his leg with his free hand. "Your husband was an idiot. You're not old or used up, and I can't imagine any man not wanting you." There was electricity in the air between them as they continued to hold hands and study each other.

"You can't?" She hated how desperate she sounded, but she needed to feel desirable and needed.

"Why the hell do you think I've been staying away from you?" His stormy gray gaze was so intense.

"I figured you didn't like me all that much." She licked her lips.

"The problem is, *Anna*," he said her given name for the very first time with the soft gravel tone she'd come to adore. "I like you too damn much."

"Well, *Sully*," she responded in kind, and then channeled her aunt, shocking them both by finishing with, "prove it."

SULLY COULDN'T SEE STRAIGHT, his mind exploded with feeling as he held Anna in his arms. The truth was he hadn't thought about anything, period. He'd just reacted. One minute she was challenging him to "prove it," and the next thing he knew she was lying beneath him on the couch. He pressed his lips to hers again, tilting her head to the side and slipping his tongue inside her sweet mouth. He had wanted to kiss her for so long now, he'd just never dreamed the opportunity would ever happen, because he hadn't planned on letting it happen. She moaned from deep within her chest, and wrapped her arms around him as though she were starving and couldn't get enough.

He'd never felt so wanted before, and damn, but it felt good. Not thinking was probably a smart thing to do. He didn't want his doubts to creep in. Maybe it was the danger. Maybe it was the alcohol. Maybe it was their confessions. All he knew for certain was that he needed her so damn much. Too goddamned much. He drank from her like a man dying of thirst. She tasted so sweet, like honey and bourbon and Heaven. And her skin felt like soft rose petals beneath his rough fingertips. He had to slow down. The last thing he wanted to do was hurt her, but when he tried to pull back, she hooked her legs over his and drew him close.

He groaned in pleasure, breaking away from her mouth to kiss every inch of her face and neck, keeping most of his weight off her body on his one arm while he ran his other hand up and down her torso, lingering on her breasts. So perfect. Jesus, she was perfect. She whispered his name over and over on her lips, and he thought he would surely die. When her foot hit his bum leg, he couldn't help but cry out. He bit back a wince but didn't let it stop him.

"Wait," she whispered.

He stilled and dropped his forehead to hers as he squeezed his eyes shut and breathed heavy. "Please don't tell me you've changed your mind, love. I don't think I could handle that right now."

She lifted her fingertips and stroked his cheek, then ran her thumb across his bottom lip. "Not a chance. I just don't want to hurt you."

He chuckled from deep in his throat. "And here I was worried I would hurt *you*. If you hadn't noticed, I'm a whole lot bigger than you."

Her smile came slow and sweet as she pulled back to look into his eyes with her magnetic gaze. "Oh, I noticed how big you are. I meant I didn't want to hurt your leg. There are more positions than one, you know."

"It seems Miss Anna Wilks has a sense of humor as well," he said jokingly but with a voice that had grown husky. "I'm all for trying out other positions if you are. What's your pleasure?"

She kissed him softly. "You. Just you."

He took a moment to kiss her deeply, trying to show her

what he couldn't bring himself to say just yet. "I need you, baby," he finally broke away to mutter.

"I know." She ran her hands through his hair. "I need you, too."

Without another word, he rolled off of her and helped her to her feet. Standing before her, he dropped his towel. She took a moment to admire him, and then she bit her bottom lip in the way he'd come to love and slowly unwound the sheet that covered her.

"You're beautiful," he said in wonder, because it was true. Full breasts, beautiful curves, and silky skin. "I..." He clenched his fists by his sides, longing to touch and taste every inch of her, but he didn't want to frighten her with the intensity of what he was feeling right now. He'd been with plenty of women to fulfill his needs, but he'd never allowed sex to become personal. But this wasn't just sex. This was making love. All he knew was that he had never wanted anyone as much as he wanted Anna Wilks, and that scared the hell out of him.

"It's okay, Sully," she said softly as though she'd read his mind. "I want you just as much." She reached out and pushed him gently until he fell back on the couch, then she climbed on top of him, straddling him as she drew his mouth to her breast. He closed his eyes, wrapping his arms around her. Maybe it was okay to give in. Maybe it was okay to let someone take care of him for a change.

Maybe it was okay to feel again.

15

A nna slowly lowered herself until Sully was deep inside her. She cried out at the feeling of being one, the feeling of being complete, the feeling of finally being home. Sully ran his hands up and down her back and through her hair, and then settled them on her hips. For a moment they didn't move, just held each other tight and felt what it was like to be needed and wanted and loved. Anna couldn't help it. A small sob slipped out.

Sully froze. "What's wrong, baby? Did I hurt you?"

He leaned back and took her face in his hands, stroking her cheeks and wiping her tears away with his thumbs. His expression was one of concern mixed with adoration and something she was afraid to name. Afraid she would be wrong and her heart would get broken. Her own husband had never looked at her this way, or held her so tenderly, or loved her so completely. His betrayal had been bad enough, but something told her she wouldn't survive losing Sully.

Yet he wasn't even hers to lose...

She shook her head no, and touched his face with her own hands. "No, quite the opposite. Nothing's wrong. Everything's so very right. You said it yourself. I've never been good at hiding my feelings. This is all just so intense. I've never felt anything like this before. I'm just so afraid it will all disappear like a dream when morning comes, and you'll go back to not liking me and run away. I don't think I could bear that."

He relaxed, and almost wilted with relief. Running his hands over his face and then through his unruly brown curls, he took a deep breath and seemed to make up his mind about something. "I'm not good with feelings. Never have been. But I can tell you this." He looked deep into her eyes. "I've never felt this way either, and it scares me to death. I can admit that, but I'm not running." He kissed her so softly more tears slipped from her eyes. "I'm not going anywhere, baby. Whatever this is, we'll figure it out together, one day at a time. Think you can handle that?"

She sobbed and kissed him back, nodding her head as her heart filled with hope and happiness. Then she whispered in his ear, "Think you can handle finishing what we started?"

He stirred within her and started moving her hips as he nuzzled her neck. "Finish? Baby, we've barely gotten started. I don't plan on letting you sleep tonight or any night soon."

True to his word, they moved together in unison, slowly building with intensity, urging each other on until they both exploded on a sea of pleasure. Waves of physical feelings as well as deep emotions swept over them as they cried out to each other. After she collapsed on his chest, he lay on his back on the couch and drew her down on top of him, pulling the blanket from the back of the couch down over them.

Anna loved the feeling of his warm, naked flesh pressed against hers. Erik had never liked sleeping naked. Had never liked snuggling, period. Anna had always thought it brought a couple even closer, especially after making love. But lovemaking had only been about conceiving a child for Erik. The task had become so mundane, the romance had disappeared from their relationship a long time ago. In fact, she wasn't sure it had ever really been there to begin with. She had loved the idea of growing up and moving out of her parents' house. Moving on to the next phase of life, which for her had always been about getting married and having babies.

That was why this time was so much more fulfilling with Sully. He wasn't her husband, and they didn't have to worry about having a baby, so there was no pressure. Just pure pleasure. They weren't together because they had to be, they were together because they *wanted* to be. She kept stroking her fingertips over his chest, loving the feeling of the soft hair that covered him. Loving the rise and fall of his chest and the security it brought.

The fact that he felt the same way she did, and was afraid too, made him seem human and approachable. His vulnerability made this whole evening that much more special. She truly believed everything happened for a reason. She was meant to be with Clay Sullivan. She just knew it in her very soul. Yes, he was still damaged and had a lot to work through, but so was she. He wasn't a kid anymore. He had her. And she didn't have to be alone because she had him.

Maybe together they could finally heal.

Her head was on his shoulder with her face in the crook of his neck, her breasts pressed against his chest, her legs straddling one of his, his thigh pressed intimately against her groin, and the length of his pride and joy snuggled against her side. She bit her bottom lip on a smile, wondering if he'd fallen asleep. Growing bolder, she let her hand slide lower and lower until she brushed the top of his penis.

She heard his swift inhale of air and felt him stir beneath her fingertips. If he wasn't awake, he would be soon, and she wanted him to know that she wanted him as much as he did her. She took him in her hand and stroked the full length of him. The hand that was wrapped around her back dove lower in a direct path to pure pleasure, over her bottom, sliding two fingers straight to the heart of her womanhood.

She lifted her head on a cry of pleasure, which he captured with his mouth, thrusting his tongue deep. Her whole body vibrated with need as tingling sensations coursed through her. Without breaking contact with her lips, he lifted her hips as though she weighed nothing at all, and slipped inside her in a single movement until he was buried deep. Sensations exploded once more. They rode the wave of bliss together until it finally crested, bringing them back to the shore of happiness.

"This is crazy. It's like I'm in the middle of a dream," she said when she could finally breathe again, lying on top of him with him still deep inside her, where she planned to keep him for the rest of the night.

He pushed the hair back from her face and looked at her in a way that made her toes curl even though she'd just been more thoroughly satisfied than she had ever been in her life.

"I know, but I can't get enough." He nipped her chin with his teeth and then kissed the spot. Sliding his hands down her back, he rested them on her bottom, holding her to him tight. "If this is a dream, I don't want to wake up."

"Maybe we don't have to," she said. "At least not tonight." She wiggled her hips, half kidding, half hopeful.

"I was hoping you would say that," he said and kissed her again, unbelievably stirring within her once more. For the first time in a long time Anna Wilks was truly happy. She would be there one hundred percent for Clay Sullivan. She simply had no idea when she made that silent vow how very soon he would need that strength.

∽

"YOU READY?" Sully asked Anna the next morning.

They had made love countless times throughout the night, sleeping for brief periods in between, and then making love again just an hour ago. Yet looking at her now, he still wanted her. Wanted to be buried deep inside her and stay there forever. He began to wonder if it would always be this way. He'd loved Cindy, but they had been kids. He was older and wiser now, and Anna was all woman.

"No." She laughed, hugging him and burying her head in his chest as though she never wanted to let go. She smelled so good. "This cabin is a magical place where dreams come true."

He dropped his pack immediately and wrapped his arms around her, resting his chin on top of her head. He felt like he could hold her forever and never grow tired of it. "Me neither," he replied, "but if we don't head out now, they will send a search party our way." He glanced around the cabin that wasn't his, yet would always feel special to him now. "I don't want to taint the memory of this place. It really is magical, isn't it?"

"You're magical." She leaned her head back and stared up at him so lovingly, his heart warmed all over again. And then she kissed him softly.

"And you're a dream come true." He kissed her back just as softly.

"How did I get so lucky?" She grinned up at him.

"I'm the one who found an angel." He kissed her nose. "You're stuck with an ornery devil."

"You're not so ornery. Besides, I kind of like your pitchfork." She winked.

"Yeah? Hold that thought until tonight. I'm pretty positive I can make it rise to the occasion and keep your halo grounded."

"Oh my." She stepped back and donned her backpack, her cheeks tinted an adorable pink. "If we don't leave now, Mr. Sullivan, I doubt we ever will."

"Regretfully, I do believe you're right, Miss Wilks." He groaned and grabbed his pack, then led the way out the door.

The sun had just risen, the remnants of the storm all but forgotten. The peaceful forest stirred to life with sounds of animals scurrying about as they foraged for food, stirring up the scent of wood and pine needles. They made their way back to the path and down the mountain to the valley below. He hated the thought of returning to reality, especially in Mystic Valley. Now that he had discovered the beauty of Anna, he didn't want to share her with anyone. He'd punished himself for so long, obsessing over finding out what happened to Cindy, feeling like he didn't deserve to be happy. But then Anna Wilks had come along and changed his life. Maybe it was finally time to put the past behind him and allow himself to live again.

They reached the bottom of the forest. He stopped just before the exit and turned around to kiss Anna. He didn't say a word, just took her hand in his in a gesture meant to show her this wasn't the end. He hoped like hell it was the start of a new beginning. She seemed pleased and squeezed his hand back as though she would follow him anywhere. They stepped out of the forest by their cars and stopped short.

A crowd of people were gearing up to form a search party. When everyone spotted Sully and Anna, a cheer went up. Chief Tess Fitz raised a brow at their joined hands, looking a little disappointed, while Officer Drew Jones's shoulders wilted in defeat and resignation. Diego and Lynn came charging over to them, followed quickly by Sarah and Bobby, pushing Sully and Anna apart as each group hammered them with questions. They took a moment to answer the questions, but their gazes kept finding each other in a silent message that reminded each other they were a united front. In this together, for whatever it was and however long it lasted.

He just had no idea his world was about to turn upside down.

Chief Fitz shooed everyone back so she could talk to Sully alone. She eyed Anna, but Sully took Anna's hand once more and said, "She stays. Whatever you have to tell me, I want her to hear."

"Fine, that's your call," the chief replied, all business now, "but you might want to sit down for this."

He felt his face pale, and Anna gripped his hand harder to let him know she was there, no matter what. It gave him strength. "I'm good," he said. "Just tell me the news."

Tess stood straight and tall, not giving anything away by her expression. But when Drew stepped silently forward beside her as though to lend support, Sully began to worry.

"Jesus, Tess, what the hell is it?" he finally blurted, no longer able to stand the waiting.

"We found Cindy Taylor."

SULLY PACED BACK and forth in the lobby of the police station while Anna stood off to the side helplessly. He'd let go of her hand the moment he found out Cindy Taylor was still alive. Anna didn't know how to process that. She tried not to read too much into it. The news was shocking for all of them. He had said he wanted her to come along, but she wasn't sure why now. She suddenly felt like an intruder, an outsider, someone who didn't quite belong. He hadn't stopped pacing, hadn't talked to her, had started shutting her out just like he used to, just like she'd feared he would do again.

They had shared such an incredible night together. Something magical and beautiful had happened between them, and he had said he wanted to see where it could lead. But that was before the love of his life had returned from the dead. Over twenty years had gone by, but Anna had seen his face after hearing her name. He still loved Cindy. They were just waiting for Chief Fitz to finish talking to her before bringing Sully in.

The chief poked her head out the door. "She's ready for you, Sully." Tess glanced at Anna questioningly.

Sully started walking through the door, then stopped as though just now remembering her. He shot her a distracted glance and asked, "You coming?" as more of an afterthought.

"Sure," Anna said with a smile that felt forced. What was she doing? she wondered, but she followed him anyway.

They entered the interrogation room and sat down at the table across from a young woman about their age. Cindy Taylor. She was alive and well and beautiful, Anna admitted, with her golden-blond hair and vibrant blue eyes. But then anger surged through Anna on Sully's behalf. He might still love this woman, but Anna was "in love" with him. He might never feel the same way about her, but that didn't stop her from hurting for him.

Where the hell had Cindy Taylor been all these years?

"Hi, I'm Hope O'Malley." The woman held out her hand to Sully and smiled a little shy uncomfortable smile. "And you are?"

He frowned, staring at her with a confused hurt look that tore at Anna's heart. He shook Hope's hand, holding on tight and not letting go. She tugged and he finally released her, looking a little embarrassed. He cleared his gruff throat. "Clay Sullivan. I just... I can't believe you're alive. After all this time of never hearing from you. I get that you were mad at me, but what about your family? They didn't deserve to suffer for all these years. And why are you calling yourself Hope O'Malley when your name is Cindy Taylor?"

"Because, Mr. Sullivan," she said with a calm, patient voice as though she had given this explanation many times already, "up until yesterday I didn't know that I *was* Cindy Taylor."

He blinked, looking shell-shocked. "How is that possible?"

"Twenty-two years ago I was in a bad bus accident." She folded her hands on the table in front of her and stared at them as she talked. "I woke up in a Detroit Michigan hospital, having no idea who I was or where I had come from. Bus routes run all over the place with connections and multiple stops. I could have come from anywhere. The doctors had hoped my memory would one day return, but it never has." She looked up and smiled a little. "That's where I got my name. They called me Hope, never giving up on me: hope I would survive, then hope I would wake up, then hope I would remember. It just sort of stuck since I had to call myself something. I still don't know anything about my past," her eyes met his, "and I'm sorry, but I don't know you."

He looked pained at her words. Staring down at his own hands resting on the table as though he couldn't quite look at her, he said in barely more than a whisper, "What about the baby?"

She inhaled a sharp gasp. "You were the father?"

He lifted his gaze to hers and nodded slowly. Chief Fitz's normally blank face registered her shock, and Drew's frown revealed his disapproval. Anna wanted to reach out and take Sully's hand but was afraid he wouldn't allow it. So, she did nothing. Just sat there helplessly, not sure who to look at or what to do, feeling useless.

"They said I miscarried during the accident. I must have barely been pregnant, but I always wondered if there was someone out there who would miss me. Who would care that I'd lost our baby."

"I cared about you," Sully said, and Anna didn't miss that he left off a response regarding the baby. "Just not enough to keep you from running away that day."

"Is that what happened? I ran away? Why?"

Sully was nothing, if not honest. He looked her in the eye and said, "You wanted the baby. I didn't. You ran away. I let you go. No one ever saw you again, and I never stopped looking." He failed to mention she had tricked him and tried to trap him. He probably figured she'd been through enough. They all had.

"That's sad," Hope said.

"Yup." Sully's wall slammed back into place, but a small crack revealed the inner emotion he couldn't quite hide. "Tell me this much. Were you at least happy?"

Hope smiled a genuine smile that lit up her face. "I got a job at a car dealership. That's where I met Aiden O'Malley, my hero. I married him a year later, and we have three beautiful children of our own. They became my family. My life. I don't know how I would have made it all these years without them."

"I'm glad," Sully said sincerely.

"I do want to thank you," she added.

He looked surprised. "For what?"

"It was your media contacts who shared my senior picture. When I saw that picture, I knew instantly that it was me. I still might not remember who I am, but you've given me answers to so many questions. And you've given me my family back. It's going to take a while to get to know them, but I am thrilled that my children will finally get to meet their other grandparents. So yes, thank you from the bottom of my heart."

Sully nodded, looking like he couldn't speak past the lump in his throat.

"I truly am sorry I don't remember you," she said with a soft voice. "I heard we were quite the team."

"Inseparable." His lips tipped up into a small smile as he added in a quiet voice, "We loved each other."

"Just not enough," she repeated his words softly. "Well, Aiden always says everything happens for a reason. He's my soul mate. I hope that one day you find yours."

Anna was selfishly a little glad that Hope had moved on, and hoped that now maybe Sully could. But he didn't say a word in response to "soul mate." He hadn't said that he loved Anna, but then again, neither had she, even though she knew it to be true. She loved him more than she ever thought she could love anyone. Just as she knew he cared about her, but no matter how hard she tried, she couldn't shut out the voice that whispered through her mind...

Just not enough.

16

"Wow, that was heavy," Drew said to Tess after everyone left. Randy and Pam were still out at their desks, finishing up work, while Drew hadn't left Tess's side since Sully and Anna had emerged from the woods.

Drew still couldn't move past the fact that Cindy Taylor was alive. Or that she had been pregnant when she'd run away. Or that Sully had known, yet hadn't done a single thing to stop her. She seemed happy, but her amnesia and her miscarriage never would have happened if Sully had stepped up and done the right thing. That's what Drew would have done.

Then again, nice guys always finished last.

That point had been proven today. Once again, he'd missed out on getting the girl. It was clear that badass Clay Sullivan had won Anna Wilks' heart. It was written all over her face and in the simple act of holding hands. Sully was harder to read, but he had seemed just as taken with Anna... until Cindy Taylor had come back into his life, that is. Now it wasn't clear where his head was at. Drew just didn't want to see Anna get hurt. Maybe she needed something. Maybe he should check on her?

Maybe he should stop hanging around in places he clearly wasn't wanted.

"You can say that again," Tess replied with a grunt, sitting on the edge of her desk, startling him for a moment, but then he realized she was responding to his comment. "Christ almighty, I didn't see that one coming," she added.

"No shit." Drew dropped down beside her, and they both just stared straight ahead at a loss for words. "Just goes to show you never know what surprises life has in store. There really are actual miracles out there. I don't think I'll ever forget the look on Hope's parents' faces. To find out their precious daughter is alive and that they have grandchildren is amazing. Hope. She really has given hope to us all that something good can come out of something tragic."

Tess didn't say anything, just looked thoughtful and vulnerable and beautiful as she sat hunched over like she carried a heavy weight on her shoulders. She looked so put together on the outside, but he'd witnessed her "bad dream." More like a nightmare, if you asked him. All he wanted to do was wrap her in his arms and be there for her. If he were honest, he would admit Tessa Fitzgerald was the person he wanted to take care of the most. She was so damned stubborn and fiercely independent, he knew she would never allow it.

"You still having bad dreams?" he asked softly, his shoulder brushing lightly against hers, and the sparks between them were as strong as ever.

In predictable Tess fashion, she sat up straight until they were no longer touching and masked her expression. "Nothing I can't handle." She hopped off her desk, brushing off her need for anyone as she adjusted her uniform which was already perfectly in place. Same as the rest of her. "Speaking of that, now that the Cindy Taylor case is closed, we'd better find something else to do to stay out of trouble." She shot him a no-nonsense sharp nod and took off.

Drew watched Tess walk out of her office to update the other officers, and thought, maybe he didn't want to stay out of trouble. Maybe he was sick of coming in last from being the nice guy. Maybe it was time he caused a little trouble of his own.

SULLY DROVE over to Anna's house later that afternoon, but she wasn't there. Neither was Sarah. Knowing Anna, she was already at The Country Store, developing the pictures from her wild adventure. He turned around and drove to the store, thinking about the life-altering events that had happened in the last twenty-four hours.

His feelings for Anna Wilks were still so raw and new, he hadn't quite figured them out yet. All he knew for certain was that they were damned powerful. He loved Cindy Taylor—or Hope O'Malley now—but he wasn't *in* love with her. There was a big difference. She had been his first love, his savior during their youth, and he would always care about her. He was just so damned relieved she was alive and happy. He still felt a lot of guilt. If it wasn't for him turning his back on her that day, then she never would have run off or gotten in that accident or lost her memory. He was still ultimately responsible for the pain her parents had gone through and for the death of his child.

Further proof he wasn't meant to be a father.

He'd made a promise to Anna that he would ride this thing between them and be open to seeing where it led. He wasn't always good, but he *was* a man of his word. He only hoped it wasn't too late. She'd gone with him to the police station, but he'd been too distracted and in shock over hearing that Cindy was still alive. And then seeing her in the flesh, looking a little older but still so much like the girl who had once been the center of his world, he'd forgotten all about Anna. It had been hard to deal with the fact that all the memories he had created with Cindy—their entire childhood—didn't exist for her, which somehow tarnished the memories for him. All he could do now was move on.

After searching his heart all afternoon, he knew he wanted to move on with Anna.

Parking his truck outside the store, a tender smile came to his face when he saw her car. Just as he'd suspected, she was inside developing the pictures she took. He was glad she had found something that made her so happy. And she was damn good at it. Her ex had really been an ass to let her go just because she couldn't have children, but then again, Sully had let Cindy go just because she could. Still, Anna was perfect for him, and he was older and hopefully a hell of a lot wiser.

He made his way inside, but kept to the back. She stood at the counter, wearing the same shorts and t-shirt she'd had on when they had left the cabin just that morning. They'd donned the only clothes they'd brought with them, having dried overnight. The rest of the morning had been consumed with recounting the details of what had happened to them to the police and the newspaper, because in Mystic Valley, Anna's disappearance and Sully rescuing her was news.

The rest of the morning into the afternoon had involved discovering the long-lost Cindy Taylor, learning about what had happened to her, reuniting her with her family, and putting the case to bed. Sully had needed time to process everything that had happened, and his sweet Anna had let him with no question asked, but he had seen the sadness and worry in her beautiful eyes, regretting that he was the one who had put it there. If she let him, he planned to make it up to her in a big way.

"Thanks so much for getting to these so quickly, Sarah,"

Anna said, gathering up her photo envelopes. "I can't wait to see how they came out."

"You're welcome," Sarah said, looking and sounding so much more confident than she used to be. "You're going to love them. You did an incredible job."

"Let's hope those magazines think so. See you at home." Anna turned around and headed for the door, running smack into Sully and bouncing off his chest.

He grabbed her arms to steady her. "Hello, Anna," he said softly.

Startled, she looked up, seeming surprised that it was him. "How are you?" she immediately asked, always putting everyone else first. That was just one of the things he adored about her.

"I'm okay. I'm glad Cindy—or Hope—is alive," he said truthfully, "but I still feel guilty as hell."

"It wasn't your fault. You can't blame yourself for her amnesia or the loss of the baby. She sounds happy, and because of you, she now knows who she is. You need to forgive yourself."

"I doubt that will ever happen, but," he stared deep into her eyes, "I *am* ready to move on if you are."

Her eyelids fluttered as though she were struggling not to cry. "But I thought you still loved her."

"I do," he said honestly. "A part of me always will. She was my first love. My childhood. But I'm older now, and we're different people. I'm not *in* love with her, and she no longer is with me either."

"You're not?"

Anna bit her bottom lip, looking so hopeful and trusting, he wanted to kiss her right there in the middle of the store. What the hell? He leaned down and pressed his lips softly against hers, and all the feelings from the night before came rushing back, reaffirming what he already knew to be true.

"No, Anna Wilks, I am not in love with Cindy Taylor. Some

auburn-haired, impulsive, clueless, frustrating, gorgeous angel has stolen my heart so completely, there's no room for anyone else."

A tear slipped out and rolled slowly down Anna's delicate cheek. "She has?"

He nodded, cradling her face and wiping her tear away with his thumb. "She has. I don't know what she sees in me, or how she's so patient and understanding, or why she's willing to put up with my ornery ways, but she miraculously is. That's why she's my angel. I think God sent her here to save me from myself. He must have known I was halfway to Hell."

"Or he knew she would really like your pitchfork." Her smile came slow and sweet, but he swore he saw a bit of the devil within her as well.

He threw back his head and laughed the first real, full belly laugh in a very long time. "What am I going to do with you, Anna Wilks?"

"I can think of a few things." She stared at his lips.

He felt himself stir and he bit back a groan. "And I want to hear all about them later, at my place, over dessert. But first we have to eat."

"Why, Mr. Sullivan, are you asking me out on a date? Are you sure this isn't just a thank-you dinner?" She teased.

"Make no mistake, darlin', this *is* an official date. That's what moving on involves." His tone turned serious. "When I said I was all in, I meant it." He kissed her softly and then winked. "But there's nothing that says you can't thank me later."

I AM AT PEACE. *Scared as shit about what the future will bring, but still at peace. I don't regret not having chemotherapy or radiation. My cancer was too far along, so all the treatments would have done*

was prolong my life, not save it, and at what cost? I would have been so sick that I would have missed out on such grand adventures, or spending quality time with my sweet Jordanna. I only wish I hadn't wasted so much time. If only I had lived my entire life instead of just the last year, checking off all the things on my bucket list. But I have no regrets. I am happy, and my little Jordanna is seeing what it's like to be courageous and daring and free. She is more like a daughter to me than if I'd had one of my own. More my daughter than her own parents. All I can hope for is that she will read this one day and live her life to the fullest. It's never too late to start living.

Even if you simply start with baby steps.

ANNA CLOSED her aunt's journal once more. Her smile came so much easier these days. Her aunt was right. It was scary not knowing for certain what the future might bring, but it was worth the risk. If she hadn't put herself out there and taken a chance on happiness, then she never would have started living. She hadn't been living when she was with Erik. She had been existing. And all that had gotten her was a barren, broken heart.

Anna was in heaven these days. Sully had been amazing. When he wasn't at her house, she was at his, or they were somewhere in town together. Everyone had come to know them as a couple. Sully still hadn't forgiven himself, but he had warmed up considerably, finally letting people in. They'd gone to the county fair in August, and now that it was September, they were gearing up for the Fall Harvest and Apple Festivals.

Anna's front door opened, and Sully walked in carrying her mail, wearing his usual jeans and t-shirt, minus the sport coat, since it was steaming hot outside today. He had promised he would stop by on his lunch break, and Sully always kept his promises. Dropping most of the letters on her kitchen table, he held one envelope behind his back. "What do you want more than anything in the world?"

"You," she said easily, wrapping her arms around him, standing on his boots with her bare feet. He'd gotten a haircut and he'd shaved, but a shadow was already tinting his cheeks, making him look as dark and sexy as ever. He smelled like the outdoors mixed with paper and ink, which somehow worked for him.

"Done, and nice try." He kissed her lips as he held the envelope high above his head so she couldn't reach it. "What else do you want besides me, which you already have, by the way?" He winked.

"Darn you're good." She stepped down and crossed her arms, then tapped her foot, trying to figure out what he was getting at.

He gave her a look that said he knew he was good, and then hinted, "Come on, baby, it can't be that hard to imagine what that dream would look like."

Her jaw dropped open, then she clamped her hands over her mouth. "Oh my goodness, is that...?"

"It is." He wagged his eyebrows. "Do you want me to open it?"

"No! Yes! I don't know..." She started to pace. "What if they say no?"

"Then you try again," he didn't even hesitate to say. "You and I both know the publishing business is bloody brutal. Pictures, words, songs—it's all hard. It's hard to get published, and even harder to stay published. But you don't give up, period. Publishing your dreams is only a little bit about making money, but it's mostly about seeing a part of you come to life. If it's no, then you try and try again, until you get it right and they say yes. And in the meantime, you still work for me."

"Okay," she said quietly while biting her bottom lip. "Open

the stupid envelope, already. I can't take the pressure of not knowing."

"You asked for it." He lowered the envelope and opened the back. He was so big and so strong, yet he looked as nervous as she felt. He unfolded the letter and stared at it with such stern concentration, that she couldn't tell what it said. Finally, he raised his eyes to hers. "I knew you could do it, babe. They want you. You're in."

She launched herself into his arms and he caught her easily, kissing the breath right out of her and touching as much bare skin as he could, which was a lot considering she had on a pair of short shorts and a skimpy tank top, with her hair piled high on her head in an attempt to beat the heat. Her old house didn't have air conditioning, and she preferred to leave the windows open anyway.

"I think it's time to celebrate," she said breathlessly.

"I was hoping you would say that. We'll have dinner and champagne tonight, but right now, I have something else in mind."

"I was hoping you would say that." She laughed softly, already kissing his neck.

He chuckled, still holding her in his arms as he carried her off to the bedroom.

An hour later, they emerged fully dressed and more than satisfied. He kissed her goodbye, getting ready to head back to work, but he stopped by the door and paused, suddenly looking unsure and vulnerable. "One more thing."

"Yes?" she asked. "Anything for you."

"Well, I brought something else along today."

She eyed him curiously. "What's that?"

"My toothbrush." He pulled a toothbrush out of the inside of his coat.

She arched an eyebrow. "Okay, what does that mean?"

"That I think it's time."

"For what?"

"For us to move in together." He held up his hand to stop her from saying anything. "Just think about it, okay?"

She nodded and watched him leave as her heart filled with joy. There's was nothing to think about for her. He still hadn't said he loved her, but he was definitely moving forward and living his life.

Baby steps, she thought. *Baby steps were just fine.*

"As you can see, we're all a bit concerned, Chief Fitz," Mayor Wilcox said. He twirled his hat around in his chubby hands, beads of perspiration dotting his bald head. It was September, but the temperatures hadn't cooled yet. Indian summer was upon them.

"No offense, Chief, but Drew never acted like this before you came to town," Officer Pam Calloway said, as though her preface made her statement okay. She swiped her gray hair to the side and walked over to stand by the mayor in a united front. They still hadn't publicly claimed they were a couple, but it was obvious to everyone that they were sweet on each other. They didn't even really hide it anymore.

"I have to agree with them, Chief," Randy said from behind the dispatch counter, still looking nervous every time he was around her. "Drew's been acting out of character for weeks now."

"What has he done this time?" Tess asked, feeling the start of a headache coming on.

"It's more like what he *hasn't* done," the mayor said. "Drew is our hero. This town counts on him to uphold the law, take care of his parents, and be there whenever anyone else needs him."

"Did you ever think you're all putting too much pressure on him?" Tess asked, and they looked shocked. "The only reason Officer Jones does all of those things is because he can't say no to anyone."

"That's not true," Pam said with a frown. "It's in Drew's nature to help people. He thrives on it."

"True," Tess said, but then added with a serious tone, "and this entire town takes advantage of that."

"I beg your pardon," Mayor Wilcox sputtered.

"Beg all you want, it's still true, and you all know it." Tess stared them each in the eye, feeling protective of Drew for some reason. She shouldn't care what people thought about him or did to him, and yet she did. More than she cared to admit even to herself. "Drew is way too nice for his own good."

"Not anymore," Drew said as he came strolling into the office, out of uniform, in a pair of jeans and a black t-shirt with his badge clipped to his belt.

"Whoa," Randy said, his lips parting in awe and a little bit of envy. He idolized Drew, which was dangerous for Tess if Drew was going to start becoming defiant.

"What do you think you're doing?" Tess asked Drew, trying not to think about how good he looked in plain clothes. He was an officer of the law, and she was his boss. Normally, he was her righthand man in enforcing her rules. Now was not the time for him to start blatantly disregarding them.

"Showing up for work," he responded with a cocky smile.

"Not without your uniform and late, you're not," she said, crossing her arms in front of her and lifting her chin high.

"Suit yourself." He saluted her and headed for the door.

"Where are you going?" she sputtered. This was *not* going

according to plan. Damn him for pushing her buttons. She had enough on her plate without having to worry about him.

"I could use a day off," he said and kept walking.

"Careful, Jones, or you're going to get more than a day off," she warned.

"Careful what you wish for, boss. It's your funeral." He winked and then left the building.

Her jaw was hanging wide open, and damned if she could get it to close.

"You see," Pam said. "That just ain't right. You done messed that boy up in the head somehow, like I knew you would. You ruined him, and now everyone else is going to fall apart. This whole place is going to fall apart." She shook her head, wearing a disapproving expression. She had warmed up somewhat to Tess being chief, but this sounded like a setback for sure.

Tess didn't exactly know how to handle it, and then suddenly she knew what she had to do. "I'll talk to him," she finally said. "Trust me, this won't happen again."

"You do that," the mayor said. "Because at the end of the day, the council is responsible for your job, and they aren't happy. They let the Cindy Taylor incident slide because the ending turned out okay, but you need to focus on Mystic Valley. Drew is a big part of our Fall festivals. This town, not to mention his own family, are counting on him to help. We can't have our police department falling to pieces."

She let the Cindy Taylor comment slide and tried not to grind her teeth. "You're right, and that's makes two of us who aren't happy. I'll take care of Drew, you can count on that," Tess said, as she grabbed her keys and headed out the door.

Goddamn Drew. What the hell was he thinking, blowing everyone off? Saying no to people who took advantage of him was one thing, but he'd blatantly ignored Tess's rules, pretty much operating on a life-according-to-Drew motto. Ever since Cindy's case had ended, they'd been wrapping up petty squabbles among the town folk while looking for a new case to jump into. Or she had, anyway, because she needed something more to do than write parking tickets and handle minor domestic disputes.

Drew, on the other hand, had slowly been slipping into this bad-boy persona, blowing off work, ignoring the citizens, and defying her rules. And for what? Just to piss her off? Well, she'd had enough. One way or another, she was going to find out what had happened to make him do a one-eighty. And then she was going to put an end to it once and for all.

She drove all over town, with no luck. He wasn't at any of his usual spots, or even at his home. Finally, she took a chance that maybe he was at the lake. The only other thing he'd mentioned that he liked to do for pleasure—when he wasn't doing every-thing else for everyone—was go fishing. He had said he could use a day off, and the weather was still warm. She drove a ways until she reached Mystic Lake, and couldn't believe her eyes. Sure enough, Drew was in his old pickup truck. At least he hadn't brought the company vehicle.

Pulling into the deserted parking lot, she parked right next to him under the shade of a big tree. He had the tailgate dropped down and was sitting on the back of his truck bed. He actually had a pretty sweet setup. He had a thick blanket thrown down, with soft music playing from a boom box, and a cooler of food and drinks. He didn't so much as flinch when she got out of her car, almost as if he'd been expecting her. Had planned for this moment. He just cast out his fishing line and slowly reeled it in a little, while singing along to the music in a rich, smooth voice that was surprisingly good. Actually, not so surprising since he was pretty much good at everything he did, which somehow made her even angrier.

"What the hell are you doing?" she asked in her most stern voice, with her hands on her hips.

He didn't look intimidated in the least. In fact, he looked hot. She clenched her jaw. He had taken off his shirt and sat in all his golden, naked-chested glory and faded torn jeans, as if he didn't have a care in the world. "Whatever the hell I want to," he finally replied with a slight smirk of his lips, turning his baseball cap around backwards, which made him look even sexier.

She ground her teeth and tried another tactic by climbing onto the back of his truck with him. Staring out at the water, she took several slow deep breaths until she felt calm. "Why are you doing this?"

"Don't you know?" he said, still not looking at her, but his smirk was gone, replaced by a quiet sincere expression. As though whatever he had to say was of the utmost importance.

"No, honestly, I don't." She sighed, her shoulders drooping a little. He confused her. She didn't like feeling confused. It clouded her judgment when she had learned the hard way to always be ready and keep her senses sharp. "I know I try to act tough, but the truth is, I'm scared to death underneath."

He stilled at her words and listened patiently.

"Being a cop is all I know. Ever since my accident, I've been gun-shy. I really thought I had earned this job. To find out my father secured it for me makes me feel like a failure. I'm so angry and frustrated with him. I know my father and brothers are just trying to protect me, but I want to make it on my own. I *need* to be independent. I'm terrified if I can't be a success in a place like Mystic Valley, then I never will make it anywhere else. You've been my righthand man." She took a breath and said the words she never thought she would say again, "The truth is, I need you."

"Did you love him?"

She blinked. Where the heck did that come from? "Who?" At first she thought he meant Sully.

"Your partner. The one who died," Drew said so calmly, still staring out at the water. "Did you love him?" He looked her in the eye finally, and the impact was powerful, the hazel color so warm and sincere.

Tess hadn't been expecting to talk about that day. A lump filled her throat. "Why do you want to know?" she asked, stalling, trying to figure out how to get the conversation back on track, how to reestablish control.

"Why do you think I've been acting like this?" he said.

She shrugged, at a loss for words.

"To get you to notice that I *am* there for you. Professionally and personally. I always have been. All you have to do is let me help you."

She tore her gaze away and stared out at the pristine water of Mystic Lake, surrounded by beautiful trees and flowers in a safe haven. Drew would protect her. She could trust him with her heart. She just couldn't trust herself, and she would die if anything bad happened to him because of her.

"I-I can't let you be there for me personally." Her voice hitched, and she hated the weakness he brought out in her. She didn't want to need anyone ever again. She couldn't afford to.

He dropped his pole to the ground and turned to her, taking her face in his hands and making her look him in the eye. "I'm not him, Tess."

Her lips trembled. "I know, but still—"

"But nothing," he growled, and swooped down to cover her mouth with his own, shocking the sense right out of her.

Chills coursed through her body, and she couldn't resist the pull of him. She melted into him, wrapping her arms around his neck. He tilted their bodies, laying her back on the blanket with him half on top of her as he deepened the kiss. For once in her life, she didn't think. She needed this. Needed him. Consequences be damned. Cold, harsh reality would return soon enough.

He stripped them both of their clothes, all while kissing any thoughts of resistance right out of her. Neither one said a word as they caressed and stroked each other to the brink of insanity, and then he entered her in one deep powerful thrust, claiming her in a way she had never been. She sucked in a breath and opened her eyes, floored at all she was feeling. He stared down at her with such passion and emotion, she was terrified of what it could mean, yet terrified of what she would do if he stopped.

But he didn't stop. He kept loving her with his eyes wide open and locked onto hers, witnessing all of her secrets as they both died a little and he sent her to heaven. This was a dream. A wonderful dream and something she had desperately needed, but eventually they would have to wake up. One of them would have to come to their senses before someone got hurt for real. But not now. Not yet. Not until they soared together in an explosion of sensation. When they floated back down to earth, he held her in his arms like he never planned to let her go.

After they had both finally caught their breath, she gave him one more chance. "So, Officer Jones, does this mean you'll return to normal duties?"

He actually seemed to consider her words, and then he said, "No, I don't think so. Something tells me your feathers need to be ruffled a time or two for any of us to get the best of you. Besides, I kind of like being the bad boy."

And there it was. Cold harsh reality at its finest.

"Is that right?" She sat up and swiftly put her clothes back on in an orderly fashion, as though he hadn't just completely altered her universe.

He sat up, staying defiantly naked, and looked at her with a hooded gaze. Really looked at her, right down to her soul.

"That's right. So tell me, Chief, what are you going to do about it?"

She looked him straight in the eye and said firmly, "Fire you."

~

"MORE GREAT PICTURES from the Harvest and Apple Festivals, Anna," Sarah said as she came home and dropped the envelopes on the living room table. "You really have a knack for taking pictures."

"Thanks." Anna smiled at Tess and gave Bobby a big hug before he bounded off to the kitchen for milk and cookies.

"What's wrong?" Sarah asked with a frown. "You don't look so well."

"I'm sure it's nothing. Maybe something I ate last night. Neither Sully nor I are very good cooks. We never should have experimented with seafood. I'll have to ask him if he's feeling off later when I see him."

"I just ran into him at the store, and he looked fine." Sarah's face puckered in concern. "If it was something you ate, then both of you would be sick."

"Maybe I have a summer flu, then." Anna shrugged. "I'm just feeling a little off. I'm a bit dizzy and I have a headache."

Sarah's face paled, her amber eyes looking huge. "You need to go see the doctor right away, Anna. What if something's wrong?" She started to pace, waving her hands about as she talked, growing more hysterical than Anna. "You can't mess with headaches. What if you have a brain tumor? You're so much like your aunt." She stopped and stared at Anna, looking like she was ready to pass out. "I can't lose you, Anna. I just can't."

Anna tried to stay calm for them both, even though Sarah's words were alarming to say the least. Anna had always been so much like her aunt; she had chosen to follow in her footsteps. She simply hadn't ever considered she might *literally*. The first thing she thought of was that Sully couldn't go through her dying. He couldn't lose her like he had Cindy. And Sarah didn't have any family. What would she do without Anna?

Anna took a deep breath, deciding not to panic just yet. "I'm sure it's nothing. I'm probably just getting my period. They are so irregular these days, I'm sure that's what it is. I always get headaches with my period. If it makes you feel better, I'll make an appointment with Doc Burns."

"Today, make it today. Right now. Here's the phone." Sarah yanked the phone off the table and thrust it at Anna.

"Okay, okay, but you seriously have to calm down before you're the one who ends up admitted to the hospital."

Anna took the phone and called the doctor's office. Doc Burns happened to have a cancellation and could squeeze her in if she went right now. She told Sarah, who stated immediately that she was going with her. Anna was pleased, because no matter how brave she acted on the outside, she was secretly terrified on the inside. She suddenly understood how her aunt must have felt. Anna still had so much living to do. It would be so unfair to take it all away now. She wasn't even close to fulfilling her own bucket list, and then there was Sully. She couldn't bear to think of life without him. No, she wouldn't go there just yet.

Ten minutes later, after dropping Bobby off at a neighbor's, they entered Doc Burns' office and Anna signed in. Sarah waited in the waiting room while Anna went through a series of tests. She had a cat scan of her brain, blood drawn, urine samples—a full exam basically. Now that she was fully dressed, she sat on the exam table while Doc Burns knocked on the door, startling her. It sounded like the angel of death knocking at her door, ready to deliver the news no one wanted to hear, but especially someone of her age. For a moment, she considered sneaking out the window. Maybe if she didn't hear the news, it wouldn't be real. But that wouldn't be fair to the people she cared about.

She sat up straight, not giving in to the temptation to be a coward. "Come in," she said at last.

He entered with a scary-looking stack of her test results.

She held up her hand, her heart suddenly beating furiously. Maybe she would have a heart attack and die of that first. "Wait!" She swallowed hard. She didn't want to die of anything except old age, in her sleep after living a long, full life. Her shoulders wilted as her voice came out timid and weak. "Can Sarah come in for this?"

Doc Burns was a jolly old man in his sixties, with thinning gray hair, round glasses, kind eyes, and a friendly smile. Even his practice was warm and friendly. He had a much better disposition than Erik's friend, Dr. Hamlin, had on that awful visit one year ago on another sunny day in September. If she was going to get bad news again, then at least it would come from a man with a heart.

"Sure thing, Miss Wilks." The doctor left the room and returned with Sarah moments later, after fetching her himself. Just one more thing to like about him. He added such a personal touch to everything he did.

Sarah rushed over to Anna's side and held her hand without having to be asked. She really was like a younger sister to her. Anna felt a huge lump form in her throat. If she didn't make it, Sarah would be vulnerable to Jud. She had come out of her shell and grown so much since leaving him, but Anna wasn't sure Sarah was strong enough to stay away if Anna weren't around. The thought of what might happen to Sarah and how Bobby might grow up was too much to even consider.

"Okay, I'm ready, Doc." Anna smiled bravely.

"I sure hope you're ready," he said, looking through all the tests one more time, nodding in confirmation of whatever he was seeing.

"Ready as I'll ever be, I guess." She had to be strong. Just like her aunt. She could get through this with dignity.

"I was hoping you would say that." He looked up at her with twinkling eyes. Why was he smiling? People didn't smile over bad news, did they? "Congratulations. Your tests look great. You have a clean bill of health, Miss Wilks."

"Thank you so much," she said on a rush of relief, her limbs feeling like overstretched rubber bands, but then she frowned as the rest of his words sank in. "Wait, if I'm healthy, then what do I have to be ready for?"

"Why, motherhood, my dear."

The same pain that always shot through her at the mention of being a mother hit her hard. "Unfortunately I'll never be a mother." This was a small town. After she had opened up to Sully and Sarah, she'd told a few more people, even Misty, about her infertility. She had thought he would have heard.

He looked at her sympathetically. "Of course you will." He smiled with reassurance and patted her hand. "I think you will make a fine mother."

"Maybe someday, if I'm lucky enough to adopt," she said carefully, thinking he must be growing senile to have missed the problems with her ovaries after all the exams and tests he had run on her. "I'm infertile, Doctor Burns."

He frowned. "No, Miss Wilks, you're not. What you are is perfectly healthy and very much pregnant."

Pregnant, pregnant, pregnant...

Anna felt her eyes roll back in her head, as her brain was stuck on that one word that would change her life forever. That was the last thing she remembered as she fainted and fell back on the exam table with Sarah holding on tight.

18

S ully pulled into his driveway and smiled for the first time that day. Anna's car was in a little spot right beside where he parked his. A perfect fit, like the spot had been made just for her. Same as the place in his heart that she now occupied. It had been a slow, boring, tedious week at work. Not much going on that was newsworthy these days. He cut the engine and climbed out, wanting nothing more than to hold the woman he loved in his arms.

He could admit it now. It had taken him a while to fully understand that what he was feeling was love. He hadn't believed it was possible to fall in love again and be happy. What he'd felt for Cindy had been nothing compared to the feelings that Anna brought out in him. She'd helped him heal after Cindy, and she'd shown him it was okay to forgive himself and be happy. He deserved to be happy.

They both did.

Tonight was the night he was finally going to tell her he loved her. He was *in* love with her. And he was prepared to take the next step together, whatever that may be. She'd moved her toothbrush and a few other things into his place, same as he had hers. She didn't want to leave Sarah alone at her house, and he didn't want to sell his mother's place to just anyone, but there had to be some kind of compromise. All he knew for certain was that he wanted to wake up next to Anna for the rest of his life.

Opening his front door, he was greeted with the most amazing aromas of beef pot roast, mashed potatoes, gravy, cooked carrots, and fresh-baked bread. He could get used to eating a home-cooked meal made with love for him, and preparing one in return, but he especially liked the idea of heating up the kitchen together.

He set his briefcase on the table by the door and smiled tenderly when he saw Anna stirring the pot of gravy with her back to him. The heat had finally broken, and the first cool breeze of Fall drifted in through his kitchen window. She'd left it cracked open, hating to be cooped up like she had been back in the city. She wore a pair of soft cotton, flowy lounge pants in red—his favorite color—with a long-sleeve white t-shirt that was just begging for his touch. She'd scooped her hair into a messy bun while she cooked, but she'd left her feet bare. He loved went she went around barefoot with her pink painted toenails.

It was sexy as hell.

He took a moment just to admire her, his heart swelling with so many things he couldn't wait to tell her, but first he needed to hold her in his arms and feel her heartbeat against his. He wrapped his arms around her and gently kissed her neck. She let out a cute little squeal and jumped, but then spun around in his arms to give him a welcome kiss, which turned into a let's-skip-dinner-and-go-straight-to-dessert kind of kiss. They broke apart for air and he rested his forehead onto hers, thinking he would never grow tired of her kisses. Never grow tired of her and what they had together.

"Hey, there, beautiful," he said softly.

"Hey, there, yourself, handsome." She laughed. "Are you hungry?"

He leaned back and looked her in the eye, knowing his desire was blazing hot already. "Can't you tell?"

Her cheeks flushed a dusty rose—another thing he adored about her—and she rested her hands on his chest until he felt the heat from her fingertips. "Dessert will come soon enough," she said in a voice just as husky as his. "Let's eat before everything gets cold."

"Thank you for making dinner." He reluctantly pulled away from her and helped bring everything to the table, grabbing a bottle of red wine along the way.

"You're welcome. I was happy to return the favor after you cooked last night. So how was work?" she asked, while they sat down and he poured the wine. She held her hand over her glass in a gesture of "no, thanks," so he set the bottle down.

"It was okay. Things are too damn quiet around here lately. I might need to stir up some drama before I go insane," he said jokingly, but then frowned when she averted her eyes. "You okay?"

"I'm fine." Her gaze met his and she smiled brilliantly, making him relax. She truly did look fine. She looked amazing, in fact, her cheeks glowed with good health.

"Good, I'm glad to hear it. How's work for you?"

He dug in and ate with gusto as he listened to her go on passionately about the latest group of pictures she'd taken. She still took nature shots, but these days she checked the weather and brought a GPS along at his insistence. He couldn't bear the thought of losing her for good this time, and she seemed to sense that, because she hadn't protested one bit. He could listen to her talk all day, loving the way her voice got all excited and breathy sounding when she was passionate about something, which made his body stir once more.

He sat back and took a hefty drink of his wine, pushing the thought of dessert aside. They needed to talk first. "The food was delicious, but now that we're finished, there's something I want to talk to you about." He rubbed his sweaty palms on his thighs, suddenly nervous. He didn't open up very easily because sharing his feelings and baring his soul was hard for him. But she made him want to. She made him want to do a lot of things.

"Funny you should say that. I have something I want to talk to you about as well." She looked just as nervous as him, which was uncharacteristic for her.

"Ladies first. Mine can wait." He'd rather she got off her chest whatever was bothering her, so he could make it all better by telling her that he loved her.

She bit her lip. "You sure?"

He nodded. "Absolutely. You can tell me anything, you know that." Maybe she was going to tell him she loved him first. Neither of them had said the words, though he was pretty certain she felt the same way he did. Not wanting to steal her thunder, he was more than happy to let her go first. Then maybe saying the words back to her would be easier.

She took a breath and smiled, relaxing a little. Letting her gaze meet his, she said, "I went to the doctor's office today."

Panic surged through him at her unexpected words and the terror they brought. He'd felt the same way when his mother had told him she was sick with breast cancer. "What's wrong? Are you ill?"

Anna quickly squeezed his hand. "I'm fine. I was afraid the seafood had made me sick, but nothing's wrong with me. Sarah went with me to Doctor Burns, and it turns out that everything is alright. I found out some great news today. In fact, it's a miracle. You see, because I never thought this could happen to me in a million years. I mean, I had hoped and dreamed for so long that it could be possible, but then they told me it wasn't possible and could never happen. That's what makes this news so special."

With each word she spoke, he could feel the color drain from his face. He found it hard to swallow, his throat suddenly bone dry. Air. He couldn't get enough air. His head started to spin and his vision blurred a bit. She stopped talking and reached for him, but he pulled his hand away before she could touch him.

"What are you saying, Anna?" he could barely get the words out.

She swallowed once and looked at him with suddenly wary eyes. "I'm pregnant."

And just like that his world bottomed out from beneath him.

"Please, say something, Sully." She wrung her hands before her.

All he could see was Cindy's face twenty-three years ago. She'd worn the same expression. One of guilt and worry and fear... and a grain of hope. Anger surged through him at the injustice of it all. Why would God put him through all of this again? Anna had known just like Cindy did that he didn't want children. He was a man now, not a young kid, but that didn't change the fact that he was terrified he would be a horrible father. He'd opened his heart and allowed himself to fall in love again, only to be blindsided once more. He couldn't go through this again. It was all too much.

"Sully, speak to me, please. You look like you're about to pass out." She sounded ready to cry. He could hear the vulnerability in her voice. He wanted to take her in his arms and make it all okay, but he couldn't because it *wasn't* okay. None of it was. He was afraid none of it would ever be okay again.

He shook his head. "How? Why? You told me you were infertile." He finally looked at her and let all his anger and doubt and sense of betrayal fill his eyes.

Pain flashed through hers and she literally flinched, sucking in a breath as her tears began to fall. That was nearly his undoing. He didn't want to hurt her, but he was dying inside. His fear suffocating him.

She pulled herself together and lifted her chin a notch, looking so small yet so brave. "Well, it turns out I'm not. I certainly didn't deceive you if that's what you're thinking." She sounded offended.

"It doesn't add up," he said more to himself than her, thinking aloud, trying like hell to make sense of it all, but he couldn't. Nothing made sense to him. "If you had thought for even one second that you could conceive a child, then you should have told me. I would have used protection. You knew how I felt about it."

"And you knew how I felt about not being able to conceive. I was devastated when I found out I was infertile. I don't know how I got pregnant. It has to be a miracle. I lost everything because I couldn't conceive after trying for years. For the past year now, I have gone around feeling broken, knowing a part of my soul was missing because I couldn't have a baby. Then I met you and started to live again." Her voice broke.

After a moment, she continued, "To find out I'm pregnant now is an absolute miracle. You're not the boy you were. You're a man. A good man, even if you don't believe it. I want to spend my life with you. Have a family with you. Can't you see this is your chance to do things differently the second time around?" Her voice filled with emotion and her eyes with hope as she said, "I love you, Clay Sullivan. With all my heart and soul. Together, forever, remember?"

He might not be the boy he was, and he wouldn't lie this time and say he didn't love her too. He just couldn't bring himself to tell her that he did, because it wouldn't matter anyway. His fear of failure ran too deep. He looked down at the table. "Forever wasn't a package deal. I can't be a father. I won't do it. I'm sorry."

She sucked in a breath on a sob, then stood and threw down her napkin as she said with a voice riddled with pain, "Yes, you are." And then she was gone, taking all the light and happiness and love in his heart with her, leaving him to clean up the mess.

He briefly wondered if he would spend the next twenty years cleaning up the mess his life had become in a single instant, but one thing was certain. He was through with ever opening up his heart again. All it brought was heartache.

"Dammit!" He pounded his fist on the table, grinding his teeth to stop the lump in his throat from choking him.

Walking away hurt so much more this time around. He'd been so happy. So ready to commit to her, but he couldn't. His hand shook with just the thought of having a baby. Her child would be so much better off without him in his or her life. He believed that Anna didn't know she wasn't infertile, but that didn't stop him from feeling betrayed. Something didn't add up, and he wanted answers.

Two weeks later Anna drove her brand-new SUV off the car lot and headed for home. She had traded in her Mercedes for a vehicle she would feel safe in during a Vermont winter. One that would protect both her and her baby. She still loved saying that word, still in awe over the fact that she had an actual baby in her womb. It truly was a miracle. One that should bring her nothing but joy, yet her smile slipped into a sad little frown. She hadn't seen or spoken to Sully since the day she told him he was going to be a father. He had left immediately left town, supposedly on business, or so his office had said. But Anna knew the truth.

He was running scared.

Her throat filled with the lump that was lodged there most days when she thought of Clay Sullivan. The love of her life. What she had felt for Erik had been nothing compared to what she felt for Sully. What she still felt for him and probably always would. She didn't regret loving him so much it hurt, and no matter what he said or didn't say, she knew he loved her too. They'd gone through too much together. Had shared too many special intimate moments. Their love really was a special kind of love that doesn't come along very often.

Yet he'd thrown it all away.

All because he was afraid he was going to be a failure as a father. Sully wasn't his father. She had seen how he treated Bobby. He was wonderful with him. The boy worshipped him. And Sully had such a big heart. He really cared about people, he just didn't want to admit it. That way he wouldn't get hurt. She never did find out what he had wanted to tell her that wonderful, awful, fateful day that would haunt her for the rest of her life. But she decided she wasn't going to give up on him. She was a very patient person, and Mystic Valley was a small town.

He couldn't avoid her forever.

She pulled her new truck into her driveway and went inside. Sarah and Bobby were there. Sarah had been fantastic. Thrilled for Anna, pampering her, and sharing in her joy. Sarah had cooked a chicken casserole that smelled delicious.

"You're the best," Anna said as she took off her coat and sat down to eat. "You didn't have to do all this, you know."

"I know. You deserve to be pampered." Sarah was pleased, and Anna knew it was her way of thanking her for taking care of her when she had needed someone the most. She had put on a few pounds, the color in her cheeks much better, but the biggest difference was in seeing her hold her head high. She had confidence, and with it, she began to blossom into a strong, independent woman.

"Well, thank you." Anna took a bite and the flavors of cheese, vegetables, rice, and seasonings all mixed with tender chicken breast melted in her mouth. Then again everything tasted amazing lately. At night, anyway. During the morning, all bets were off. She didn't touch a thing except saltine crackers and decaf tea, reminding her she had a long, bumpy road ahead of her.

"Besides, we're in this together." Sarah reached out and squeezed her hand. "You're not alone, Anna. I hope you realize that."

Anna fought another lump in her throat, feeling so emotional lately. She wasn't due until May and was barely pregnant, but the hormones were soaring already. She'd read the first trimester was the trickiest, and she just prayed she didn't do anything that would cause her to miscarry on her one and probably only chance to be a mother.

"I know," Anna replied when she could finally speak. "We're a family now."

"Speaking of family," Sarah said. "Did you tell your parents yet?"

She knew the whole story and had encouraged Anna to reach out to them time and again. Anna had resisted for a while because she wasn't ready, but the more she read her aunt's journal, the more she had come to understand herself, as well as why her father acted the way he did. He'd been raised that way by his own father.

"Yes," Anna replied easily. "I still love my family, they just infuriate me sometimes. Space is a good thing for us. We're working on our relationships. It's slow going, but there is some progress. Mostly on my mother's part. My father is a proud, stubborn man. He doesn't forgive or forget easily, and he never admits he's wrong, but I *do* know he loves me. He'll come around in time."

"What was their reaction to the news? They must have been stunned."

"They were shocked. Thrilled to know I can have children, yet already trying to marry me off to someone at the yacht club. Can't have me running around pregnant and raising a baby alone, Heaven forbid. Of course, they want me to move home immediately."

"Are you going to?" Sarah looked worried, even though she tried to hide it.

"No, absolutely not. My aunt's journal has taught me that it's okay to be on my own. I don't need a man to make me happy or complete. Only I can do that. Not that a man wouldn't be welcome in my life, I've just learned I'm okay as just me. Anna Wilks. I'm going to be fine, and I will raise this baby alone if it comes to that."

"If?" Sarah raised a brow in question. "Does that mean you're not giving up on Sully completely?"

"I'm not ready to give up on him just yet. Truthfully, I don't know if I'll ever be able to give up on him. He's a part of me now. Forever." Anna rested her hand on her stomach and smiled tenderly.

"Good," Sarah said firmly. "Sully is a good man. Stubborn and pigheaded and too proud for his own good, but still. Men like him don't come around very often."

This time Anna squeezed her hand. "I agree, he just doesn't know it yet, but that's his journey. He has to figure out who he truly is, now that his quest to find out what happened to Cindy Taylor is over. But until he gains closure on his past with his father, he will never be happy. He just needs time, but I'm not going anywhere."

"I filed for divorce," Sarah said in a quiet, sad voice.

Anna wanted to say good for you, or it's for the best, or screw Jud, but no matter how he had treated Sarah, it was obvious she loved him. She probably always would as well. The heart didn't care whether it was right or wrong or healthy or not when it came to choosing a person's soul mate. As hard as it was, Sarah had found the courage to walk away. She once told Anna Jud hadn't always been abusive. That had started after falling on hard times and turning to alcohol. He had loved Sarah too, and would one day come to realize all he had lost. Anna just hoped Sully didn't wait until it was too late before he lost his own future. She might not be going anywhere right now, but she wouldn't wait around forever.

"You aren't alone, either," Anna said. "You'll always have me. You, Bobby, me, and the baby. One big happy family."

"Thanks." Sarah sniffed and dabbed at her eyes. "For everything you've done for me. I'll never forget it."

"Same here."

"Well, I better clean this mess up. I have to give Bobby a bath and put him to bed soon."

"Here, let me help," Anna said, getting to her feet, even though Sarah protested. "I'm pregnant, not sick, remember?" She laughed, and Sarah reluctantly agreed.

It didn't take them long to finish the dishes, and then Sarah headed off to round up Bobby. Poking her head around the corner she said, "Oh, by the way, a large envelope came for you today. It's over by the phone."

"Thanks," Anna replied. "It's probably from another magazine."

At least Anna had that, since she didn't have a clue if Sully would let her continue to work for him anymore. The October leaf peeper weekends were coming up as well as the winter carnival. Maybe by then Sully would change his mind and come around. She grabbed the envelope and carried it to the living room. Sitting on the couch, she stared down at the envelope and looked at the return address. Her heart skipped a beat.

It was from Sully.

What on earth could he be sending her in such a big envelope? Maybe he found it easier to express his feelings in a letter, but then again, this wasn't a letter-sized envelope. This was a large manila envelope. She tore the flap open and pulled out the contents. Her heart squeezed when she saw his handwriting, so bold and masculine, heavy on the pen, like he'd forced his hand to write the words. If only he would listen to his heart instead of his terrified mind, they wouldn't be going through any of this.

Anna,

   This doesn't mean I've changed my mind. I just had to know. To try and make sense out of this whole mess. What I found was shocking. You getting pregnant wasn't a miracle, it was all because of a lie. It doesn't make me feel any better to know the truth, but I'm hoping it might at least give me closure. I felt you had a right to know as well.

   Good luck,

   Sully

HE HAD CROSSED out whatever term of endearment he had originally written and settled on good luck. She squinted and thought she made out a capital L as though he'd originally written Love but then thought better of it. She sighed, saddened by his words. There was nothing left to do but start reading. One gasp after another slipped out of her mouth as she read page after page of evidence. Sully had used his connections as well as a private investigator to get to the truth. It turned out Anna and Sully hadn't been the only ones keeping secrets.

Erik had a secret as well.

Anna had known that Erik went to college with Dr. Matthew Hamlin. What she hadn't known was that the doctor was addicted to pain meds. Erik had found out and was black-mailing Matthew. No wonder Matt had looked so much older and had lost weight. It was hard keeping that secret, not to mention lying. It turned out Anna had never been broken at all.

Erik was the one who was sterile.

Erik was the last male in his family and determined to carry on his family name. He would rather she think he was unfaithful than to let anyone know he was less than whole. So when he'd come across one of his students that he was close to and saw her crying, he asked her what was wrong. She had just found out she was pregnant, but had no idea who the father was. She was terrified that she wouldn't be able to raise the baby alone and stay in school. That's when he made her a deal too good to pass up. He would marry her and take care of her for the rest of her life if she would say the baby was his.

Anna felt sick inside. How dare Erik make her feel less than whole? He let her go on believing she couldn't have children and that no man would ever want her. She'd actually blamed herself when it had been him all along. Anger surged through her for all the time she wasted. She was thirty-five now. Pregnancy could be risky at her age, and she might never have the chance to have another child. All because her ex-husband had lied to her in the worst way imaginable.

The papers she held fluttered to the coffee table before her, and her anger flew away with the evidence as her hand settled over her abdomen. She had to focus on the fact that she *was* pregnant now. She had been given this miracle. She would have no regrets. No looking back on what could have been. Erik had been so desperate to carry on his family name, he'd lied. They could have adopted, but it was clear he didn't really care about having a child at all unless the world thought it was his flesh and blood. He only cared about the legacy he would get to leave, as well as his studly reputation.

She should expose the truth, but revenge took too much energy, and frankly he didn't deserve another ounce of her time or energy. And Sully had been blessed with a miracle twice, yet he had turned his back on that gift both times out of fear. She had once thought he was so big and strong and brave, but he wasn't brave at all. He was a coward. No, she wasn't angry at either of them. She was through with wasting another thought on men who didn't have a clue about the gifts that were right in front of them. From here on out, she was on her own. It was their loss, not hers. It would be hard to shut off her feelings, but she vowed not to feel anything more for either of them ever again, except for maybe one thing...

She felt sorry for them both.

19

It was mid-January now. Anna was five months along already. The morning sickness had finally stopped, and life was good. She was starting to show now and had just bought the most adorable maternity clothes. Most women she knew hated maternity clothes, but Anna had been thrilled at the chance to wear them. Every aspect of being pregnant thrilled her. The only part that saddened her was going through it alone.

Thanksgiving and Christmas had been hard. Her family was upset when she refused to spend the holidays with them, but she wasn't ready yet. This year was all about her for once. She didn't need the drama or stress and wouldn't do anything to jeopardize the health of her baby. So she'd spent a lovely time with Sarah and Bobby and tried not to think about Sully's absence.

She lay on the exam table in Doctor Burn's office with a pillow behind her head and cold, wet gel all over her exposed abdomen. The ultrasound technician used a white wand attached to a cord that was hooked up to a monitor. She moved the wand expertly all over Anna's stomach, stopping and pressing it at certain spots while she clicked a keyboard and took pictures and measurements.

Seeing her baby on the screen would never get old for Anna. She smiled tenderly, holding back the tears of joy that filled the emptiness in her soul. And the tears of sadness for all that Sully was missing. He should be here right now, but he wasn't. Her vow not to think of him anymore had been a joke. Everywhere she went, she seemed to run into him.

He always said hello and asked how she was, but every time the conversation got too lengthy or took a turn toward anything intimate, he made an excuse and left. It was almost as if he just needed to know she was okay, but didn't trust himself to get too close. His fear was bigger than the both of them, and she didn't have the energy to deal with the emotional rollercoaster she was on. Her hormones were all over the place these days: laughing, crying, starving... you name it, she felt it.

"Good strong heartbeat," Doc Burns said, as he stepped into the room with his lab coat and stethoscope and looked at the screen while the ultrasound technician finished up. He adjusted his glasses and smiled. "Good size, too."

Anna beamed. "I wouldn't expect anything less, considering who the father is," she said before thinking. Her smile slipped a little.

"How is Sully these days?" Doc asked gently as he looked at her.

She shrugged, ignoring the ache in her throat. "I wouldn't know. We say hello in passing, but that's about it."

"I saw him last week. He's looking a little haggard. Lost some weight. I said as much to him, but you know Sully. Stubborn as the day he was born. He brushed off my concern, saying he was fine." Doc shook his head sadly. "Boy's been through a lot over the years."

"We've all been through a lot, Doc. That doesn't excuse his behavior." She clenched her jaw.

"Give him time. He'll come around."

"It's his loss if he doesn't," she said matter-of-factly, and meant it.

"That's right." Doc squeezed her hand and nodded, then his face brightened a bit mischievously. "Want to know what you're having?"

Anna's heart flipped at the thought of that. Part of her was dying to know, but another part loved surprises. She thought of her aunt and her excitement for life and made her decision. "You know, there are very few surprises in life. It's like at Christmas. The anticipation of having to wait to open your gifts is so hard, but the joy and excitement on Christmas morning is something that can't be replaced. I want the birth of my baby to be as special as it can be. So no, I'm going to wait."

"Good for you." He looked pleased. "We'll be surprised together."

"Thanks, Doc."

"In the meantime, keep taking your vitamins, drink lots of water, eat right, and get lots of rest." He looked over the top of his glasses with a no-nonsense expression.

"Always." She held up her hand, making a scout's-honor sign.

"Any questions?"

"Yes. When should I feel the baby move?"

"It depends. With a first baby, you might not recognize the little flutters for a while. It should be any time now. At first it will feel like a butterfly's wings, but soon you will feel the poke of a kick, and at the end, you'll be pushing a foot out from under your ribs. Careful what you wish for." His eyes twinkled. "The excitement might wear off eventually."

"Somehow I doubt that," she said dreamily. "I've never looked forward to anything more."

A FEW WEEKS LATER, Sully and Diego and Lynn were covering the winter carnival. They'd had a doozy of a snowstorm the night before, but today dawned sunny and bright, the temperatures unusually warm for a change. The entire town had turned up to help dig out the area for the festivities. There were tents with food and music, a chili cook-off contest, snowmobile and cross-country ski races, sledding competition, and even an ice sculpture contest.

Once again Lynn was interviewing the people while Diego took pictures, which he wasn't too happy about. Sully couldn't bring himself to work with Anna anymore. It was too painful. He'd told her he was sorry but he couldn't be a part of their lives, yet he'd be damned if he'd been able to stay away. She was so small and vulnerable, and now that she had started to show, he was scared to death for her. Protective instincts surged through him every time he saw her, and all he wanted to do was scoop her up into his arms and take care of her.

He worried about her every day, but especially this time of year. The storms had hammered their town this winter, and they were only halfway through. He felt like a stalker, but couldn't help following her around, checking up on her, making sure she was okay. He'd tried to be discreet, but he'd had a feeling she'd seen him several times. It killed him that Superhero Drew came to her rescue time and again. That should be Sully.

He was jealous as hell.

He'd spoken to her a few times because he missed her so damn much. Missed her sweet voice and soft smile and gentle touch. The way she had looked at him the day he'd walked away would be burned in his mind's eye until the day he died, and he would forever regret the pain he had caused her. But every time he felt the urge to tell her he was sorry and beg her to take him back, fear choked down his words and he walked away. The fear was so bad he experienced panic attacks like he had during the war. He couldn't sleep, couldn't eat, could barely function most days, but fear was a powerful beast and bigger than he was.

"Hey, Anna's here," Diego said from beside Sully. He looked relieved. "She has her camera, thank God." He started to walk toward her, but Sully stopped him by grabbing his arm and shaking his head no.

"She's not here to take pictures for the newspaper."

"Come on, man," Diego grumbled. "Our sales have gone down since she stopped working for you. The town is more pissed off with you now than after Cindy Taylor. They adore Anna Wilks, if you haven't noticed."

"So I've seen." Sully clenched his jaw when he spotted Drew heading straight for her with a besotted look on his face, and her beaming smile spoke volumes. She looked adorable in an enormous white puffy coat with a big hood and matching mittens.

"It's not too late, you know," Diego said in a serious voice with a sincere look on his face. He patted Sully's shoulder. "Everyone can see she still loves you. No matter what you say, I know you love her too."

"Doesn't matter." Sully looked back at Anna gazing up at Drew, her hands moving as she talked excitedly. She slipped, and Sully's heart jumped into his throat. He took a step toward her, but Drew caught her, then looped her arm through his and didn't let go. Sully's stomach bottomed out. "She doesn't need me," he said painfully. "I made sure of that."

"Yeah, but you need her. More than you know, man." Diego hoisted his camera. "Tell her you love her. The last thing you want is to go to your grave, burying another secret." Then he walked off to shoot the rest of the carnival.

Sully thought about Diego's words. He was right. Diego was always right. Sully wanted to tell Anna how he felt, but he didn't know how. He didn't know how to make things right between them. All he knew was it was killing him living without her.

"WHAT WOULD I do without you, Drew?" Anna looked up at Drew's handsome face with great fondness.

Drew was her rock. He'd been there for her, time and again, all winter long, thank goodness. They weren't kidding when they'd said winters in Mystic Valley were crazy scary. She was so glad Sarah and Bobby lived with her. It would have been hard keeping up with shoveling and salting her driveway and porch, knocking down icicles from her roof, hauling in wood and stoking the fire, and everything else that went along with living in an old house during a stormy winter. And of course, Drew had checked on them every day.

"Lucky for you you'll never have to find out." He kept her arm tucked securely in the crook of his. "How were the roads getting here? I worry about you driving alone."

"Slippery, but I went slow. And I had Sarah and Bobby with me. They're running the chili cook-off contest. She's a great cook. I blame her for how big I'm getting."

"Oh please, there's nothing to you. You're barely showing." He patted her belly, but there was nothing intimate about it.

Drew felt secure and comforting and safe. Safe was good these days. She struggled to keep her gaze from wandering in Sully's direction. She had seen him the second she'd arrived. He was like a magnet, always pulling her to him, but she had to stop wanting what could never be. He'd made that crystal clear.

"You look adorable by the way," Drew added.

"You're such a good liar. At the rate I'm going, I'm sure I will look like a whale, but I don't care." She covered her belly with her mitten. "I love it all."

"You glow, Anna." His hazel eyes were so sincere. "There's something very beautiful about a pregnant woman. My sisters had that same glow."

And there it was. The word "sister." No matter how close they got, Anna never felt like anything more than a sister to Drew, but that was okay. He was the brother she'd never had but had always secretly wanted. "Well, thank you. I feel wonderful. Doctor Burns said everything looked great and... oh my gosh." Her breath caught in her throat.

Drew stilled and grabbed her arms, facing her. "What's wrong?"

Anna stood still, not daring to move or speak. She didn't want to do anything that might make it stop. Looking down at her stomach, she kept her mitten over her tummy and concentrated. "There it is again!"

"There's what again?"

A tiny flutter, deep inside her womb, flitted about. She'd never felt something so amazing before. The realization that she had a tiny little living human being inside of her swept through her, taking her breath away. "Doctor Burns had said it would feel like butterflies. He was right."

"Butterflies?" Drew's eyebrows puckered with lines of worry.

She looked up at him in awe, feeling moisture gather in her eyes. "I just felt my baby move for the first time."

Drew's face softened. He looked down at her stomach, and she could swear his eyes grew a little misty too. He covered her hand with his own as he said, "That's wonderful, Anna." And then he hugged her, making the moment even more special. Yet she couldn't help wishing she was wrapped up another pair of big strong arms.

Anna stood there, letting Drew embrace the moment with her, when she glanced to the side and caught sight of Sully. She blinked in surprise. He was walking toward her, his face an unreadable mask of intensity as he looked like he was on a mission. His hair was longer, his face covered with a darker shadow of whiskers, with a heavy tan sheepskin jacket, gloves, hat, and boots. He looked like a scary lumberjack as he charged toward her, his limp barely noticeable. She pulled away from Drew, whose gaze followed her own. But then he frowned, and Anna knew why.

Tessa Fitzgerald.

Chief Fitz intercepted Sully. He looked distracted for a moment, but then focused on her as they talked. When he looked back at Anna, Drew stood solid by her side with his arm around her shoulders protectively. Tess followed Sully's gaze, and she noticeably stiffened. Sully's shoulders seem to droop as if whatever had driven him a moment ago was too heavy a load. He and Tess turned and walked away, leaving Anna with a feeling of longing and disappointment. She couldn't keep letting him disappoint her.

Looking up at Drew, she said, "You ready to get out of here?"

"You have no idea," he said, staring after Tess with the same look of longing and disappointment that Anna had just felt, and in that moment, a bond formed between them.

20

I t was Valentine's Day. February 14th. Five months had gone by with Tess ignoring him. Drew ground his teeth, infuriated every time he thought about it. He still couldn't believe she'd fired him, especially after what they had shared in the bed of his truck. Making love with her had been more powerful than anything he'd ever experienced. He'd always known he was attracted to her, but the moment he had entered her intimately, he'd never been more sure of anything.

He was crazy in love with Tessa Fitzgerald.

The feelings she brought out in him were overwhelming. People always told him he loved fast and he loved hard, which was true. After losing everything in the fire and nearly losing his life, he didn't see the need for holding back. He admitted he came on a bit strong and scared most women off, but this time was different. He had never felt this way about anyone. He now knew for certain that what he felt for Anna Wilks was more of a brother-sister relationship. He adored her and would always be there for her, looking out and making sure she was okay, but he would never love her like he did the incredibly annoying, head-strong, pain-in-his-ass, gorgeous Tessa Fitzgerald.

Mayor Wilcox and the town council were furious with Chief Fitz for firing him, but she was too damned stubborn to admit she'd acted hastily. Drew knew she would take him back if he agreed to follow all of her rules. Normally, he wasn't a rule breaker, but this wasn't about breaking the rules. This was about getting through to her. She was terrified of letting anyone get close to her ever since her partner had died. Drew knew she had loved Simon and killed in self-defense to save her own life. No one could fault her for that, but she couldn't seem to forgive herself for some reason. She refused to acknowledge that she and Drew were a team, and he'd be damned if he would be her lapdog.

He'd just never imagined this standoff between them would last five months.

"Earth to Drew," Anna said while sitting across from him at Deb's Diner, her hair hanging in soft waves over a burgundy long-sleeve maternity shirt.

He'd been looking out for her over the past five months, since Sully had flown the coop. That was another sore subject for Drew. How the man could live with himself knowing Anna was six months pregnant with his child was beyond Drew. Drew might not have gone back to following Tess's rules, but he *had* gone back to helping people. It was a part of who he was, and he enjoyed it. End of story.

If he were Sully, he would have rejoiced in the fact that the woman he so obviously loved was nurturing their baby within her womb. Anyone who saw the two of them together could tell they were madly in love and meant for each other. Why, Drew didn't think he would ever understand. They were polar opposites, but then again, so were he and Tess.

"You looked miles away. Where did you go just now?" Anna added, looking at him curiously while she ate a chicken sandwich and a salad, accompanied by a glass of milk.

She looked lovely. Glowing with health and so happy to be pregnant. All of Mystic Valley had come to adore her. The sadness that had once filled her eyes had disappeared for a while after getting lost in the woods and rescued by Sully. Drew hadn't thought they even liked each other, but when they had emerged, it had been obvious to everyone that something powerful must have happened. Except now her sadness was back. Not as much as it had been before, but enough to make Drew angry at Sully all over again for putting it there.

"Sorry," Drew said, pushing his fries around on his plate. All these depressing thoughts had made him lose his appetite. He dropped his fork and scrubbed a hand over his buzz cut. "Just thinking about how fast time flies."

"You can say that again." She laughed and rubbed her stomach. "I love being pregnant. I'll admit the first trimester was rough, but now I feel great. I adore every aspect of being pregnant and don't want it to end. I love feeling this tiny little miracle that I helped create move and grow inside of me." Her eyes grew misty, her love and adoration so apparent, it was obvious her child was going to be lucky to have her as a mother. Drew's own parents had been the same. Every kid deserved to be treated that way.

"You look beautiful," he said to her, and meant it.

She smiled and for a moment they stared at each other as though both reflecting on what if... yet neither needed to say a word. They both seemed to realize they were destined for another, but that didn't mean they couldn't have a special relationship of their own. Ever since the winter carnival, a bond of being the *unloved* ones had formed between them, and they both inherently knew they would always be there for each other.

"Thank you, Drew." She reached out and took his hand in her own. "For everything."

And of course, that's how Sully and Tess found them as they

entered the diner for lunch. Sully and Tess took one look at them and their joined hands and then turned around and left the diner, their heads close together as though conspiring about something.

Anna slowly pulled her hand away from Drew's and let out a sigh that said it all, no words necessary. "I still can't believe she fired you."

"And I can't believe *he* fired *you*."

"I took pictures of the October leaf peepers anyway, as well as the November antique shows, and of course the winter carnival. I just didn't give them to Sully." She shrugged. "It's his loss," she said, and Drew knew she meant so much more than mere photographs. "I made copies for all the locals since they wouldn't be seeing themselves in the paper—at least not the way that I capture them—and I even sold a few to the magazines that like my work."

"Good for you," he responded with a grin of satisfaction and admiration. She never ceased to amaze him. So strong, so brave, so beautiful—Sully was a damn fool. "Chief Fitz wouldn't let me help out officially with any of the events, but that didn't mean I wasn't there unofficially, volunteering for pretty much everything."

"I know, and I'm grateful. I'm sure everyone else saw and is grateful as well." Anna laughed softly. "I also saw you break up several situations that could have turned into serious altercations. Unofficially, of course."

"Of course." He chuckled back. "Just acting as a concerned citizen."

"Please don't stop." She looked him in the eye. "This town needs you." She paused for a moment. "I need you."

"Don't worry, Anna," he said, with emotion clogging his throat.

He grew up in a family of women who had taught him at a

young age that he was still a man even if he showed his feelings. He was comfortable in his own skin, and felt sorry for those who weren't. He'd been taught that shedding a tear wouldn't make him any less of a man. Not showing how he felt, however, would be a damn shame. Those were words he lived by, whether those around him could handle that or not wasn't his concern.

"I'm not going anywhere," he continued. "I would no sooner abandon this town than I would you. I need you too, you know. Every damn day."

"I know." She inhaled a deep breath and let it out slowly. "We're a couple of big ole saps in love with two numbskulls who are too thick-headed to realize what is right in front of them. All because of fear."

Drew blinked. He hadn't told anyone how he felt about Tess, yet leave it to Anna Wilks to see right through him. Then again, neither one of them was any good at hiding their feelings. "You're amazing. Things would be so much easier if you and I were in love."

She laughed out loud at that. "Yes, they would, my dear. Yes, they would, indeed. And we would be awesome."

"We would, wouldn't we?" He couldn't help grinning from ear to ear. "We would set this town on fire, showing them how it's done."

"Absolutely." She took his hand once more. "I do love you, you know."

He winked. "Me too. Always."

"Well, Romeo, I think you better take me home before I explode."

"Bathroom or food?" he asked, having grown up with sisters.

"Both!" She groaned. "Be glad you're not a woman."

"Amen." He helped her to her feet, paid their check even though she protested, and then drove her home.

"Sarah's not home yet," Anna mused. "Maybe she took

Bobby out to a special lunch since it's Valentine's Day. He's probably missing his dad a little. Jud might have been awful to Sarah, but he had never harmed his son. She's such a great mom."

"And you're going to be just as great." Drew ran around and helped her into the house, standing by the front door until she was safely settled. "Call me if you need anything, okay? I'm always around, and trust me, I have too much time on my hands these days. I need the distraction."

"I will, and thank you, Drew." Anna kissed his cheek. "You truly are wonderful. If Tess can't see that, then it's *her* loss."

"Right back at ya, babe," he said and tweaked her nose, then headed to his truck.

Drew climbed inside and then waited, but Anna didn't lock her doors any more than the rest of them did. Mystic Valley was a peaceful place where people didn't worry about their neighbors. He frowned, not sure why, but for some reason an uneasy feeling had settled over him. He was glad she had stayed here even after Sully had abandoned her, and that Drew got to be a part of her life. He planned to stay a part of her life, whether Sully liked it or not.

Her child would have a male role model, the same way he had picked up the slack with Bobby. Sully hadn't just abandoned Anna, he'd turned his back on Sarah and Bobby, and that wasn't right. Uncle Drew. He liked the sound of that. He was a great uncle for his nieces and nephews. What was the harm in adding a couple more? He vowed this child would know he or she was loved, one way or another.

Drew put his truck in drive and had just turned onto the main road when he decided he'd had enough. He might not be actively on the force, but that didn't mean he wasn't aware of everything that happened in Mystic Valley. This was his town, and it always would be, unofficially or otherwise.

Drew didn't think twice. He knew what he had to do...

Consequences be damned.

TESS WAS JUST GETTING ready to leave the station and go out on patrol, considering they were one member short. Randy was holding down the fort and Pam was out on another call and don't even get her started on Drew. He didn't work for the police department anymore, the stubborn ignoramus. All he'd had to do was follow her rules, and everything would have gotten back to normal. But no, the stupid fool had called her bluff. He wasn't willing to bend, and now the entire town was royally pissed off at her.

Dammit! Why had she let down her guard and slept with him?

She should have known it was a stupid, idiotic move. She'd thought sleeping with him would just fulfill a fantasy, but she was so wrong. She had been shaken to the core and didn't know how to handle all she was feeling. That's why she'd blurted impulsively that he was fired. She'd known there was no way she could work side-by-side with him after the way he had made her feel. But then it had backfired. She'd made everyone in town angry at her, and her approval rating had plummeted. Maybe if she brought down Jud, she would stand a chance of gaining it back. She'd never had enough evidence before. All she knew for certain was she had to at least try this time. And part of her was relieved that everyone but her had been busy today.

Fewer people to worry about in the line of fire was a good thing.

She headed to her SUV out back by the trees. A sudden eerie quiet enveloped her. She didn't see any movement or hear any noise, but that didn't mean anything. Eerie quiet could be deceiving. The hard knocks of life had taught her that. Her heart started pounding, and feelings of déjà vu inundated her. She breathed deeply, refusing to let them take over. This wasn't the Boston harbor. Simon wasn't with her. No one else's blood would be on her hands. She could do this. She hit the remote start and had just about reached her vehicle when a hand wrapped over her mouth and pulled her behind a set of bushes.

She hadn't heard a thing. She must be slipping. Instinctively, she started to fight. Jabbing her elbow back hard, all she heard was a soft grunt, as though the culprit had been expecting that move. She stomped down hard with her heel, but her attacker stepped back just in time before having his shin scraped raw. Then she whipped back her other fist, hoping to break his nose, but he easily caught her arm in his large hand.

Wait a minute.

A typical attacker wouldn't have anticipated those moves or known how to deflect them, especially not anyone living in Mystic Valley. So who the hell was holding her? Her breath caught in her throat. Oh no, it couldn't be. She'd worked so hard to make sure those she cared about stayed out of harm's way. Damn Drew for ruining all of that. She couldn't afford to be distracted. Her breath hitched in her throat. She couldn't afford to worry about him.

"Dammit, Drew, what the hell are you doing here?" she ground out, her body relaxing in his arms and her head falling back against him.

He didn't let her go right away, just held on tight for a moment as though savoring the feel of her against him. She closed her eyes, hating that she longed to do the same. He felt so good, and it had been so long. She missed him. She could admit it, but that didn't mean that it was smart. She wouldn't allow it to change anything. He had no idea she was protecting him as much as herself. Ever since she pulled the trigger first, she wasn't at all sure of what she would do if the situation presented itself again.

He let her go and slowly turned her around to face him. "I'm here because I'm your partner. That's what partners do. They have each other's backs."

"Not anymore." She hoisted her chin up high.

"Bullshit," he said, staring her in the eye with that intense hazel gaze of his. "You and I both know it doesn't matter what title I hold, I'm still your partner in every sense of the word. I was meant to be by your side whether you like it or not."

"You're crazy," she hissed.

"About you," he said sincerely.

"Don't do that." She pressed her lips together to stop them from trembling.

"Don't do what?" He cupped her cheek, his eyes softening as they traced her features. "State the truth?"

"But you and Anna—"

"Are just friends. Same way that you and Sully are. It's obvious to everyone that they belong together. Same way that it's obvious we do too."

"What are you saying?" She was afraid to hear his words. Had been afraid she'd ruined things beyond repair, and that he would hate her for what she'd done to him. To his career. He couldn't be this kind and understanding. No one was that good.

"I love you, Tessa. I think I have from the very start." His words rang with such sincerity, she couldn't help but believe them.

"Then why have you been so difficult?" she asked curiously.

"I've been waiting for you to come to your senses."

She was already shaking her head no. He didn't know what he was saying. Loving her involved risk and heartache for most. "You can't. You don't. You just think you do."

He swooped down and kissed her on the lips, firm yet soft,

and so full of passion it said it all. He didn't have to say a word, but he said it anyway. "I do, and I always will."

She couldn't stop her tears from falling now. Maybe it was the situation they were in that made her so vulnerable. She hated feeling weak, but he always made her feel it was okay. That she wasn't less of a cop for showing emotion and being human. He always made her feel like she could do anything, which only made more tears fall.

"I can't risk you dying because of me," she finally said with a sniffle.

He took her in his arms so tenderly it made her cry harder. "No one is going to die, baby."

"They all died because of me," she added, haunted by the memory yet needing to tell someone. Who better than her Drew?

He frowned. "What are you talking about?" he asked while stroking her back. Her head rested on his shoulder.

"I shot first. Oh God, Drew, I shot first." She kept her head on his shoulder, unable to look at him.

Tess couldn't bear the thought of seeing the disgust and condemnation enter Drew's eyes, which it undoubtedly would. That's what she felt about herself every day. But she couldn't let him go on thinking he loved an awful person.

She found the courage to continue. "I had the advantage. The upper hand. They didn't even see me. I just pulled the trigger in revenge. One of their guns went off as an afterthought, and that's how I got shot in the shoulder. I didn't even realize I'd been shot at first. I was so focused on the shock and fear I saw in their eyes when they realized they weren't going to make it, because that's the same look Simon gave me right before he died. It wasn't self-defense at all, Drew. It was murder. I *wanted* them to die. I shouldn't be a cop, and I sure as hell shouldn't be the police chief." She sobbed.

He just held her for a long time, as though digesting her words. She was shocked he hadn't shoved her away. Telling him was a risk, because he might use the information against her and get her back by ruining her life like she had his.

Stunning her further, he said, "Who knows what anyone would do, given the circumstances. They had just murdered someone you loved, your partner. It doesn't make you a horrible person, it makes you human. You just need to acknowledge that and forgive yourself."

"Whether they lived or died wasn't up to me. I played God, Drew."

"It's okay, baby. You don't know what they would have done the minute they saw you and realized you were alive. There were two of them, and from the reports I read, they were cold-blooded cop killers and good at what they did. You're going to be okay, Tess, I promise you. I'm here now, and I'm not going anywhere. We're a team, you and me. No one has to die."

"But I can't take the risk." She leaned back and looked at Drew.

"Yes, you can. And you will. You can't do everything alone, and why should you, when you have people who care and are willing to help." He swiped his thumbs under her eyes, wiping her tears away. "I've been patient enough. I'm done playing games, Tess. I love you. I want you. I won't accept no for an answer. You and me, together against the world, in sickness and in health... and in work. No buts."

She couldn't believe after all she had confessed to him, that he loved her anyway. He didn't condemn her, he understood what it was like to be upset and make a mistake. She wasn't a bad person, and with him by her side, she wouldn't make the same mistakes again. He wouldn't let her. He'd made her see she didn't have to punish herself for the rest of her life. That she deserved to be happy.

"No buts," she finally said, taking a breath and getting her emotions under control as she pointed at him. "But don't think this means you're still getting away without wearing a uniform." She actually smiled.

He laughed out loud at that. "Deal."

A call came over the police scanner in Tess's SUV. A domestic disturbance was happening on the edge of town. She read the address and immediately knew it was Sarah Shaw's old trailer. The one Sarah had lived at when she was still married to Jud. She had filed for divorce, and he hadn't taken it lightly. The holidays were rough on everyone, but especially on him. This could be her opportunity to finally do some good.

"I bet it's Sarah Shaw," Tess said. "Jud must have gotten to her."

For a while Tess had thought Jud would go after Anna for pulling Sarah away. But after Sully had put the scare of the devil right through him, he hadn't caused any trouble. But now that Sully had become nonexistent and Anna was pregnant, Sarah was fair game.

"Shit!" Drew cursed. "I just realized why Sarah hadn't been home. Valentine's Day. A hard day for anyone with a broken heart to handle. But an even harder day for a drunk set on revenge." He looked at Tess. "What do you say we go teach Jud the proper way to treat a lady."

"You read my mind." Tess narrowed her eyes and focused on her job. She was a good cop, dammit, and she was through with giving Bonnie and Clyde the satisfaction of making her doubt herself. She didn't deserve that, and Simon sure as hell didn't. Tess led the way, but then paused to glance over her shoulder, owing the most wonderful, kind-hearted man— who'd refused to give up on her—everything. "Oh, and by the way, Jones?"

"Yeah?" He eyed her curiously, looking too handsome for

words and making her realize what she'd almost lost. She didn't make mistakes twice.

"I love you too," she said, with her standard no-nonsense tone when she wanted him to know she meant business. "Just don't let it go to your head."

He slapped a hand over his chest, looking ridiculously pleased with himself. "I promise you that will *never* happen." His grin came slow and sweet with a bad boy edge that still lingered, and she secretly admitted she'd come to adore. "Your head is big enough for the two of us, Chief." He winked. "Now let's go get our man."

21

"Anna, just the person I wanted to see," Sully said sometime in March as she came out of The Country Store with a large envelope in her hands.

She looked great. Glowing and healthy as her stomach was rapidly growing. He swallowed hard and tried not to let fear win out again. He hadn't seen her since Valentine's Day when she'd been at the restaurant with Drew. He'd realized when he saw them together that he didn't want to see her with any other man but him.

He hadn't forgotten Diego's words at the winter carnival. That he should get over his fear and tell her he loved her. He'd come so close to doing just that on that day, but then Tess had stopped him to talk about a news story, and the moment had been lost. Drew and Tess were together now, and it made Sully think anything was possible. That maybe just maybe he could find a way to make things work if it wasn't too late.

"You wanted to see me?" Anna looked surprised and a bit wary. She brushed her hair back, looking self-conscious, and tightened her coat around her middle as though she were uncomfortable with the way she looked. She had no idea just how beautiful she was to him.

He cleared his throat. "Diego and Lynn can't take pictures worth a damn." He glanced at the envelope she held in her hands. "I take it those are the pictures from the Maple Syrup Festival?"

She looked down as though surprised to see she was holding something. She nodded her head a little and responded, "Yes, they are."

"Well, if it's not too late—"

She was already shaking her head no before he finished speaking. "It is," she cut him off. "Too late, I mean."

"Oh," he said, suddenly wondering if they were still talking about the pictures. He let out a defeated sigh and shoved his hands in his pockets to keep from touching her.

"I already sold the pictures to a magazine," she clarified, adding softly, "I'm sorry."

Disappointment shot through him. Her words seemed to hold so much more in their meaning. "Well, maybe next time then."

"I think you were right." She started backing away. "It's probably not a good idea for us to work together." She looked pained for a minute, but then it started to rain. Protecting her package, she said, "See you around, Sully. Take care of yourself. I've got to run." She darted off to her car and left without so much as glancing in the rear-view mirror.

Diego was wrong in saying it was never too late, because clearly Sully had messed things up for good. It was probably for the best. He'd been a fool to think he could do this. Telling her he loved her would only hurt her. He'd do well to remember no matter how much he might want to try, he just wasn't husband and father material.

"You look fantastic," Sarah said to Anna at her baby shower.

She had insisted that April showers bring May flowers. As for this shower, a May baby. It was good luck. So Anna had agreed, but honestly, Sarah was the one who looked fantastic. She was glowing with health and happiness in a floral skirt and mint-green blouse. Anna was so happy for her and proud of how far she'd come.

"I'm eight months pregnant and feeling like a cow," Anna replied. "I never thought I would get this big." She laughed as she ran her hands over her big belly.

She'd worn a soft cotton, buttercup-yellow maternity dress. It was one of the few things that still fit her these days. Between Sarah's delicious cooking and Anna's cravings for pretty much everything, she'd gained too many pounds. Not a good thing on her petite frame, her mother would undoubtedly say. Her blond goddess sisters—the J's—had all carried just like her mother— picture-perfect in every way, gaining the recommended amount of weight right down to the last ounce.

It didn't bother Anna. She was enjoying every second of being pregnant, and imagined her aunt would have thrown the recommendations out the window and done *whatever the hell she damn well pleased* if she'd had the chance to have a baby. Anna silently chuckled, but then sighed. As much as she wanted to meet her new baby, she knew she would be a little sad when her pregnancy was over.

She ran her hands through her hair, smoothing the strands. It had grown past her shoulders, and she left it loose and wavy most days now. In part because it was easier to take care of, and in part because she knew Sully preferred it that way. Not that it mattered. Ever since she had run into him after the Maple Syrup Festival, he'd made himself scarce. She couldn't handle going back to work for him. It would be too painful knowing he didn't feel the same way about her. Sully was still too afraid to love. Speaking of fear...

"The thought of giving birth is a little terrifying," Anna said, focusing back on her belly. "Any child of his is bound to be big."

"Don't worry. I'm little too, and Bobby was nine pounds. I promise you it can be done." Sarah hugged her. "You're going to do great."

"Thanks so much for hosting my baby shower. It means a lot to me," Anna said.

Sarah had gone all out. Anna had insisted they use Erik's money, and Sarah had reluctantly agreed. She'd decorated the room with every pink and blue baby item she could find since they didn't know the sex of the baby yet. And she'd made so many mouth-watering finger foods that were better than any caterer Anna had ever used. She had suggested Sarah start her own catering service. After today, she would be booked for months.

"You're welcome," she said, beaming. "I'm just glad you let me invite your mother and sisters. I'm dying to finally meet them. Family is so important."

"I know. It's time. They weren't happy that I was having the party here instead of at the Vineyard, but I didn't want to make that trip this close to delivering. And I admit a part of me is nervous about going back there and seeing my father. Do you know he still hasn't spoken to me? Men! I don't get any of them."

"Amen to that." Sarah laughed.

The doorbell rang.

Sarah clapped excitedly. "You have a seat in the living room. I'll get the door." She rushed off.

Anna made her way to the living room but didn't sit down yet. She was too nervous. Most of the women from Mystic Valley would be here today, but they weren't the ones who made her nervous. This would be the first time she had seen her mother and sisters in almost a year. They had spoken a lot more on the phone, her mother and sisters actually a big source of help in answering all of Anna's questions, but they still hadn't seen each other. She looked up. Of course they were the first to arrive. Her mother was nothing if not prompt. They followed Sarah into the living room like a graceful swan followed by her darling chicks to join Anna the ugly duckling. Story of her life.

"Sarah, this is my mother, Mary, and my sisters." She listed all six of their J names, and then told them who Sarah was. She knew her mother. Introductions and proper etiquette came before hugs and kisses.

"It's a pleasure to meet you, Sarah," her mother said sincerely. "We've heard so much about you." She shook Sarah's hand.

Mary looked sophisticated and full of class. Everything about her screamed money, but she'd never treated anyone like she was better than them. That was one of the things Anna had always loved about her mother. Anna swallowed the lump in her throat, realizing now how much she'd missed her.

Her mother looked around the house. "I must say you've done a wonderful job in preparing this party, Sarah."

Sarah blushed becomingly, but held her own, no longer looking like the frightened woman she'd been not so long ago. "Thank you, Mary. I'm so happy with the way everything turned out. Anna has encouraged me to start my own catering business. I wasn't sure I could pull it off, but after today, I just might give it a try."

"As well you should, my dear. As well you should." She patted her hand, leaving her to speak with her other daughters as she turned to Anna.

For a moment they just stood there, looking at each other. But then her mother smiled tenderly and opened her arms.

Anna didn't hesitate. She threw herself into her mother's embrace and hugged her tight, once more biting back tears so her makeup wouldn't smudge before everyone else arrived.

"I've missed you, Mom."

"Me too, darling," her mother whispered, still hugging her and rubbing her back. "So very much." She kissed Anna's cheek and then finally let go.

"How's Dad?"

"Same as always. He means well, Anna, he truly does. He's just stubborn and set in his ways. You've always been special to him, just like his dear Annabeth. He's so afraid he's going to lose you too. That's why he holds on so tight and wants you close to him."

A slice of guilt settled in the pit of Anna's stomach, but she knew it was a two-way street. He would at least have to meet her halfway. "I'm not that far away, and once the baby is here, we'll visit often, I promise." Anna's voice softened. "I just needed this."

"I know, dear. It's a quaint, peaceful place. I felt that the minute we drove over that old covered bridge. I think deep down inside, your father knows too. Now let me look at you." Her mother stepped back and smiled proudly as her gaze swept over Anna with anything but reproach. "You're lovely, sweetheart. Simply lovely."

Anna melted, basking in her mother's praise, finally feeling like everything was going to be okay. "Thanks, Mom. That means more than you know."

"Just wait until Henry sees his new grandbaby. He's going to fall hard. You know how much he loves babies."

"Looks like he's going to get a big one." Anna patted her belly and laughed.

"All the more to love." Her mother smiled.

The J's finally swarmed Anna, buzzing like lovely hummingbirds as they ooohed and ahhhed over her belly. Soon after, everyone else arrived and the party went off with a huge success. She had enough baby items to take care of triplets. In true Mystic Valley fashion, they'd come through once more and taken care of their own. Anna could feel the love and support around her, and she was suddenly so thankful for Sarah, because she'd been right.

Family was so important.

THE NEXT DAY ANNA, Sarah, her mother, and sisters had breakfast at Deb's Diner. They had only been able to stay one night and were getting ready to leave now. Spring was a busy time at Wilkinson's Winery, with tending to the grapes and planting new crops. It took a lot to whip the winery into shape after a rough winter, not to mention people came out of hibernation with a powerful thirst, as her grandfather used to say, which made Anna think of her father.

She missed him too.

"That was delicious," Mary said to Anna as they gathered up their coats and got ready to leave. Her sisters were saying their goodbyes to Sarah and the regulars they'd met, while Anna and her mother shared a private moment by the front door. "The people are every bit as gracious and welcoming as you said. I can see why you like it here."

"I'm so glad you came, Mom. I needed this more than you know. Do you think Dad would approve of Mystic Valley?"

Her mother touched her cheek. "You know your father. This place might be a bit too unrefined for his tastes, but I think it's lovely. I'm happy for you. And I have to say I'm relieved you're not alone. You have a support system here. That makes it easier for me to accept. I just wish..." She shook her head as though she'd decided against saying what she had wanted to.

"What?" Anna asked, but she had a feeling she already knew.

"It's nothing, dear."

"You just wish I had a husband to take care of me," Anna finished for her.

Her mother looked at her sadly. "To love and share your life with, not just take care of you and the baby. Love is about taking care of each other. Your father might have flaws, but we all do." Her face softened. "I have loved that man since I was just a girl, and I still do."

A powerful longing hit Anna, and she realized she wanted that more than anything for herself. The problem was she knew she'd already found that with her soul mate. He just hadn't loved her enough. Knowing she wasn't worth the risk hurt.

"I knew you never loved Erik like that, but you had seemed happy at first," her mother continued. "It didn't take long to see that you weren't. I was actually relieved when you left him. I don't know anything about the father of your child, but I do know there was something in your voice every time you talked about him over the phone. I didn't have to see your face to hear how happy you were. That's all I want for you, honey. All we both do."

"I know," Anna said and meant it. "Some things just weren't meant to be. I'll be fine, Mom. I have my baby to look forward to loving. My very own family to take care of. We'll take care of each other." She gave her mother a hug. "Tell Dad I love him."

"Maybe you should tell him yourself."

Maybe he should tell me, is what Anna wanted to say. Instead, she said, "I will soon. Drive safe." She hugged the J's.

"Call me as soon as there's any news on the arrival of my

newest grandchild. I will drop everything and get here as soon as I can."

"I will." After one last hug, Anna waved them off.

They left, and she paid their bill upon her insistence. Like Sarah, her mother only allowed it because it was Erik's money. They were all on the same page when it came to using him as much as they could since he had used her for so many years. Grabbing her purse, Anna walked out the diner's door, looking down and fishing out her keys. She looked up at the last second and let out a squawk. Sully grabbed her as they collided before she could fall. He just had no idea she'd already fallen hard.

It was a full circle moment.

They just stood there like the first time they met, staring into each other's eyes in wonder and confusion. It was an unusually warm spring day. Anna had on a short-sleeve cotton dress with no coat, and Sully had left his corduroy jacket off, wearing just his cotton shirt and tie. Her belly was so large now, it pressed snugly against his own. He kept holding her and staring at her, and neither of them could speak, but she could see the longing and regret swimming in his stormy gray eyes. He'd missed her as much as she'd missed him, but would he be brave enough to say so?

Then the most wonderful thing happened. The baby kicked hard.

Sully's eyes widened, and he looked down. His Adam's apple bobbed, and he stared at her stomach with a mixture of surprise and awe and fear. "Was that...?"

"Yes, Sully. You just felt your child move for the first time," Anna said softly. "Pretty special, isn't it?"

"Amazing," he said almost to himself in the low, gritty voice she'd missed so much. He lowered his hands and placed them on her stomach. Their baby kicked again, and a small smile tipped up the corners of his mouth. "He's a strong one."

"What makes you think it will be a boy?" Anna asked, almost afraid to speak and ruin the moment, terrified to scare him off.

He shrugged. "I don't know. Just a feeling."

Anna carefully placed her hands on top of his in a united front, holding them to her stomach, desperately trying to connect them all together as a family. Trying to show him what could be, and that with her by his side, being a father didn't have to be scary. They could do this if they had each other.

And just like that, the moment was gone. Sully dropped his hands and took a step back. He met her gaze with his unreadable mask firmly back in place. "I know what you're thinking. Don't go there. Nothing has changed."

"I don't believe you, Sully." She shook her head. "You can't tell me you didn't just feel something when you felt your baby move. I saw it in your eyes."

"You were right, and I was wrong. Babies are a miracle. A gift. I can see that now. And you will be a great mother." He looked sincere but sad. "That doesn't change the fact that I can't be a father. I won't risk ruining this child's life by being in it."

Instead he would risk breaking her heart by not being in hers.

He clenched his fists and swallowed several times before finally saying, "I'm sorry, Anna. I truly am." Then he turned around, got into his truck, and drove off without looking back.

Running away again.

22

W ell, this is it. The end of my journey. The cancer is getting worse. I'm growing confused, and the medicine that relieves my headaches makes me loopy. Henry is getting worried. Poor Jordanna, that smart little cookie, is asking way too many questions. They all still see me as wildly independent and strong. While Henry might not like it, I can tell a part of him admires what I'm doing, he would just never admit it because he's not free to do the same. I know what the future brings for cancer patients. And I especially know what it does to their families. Time has run out for me. I'm not afraid to die, but I am afraid of being in pain and helplessly withering away while my family hangs on with breaking hearts as they pity me. To me that is worse than dying. So I know what I must do. I'm going on my last grand adventure today. Sky diving. I can just imagine what it's going to feel like to be high above the clouds totally free as I touch a little piece of heaven before falling through the sky. I am going to enjoy every last second of this final wild ride called life. And then I'm going to die on my own terms, dammit.

Forgive me, Jordanna, for not pulling the cord.

. . .

ANNA GASPED as she read the last page of her aunt's journal, and then her tears began to fall. Her aunt hadn't died in a tragic accident. She had chosen when and how she wanted to leave this world. She had died on her own terms after all. The selfish part of Anna was angry for not getting to spend more time with her aunt, but she couldn't help smiling. Her aunt had left this journal in a spot she knew Anna would one day find, in hopes of making her understand.

Anna understood her aunt was the bravest woman she had ever known.

She closed the journal and hugged it close to her chest, and then ran a hand over her protruding abdomen. It was May already. It was hard to believe she had lived in Mystic Valley for one whole year. So much had changed during that time. With her aunt's help, Anna had grown strong and independent and brave as well. She had learned how to survive on her own, and how to thrive at something she loved to do. This town had come to mean so much to her.

Jud was in jail for attacking Sarah, getting the help he needed. Maybe this would finally force him to become sober and get his life back on track. Meanwhile Sarah and Bobby were making a new life for themselves, her catering business now thriving. Drew was back on the force, and it was wonderful watching the way he made Chief Fitz come out of her shell. They made a great team, in more ways than one, and Anna was happy for him. Happy for them both.

Erik continued with his false life, and Anna didn't really care. She hardly thought of him at all anymore, and it amazed her how easy it was to forgive him, move on, and let everything go. It had been great seeing her mother and sisters at her baby shower. Of course, Anna's father still hadn't come around. It made her sad, but it was his loss. Thinking of loss made her think of Sully.

Ever since he'd felt his baby move at the diner, he was suddenly everywhere. He hadn't said he loved her, and he didn't want to be in their lives, yet his actions contradicted everything. Anna kept catching him watching her, always hovering nearby, but he would look away with a frown the second he realized she'd noticed him.

All winter long she kept noticing little things that had been done on her property. Repairs on the house. The driveway shoveled. Her front steps salted. The same was happening this Spring. She had thought it was Sarah, but Sarah had said otherwise. When Anna thanked Drew, he had surprised her by saying it hadn't been him, either. The only other person it could have been was Sully. Anna knew in her heart he cared about both her and the baby, though he would never admit it. He was too stubborn. He was too afraid.

He was too foolish.

Life was short. It was crazy not to make the most out of it. Her aunt had taught her that. Sully wasn't making the most out of anything. He was missing it all. Anna had once thought she would wait for him forever, but now she wasn't so sure. She wanted what her parents had, but at what price? She would give him one more chance. When she went into labor, which would be any day now, she would let him know. If he didn't show up at the hospital, then she would have her answer. Maybe then she could finally move on.

Live life on her own terms, just like her aunt.

Anna grabbed her purse and headed to Doctor Burns' office. Now that she was at the end of her pregnancy, and because of her age, he wanted to see her every day to do a quick check of the baby's vitals as well as her own. She smiled fondly, remembering just yesterday her baby had kicked up a storm, as though as anxious as she was to enter this world. Today was a much quieter day, thank goodness, because her ribs couldn't take much more pounding. Still, she was going to miss being pregnant.

Doctor Burns had just delivered a set of twins—Misty Monroe's first grandchildren—at the hospital, so his office had asked Anna to go there instead. It would be a quick visit since he would be tied up most of the day. That was the nice thing about small town hospitals. Everyone knew each other. Anna was excited to take a peek at the twins and chat with Misty, who must be thrilled. Anna didn't know if it was the excitement of seeing brand new babies or the idea of finally having one of her own, but everything changed in an instant when her water broke.

Panic gripped her by the throat, and for a moment she was terrified. She could relate to her aunt. Having a baby didn't scare her. She was ready for this. Had been born ready. But going through pain and facing the unknown about what to except was scary. She was afraid to go through it alone. The first pains started, and Anna shook off her fear. If her aunt could be brave, then so could she. She started her breathing, left a note for Sarah who was at work, and grabbed her bag that had been packed for weeks. Hesitating briefly, she made a decision.

She called Sully.

He didn't answer, but that didn't mean anything when it came to her. He was probably screening his calls. She left a message on his machine, telling him she had gone into labor. The ball was in his court now. All she could do was sit back and wait to see what he would do. Next, she called her mother and let her know. They were in the middle of a big wine-tasting party. Her mother promised to come help the second she was home from the hospital.

Anna drove herself to the hospital since her labor was in the early stages, but by the time she got there, the pains were coming much quicker and stronger, to the point where she could barely walk. She was ushered pretty quickly into an exam room, the nurses lightly scolding her for not having called an ambulance.

"Is this normal?" Anna asked Doctor Burns the second she saw him, having a hard time catching her breath. "I thought I had time. Don't first labors usually take a long time? This seems too quick."

"Every labor is different. Some slow, some fast. Consider yourself lucky." He examined her and blinked, his brows raising high.

"What's wrong?"

"Not a thing. You're very lucky indeed. Fully dilated and the head is crowning. No time for a monitor, this baby wants out now." He smiled. "Are you ready for this, mama?" He looked around, his smile fading into a frown. "Don't you have anyone with you?"

Anna smiled back through the horrific pain, reminding herself everyone said once you delivered and saw your baby, the pain would disappear. Anna focused on that. "Just me, Doc, so feel free to hurry. I'm ready to get this show on the road anytime you are."

"Well, you have me, Anna. You can count on that. When you feel the next urge to push, I want you to bear down. Think you can do that?" He gave her an encouraging look.

She nodded, unable to talk at all now. The pain was almost unmanageable, with no time for any medication, but that was okay. She wanted to experience every aspect of bringing her child into this world. Another contraction started in her back and wove its way around to the front, her stomach growing rock hard and a pressure between her thighs urging her to push. She took a quick breath and pushed with all of her might.

"Don't push through your face, Anna. Use your stomach and push hard for as long as you can. That's it, keep pushing—okay, stop." She stopped while he checked her. "You're doing great. I want you to do the same thing when the next contraction starts, okay?"

She nodded again, gripping the hands of the nurses on either side of her. They kept murmuring words of encouragement to her so she wouldn't feel so alone. She knew them all, but it wasn't the same. Anna's eyes kept darting to the door, but Sully hadn't bothered to show up. She had her answer. She should have known he wouldn't, yet a part of her had hoped he would be strong enough to prove her wrong.

Another pain hit her hard, and the pressure was unbearable. She cried out and pushed with all her might again. After going through this several more times, she suddenly felt the head slip out.

"That's it, almost done, Anna. Here we go, ah yes, there's one shoulder, and now the other, and it's a boy!" the doctor said with a huge smile.

Tears of joy leaked out of Anna's eyes as all the pain disappeared. She'd done it. She'd given birth to an angel. Everything was right in her world. Until she looked at Doctor Burns' face. He was bent over her, frowning and working frantically. He cut the cord, whisked the baby away, and started working on him while the nurses took care of her. Time stood still, and everything moved in slow motion as Anna tried to process what was happening.

She felt out of her body as though watching this scene in a movie. It couldn't be real life. Couldn't be her life. Anna's breath lodged in her throat. She felt dizzy. What was happening? Why wasn't anyone speaking to her and telling her what was going on? It was as though she wasn't even present. A ghost that no one could see or hear. Blinking through her tears, she finally managed to speak in a hoarse voice.

"What's wrong?" she asked, but no one answered her again.

What was the doctor doing? She couldn't see anything, just heard the panic in their voices as they uttered terms she couldn't understand. They worked for what seemed like forever while the nurses delivered the afterbirth, cleaned her up, and stitched her. All while Anna's eyes were glued to Doctor Burns. He spoke with a nurse who wrote something down on a clipboard.

Finally, heartbreakingly, he wrapped the baby in a blanket and carried him over to her. She could tell by the look on his face that something had gone horribly wrong. She was strong. She could deal with any hurdle her child might have to overcome. They would face it together as a team. Take care of each other, just like her mother had said. She would do anything for her baby, love him just the way he was. She'd already decided to name him Clay after his father. He deserved to have at least that much of him.

"I know something's wrong, but it's okay. I can handle it. Now, can I hold my son?" She smiled bravely, holding back any more tears.

Doctor Burns squeezed his eyes shut and took a shaky breath, then his tear-filled gaze met hers. For the first time, real panic set in. She was already shaking her head in denial. "I'm so sorry, Anna."

"Sorry? For what? What's wrong with him?"

"He was stillborn. There was nothing we could do."

Anna heard a wail of such utter despair and anguish, it startled her. It took a moment for her to realize the wail had come from her lungs. A commotion sounded out in the hall, and several people raced off to deal with the next tragedy. She would forever see hospitals as being an awful place. A place where death lived. No wonder her aunt had wanted nothing to do with them. She had died on her own terms, while precious Clay hadn't stood a chance. He didn't even get to take a single breath or open his eyes or see the love shining within his mother's eyes as she gazed upon his tiny perfection.

Tears poured down her face as the doctor placed her blanket-wrapped miracle gently in her arms and left the room to give her a few minutes to say goodbye. Pain sliced through her. How? How could she possibly say goodbye? Anna looked at his face. He was perfect. A head of dark hair and tiny little features that looked just like his father. Unwrapping the blanket, she studied him in wonder. He looked so big and healthy and angelic. She stroked his baby-fine skin and ran her fingertips over his curved little legs to touch all of his adorable toes. Wrapping him up once more, she left his hand out so she could hold his tiny fingers wrapped gently within own.

"Why?" she said out loud, looking up toward Heaven. "Why?" she shouted louder, sobbing harder, then cradled Clay to her chest as she rocked back and forth.

Why would she be given this miracle only to have it taken away from her so soon? It wasn't fair. It was cruel. She loved him more than she ever imagined a person could love anything. Her heart ached as it shattered into tiny little pieces she didn't think would ever heal. Doc Burns had said she was lucky. She wasn't lucky. She was cursed. You needed sunlight to make things grow, she remembered.

It turned out she was still broken after all.

What had she done that was so wrong to deserve this? She sobbed harder. She'd been so careful. Just yesterday she had felt him move inside her and all the tests showed he was fine. She hadn't felt him move this morning, but she'd thought he was resting up for the big event. It didn't make any sense.

Doctor Burns came back into the room.

"This was all my fault. I killed my baby. Maybe if I had been more careful. Or maybe I should have called just as soon as I didn't feel him move. Maybe I could have saved him. If only I had done something. Oh, God, I truly killed him." The doctor put his hand on her shoulder, which made her sob harder yet. She didn't want comfort. Didn't deserve it. She moved until his hand fell away.

"Anna, don't do this to yourself," he said, looking emotional as well. She looked away, unable to stand the pity in his eyes. Her aunt had been so right. Pity was worse than dying. If only it was possible, she would gladly give her life for her child.

"There was nothing anyone could do," the doctor added. "It's no one's fault. It's just a horrible tragedy, and I am so terribly sorry for your loss. If there is anything I can do, just say the word."

She shook her head. "There's nothing anyone can do."

"Do you want me to call someone? You shouldn't be alone."

"Oh, but I am alone, Doc. More than you know." He reached out and tried to take the baby from her arms, but she leaned away and hugged him to her tighter.

"Anna, I have to take him now. You have to let go."

A new wave of panic clawed at her throat, choking her. "No! You can't take him away from me," she shouted hysterically. "He's mine!" Her voice lowered to a pathetic whimper. "Please don't take him from me. I can't let go. I don't think I'll ever be ready to let go. It's not fair," she kept repeating like a broken record. Everything about her was broken, even her thoughts.

"I know it's hard, but you have to let go, sweetheart." Doc Burns tried again, and this time—after one more heartfelt kiss on Clay's perfect little forehead—Anna let the doctor take her son, who was already growing cold, away from her. She grabbed the burp cloth that had been tucked inside his blanket and brought it to her nose, inhaling his scent—the only mark he'd left on this word—and imprinted it on her brain so she would never forget him, desperate to hang onto any part of him for as long as she could.

"I love you, Clay Henry Sullivan," she whispered, as she watched the light in her life disappear through the door. Her angel was gone, leaving her in a cold, dark, empty well she wasn't sure she could ever crawl out of.

∼

A COUPLE OF DAYS LATER, Sully stood in the back of the cemetery watching the burial of his stillborn son. His breath hitched, but he swallowed hard and held back the tears, putting up the wall he always hid behind in order to survive. He hadn't cried since his mother died. Anna had named their son Clay after him. His heart ached over that. Over all he had missed. She always used to say everything happened for a reason, but he'd be damned if he could figure out a reason their son had to die. He may have said *her* son at the beginning, but he had secretly always thought of him as *theirs*. A product of the love they once shared. A love he still felt for her with every ounce of his heart. Such an innocent human being that Sully had thought he was protecting by staying away, and yet Clay had died anyway.

It didn't make sense.

Sully had watched Anna throughout her pregnancy, blossoming and becoming more beautiful with every passing day. He'd worried like hell about her through the winter, and tried to be there for her in little ways, because he knew he couldn't in the way that she wanted. She would catch him looking at her, and her eyes would soften, but he would turn away before he gave in and went to her. She was such a positive, hopeful person, he knew she hadn't given up on him, but he was damaged goods. And she was too damn good for him. That didn't mean he didn't think about her constantly. Think about them both.

He missed her so damn much.

He'd thought over time his love for her would lessen, but it didn't. He got jealous as hell whenever he saw her with Drew. At least Tess had been his ally. She had been someone he could relate to and confide in. But once she acknowledged her feelings and turned to Drew, they had become a couple. Sully envied her ability to overcome her fear and let love in. He had honestly thought he was saving Anna and Clay from himself. Being noble in a way. The last thing he wanted was to mess up their lives. But now Clay had no life at all, and Anna's was changed forever.

She looked devastated. He'd asked Sarah about her. Sarah was angry at him, too. She'd grown strong enough to tell him as much, which he deserved. If he were honest, he would admit he missed Sarah and Bobby as well. Sarah had caved enough to let him know Anna's family was coming in for the funeral, so she wasn't alone. And Doc Burns had given her anti-depressants to help, but she still didn't sleep at night. Sarah had said Anna's crying alone in the dark when she thought no one was watching was the saddest part of all.

At the end, Sully had tried to do the right thing. He wanted Anna back in his life, but he was terrified he was too late. He didn't know how to get her back. She probably hated him now, and he couldn't blame her. He hated himself, too. The funeral was finished and the burial over. The entire town had turned out, everyone in mourning. Anna was adored by all, but so far no one could console her. Nothing anyone did helped. Sully was most afraid that she would never let herself be happy and live again. Even if she didn't want anything to do with him, he at least wanted to know that she was happy.

It was a rainy, drizzly spring day. Cloudy, overcast skies, with just enough mist as though little tears from heaven were falling down in agony over the precious fallen angel. The crowd finally cleared, and people left to bring food to Anna's place. If he didn't catch her now, he wouldn't have a moment alone with her anytime soon. He needed to talk to her. Wanted to hold her in his arms and make everything okay, but he knew she would never let him. Shoving his hands in his jeans pocket, he limped forward, knowing he had to at least try.

Anna stood alone by the grave, while her family waited for her in the car. She stood with her back to him, wearing a loose-fitting black dress, her hair pulled back in a severe bun. She looked small and fragile, and it ripped him apart inside knowing she was in pain. He slowly approached her, never having been more afraid in his life. He didn't know what to say. Where to start. So he just stood there and waited. She seemed to sense that someone was behind her. Slowly turning around, she stared at him with dead eyes, her hands folded together demurely in front of her. He flinched, but not over any pain he saw in them. He was more concerned because he saw nothing at all. They were vacant. Like she had a pulse, but she wasn't alive inside.

"Now you come?" was all she said in a quiet, empty voice, devoid of emotion. No anger, no sadness, no nothing. Just stating a fact.

"Anna, I—I don't know what to say." He shook his head and blew out a breath. "There's so much I want to say to you."

"Now that he's gone?" she asked in that same neutral, quiet voice. "I imagine you're relieved. Just like after Cindy miscarried. You were right. You weren't meant to be a father." Her monosyllabic tone uttered the words as though reading facts from a book, nothing more.

Sully winced, her blow hitting its target. He was glad. He deserved it. He only wished she would shout at him, hit him, show some emotion and let it out. Her eerie calm worried the hell out of him. "I tried—"

"No, you really didn't." Again, with the calm. "It's too late now, Mr. Sullivan. Clay took my heart along with him on his way to Heaven."

"Baby, please—"

"I have to go now." She finally looked at him. Really looked at him. A flicker of the old Anna appeared for just a second, but then she said, "Goodbye, Sully."

Anna walked away, leaving him feeling like her goodbye meant a whole lot more than simple words. Sully couldn't look at his son's grave. He couldn't break down now. He had to be strong and hold it together. Survive. That's all he knew how to do. All he'd ever known how to do. He couldn't begin to consider all that he'd lost. The damage he'd done. In trying so hard not to be like his father, his worst nightmare had come true. He had turned out just like him. There, but not really present. Actually, he had turned out worse because he hadn't been there at all.

And now he'd lost everything.

23

O ne month later, Anna stood inside her parents' living
room at Wilkinson's Winery, looking out over Cayuga
Lake. She had to admit the June weather was beautiful, the hills
and trees around the lake in full bloom, the grapes on the vines
full of life. This place had always had a calming effect on her.
She hadn't thought she would ever come back here, but after
losing Clay, she had needed time to heal. Anna was the same age
her aunt had been when she died, and a part of Anna had died
along with her son. She needed to find a way to feel alive again...

Or what was the point of living?

Sarah and Bobby were holding down the fort at her house in
Mystic Valley, while Anna had let her parents take care of her for
a while. More like her mother, since her father seemed to say
and do all the wrong things, but at least he was trying. At least
he didn't look at her with pity. She couldn't face the looks of pity
from all the people in Mystic Valley, and if she were honest, she
couldn't face Sully. She couldn't look at him without thinking he
was secretly glad their son had died. She rubbed the chill from
her arms. That was just too much to bear.

"There you are, Jordanna," her father said, as he came to a

stop beside her, standing straight and tall and refined, with his hands behind his back as he stared out the window.

He'd always looked so sophisticated and powerful. He was seventy now, his hair as white as ever, his eyes so like her own. They used to have a special bond, closer than he did with any of her sisters, but all of that had changed after her aunt had died. He'd become serious and strict, but especially with her. And then when she'd become Anna like her aunt, he'd looked disappointed as though she had failed him in some way. He had shut her out, stubbornly refusing to give in, until she'd lost her son. Then he had come around. She'd never understood why he had done all that. He should have known she'd needed his strength.

She didn't respond to him now, just kept staring out the window as well.

"I worry about you," he spoke again. "You're thinner than you were before you got pregnant. It's not healthy."

"I'm fine," she finally responded, wondering why he cared so much now. She was still angry at him. If she were honest, she was angry with the world.

"You're not fine," he snapped, surprising her with the force of his frustration and anger. "I've let you wallow long enough." She gasped, but he kept going, ignoring her. "It's not helping. You need to stop this nonsense now. It's time to move on. I've arranged a meeting with a nice young man—"

"I'm not meeting anyone, Dad, because I'm not staying here," she ground out, angry over how insensitive he sounded. "Then you won't have to worry about my *wallowing* because you won't have to see me at all. It didn't bother you before, so I can't imagine that it will bother you this time." She surprised herself even more. She had never stood up to him, other than when she'd first left Mystic Valley. But she had grown stronger since being on her own, and she wasn't afraid to speak her mind now.

"I didn't get dumped by a boy. My son died. I think that makes me entitled to wallow."

"Don't be ridiculous," her father said even more firmly, almost sounding desperate. "You're not going anywhere. I forbid it."

"You can't tell me what to do anymore. I'm not a child."

"You're certainly acting like one. You never should have gone off acting crazy like your aunt. She died because of her reckless behavior. Maybe if you hadn't been so reckless, your son wouldn't have died."

It all happened so fast. Pain sliced through her at his words, and she reacted before having time to form a single thought. She slapped him hard across the face. His stunned expression matched her own, and then she burst into tears and ran from the house. Her mother looked startled as Anna ran by her across the lawn. Not stopping to say a word, she kept running, all the way through the vineyard until she came to the fort she'd made with her aunt. The only place she felt any source of comfort. Sobbing hysterically, she climbed inside and sat on her favorite rock, and the feeling of déjà vu settled over her.

Anna didn't know how long she sat there crying, but gradually a sense of peace shifted inside of her. Once again she could feel her aunt's presence surrounding her in comfort. She heard a noise just outside the fort and smiled a little. Her mother wasn't her aunt, but she had always tried to do the best she could. They had grown closer than they'd ever been this past year.

"Come in," Anna said.

Only, the person who entered wasn't her mother.

"Dad?" Anna said in shock, as he sat down on the rock across from her. "How did you find me?"

"This is my vineyard. My life. I know about everything that happens on this land. I made sure it stayed intact. For you and for your aunt," he said quietly, the red imprint of her hand still lingering on his cheek.

She pressed her lips together to keep them from trembling, then sat up straight and said, "I'm sorry."

He held up his hand, looking anything but refined and intimidating. He looked deflated and old and sad. "No, I'm the one who is sorry. Can you ever forgive me?"

"For what?" she asked, wondering if he meant his comment about her son or for her entire childhood.

"Everything." His jade green eyes met hers, and she felt the connection they'd once had return. "You're so much like her." He smiled a little. "I miss her every single day."

"I miss her too."

"That's why I've always been so hard on you. I couldn't stop her from acting crazy and dying." He rubbed a hand over his face. "The guilt I've felt for not trying harder has haunted me for years. That's why I've been so determined to keep you from making the same mistakes she did. I was terrified I would lose you too." He broke down and cried. "I couldn't handle it if I lost you. I love you so much."

Anna reached out and hugged him and told him she loved him too. He hugged her back and held her tight, rocking her slowly. She closed her eyes and allowed herself to feel protected and cherished and loved like she had as a little girl so very long ago. She'd missed this. Missed him. More than even she had realized she could.

When they finally pulled apart, she said, "There was nothing you could have done to save Aunt Annabeth."

His forehead puckered. "How do you mean?"

Anna had made a decision. Her aunt had tried to protect Henry because she loved him too. But in protecting him by not telling him about her brain cancer, she'd made him live with the guilt of thinking he'd failed her as an older brother. With the way he had been raised, the thought of not being able to protect her had been worse for him than knowing about her cancer would have been. Maybe that's why her aunt had left her the journal. She'd known it would help Anna, and she'd known Anna could help Henry when he was finally ready.

"I want to show you something." She leaned forward and pulled out the metal box, then reached inside and pulled out her aunt's journal. "I brought this with me when I went to Mystic Valley, and it helped me discover who I am. When I didn't need it anymore, I brought it back here when I returned, thinking this was where it belonged. But now I think you need it more than anyone."

"What is it?"

"Aunt Annabeth's journal." She handed it to him.

He took it in his hands so gently, as though she had just given him the greatest gift. "Thank you," he said, as if Anna had given him a piece of the sister he'd adored. In a way, she had.

"I think what's inside will explain a lot about why she changed her name and acted the way she did. She wasn't crazy. Start from the beginning and follow her journey to the end. Through her story, maybe you will finally understand."

He nodded. "Okay. Now I want to tell *you* a story."

Anna couldn't help but smile. "Don't you think I'm a little too old for that?"

"No, I think this is the perfect time in your life for me to tell you this particular story. It's a story I haven't shared with anyone except your mother. You see your mother and I didn't just have you six girls."

Anna's eyes widened, but she didn't say a word, sensing this wasn't just any story.

"We were young and so full of life and so excited when she first got pregnant. Terrified we would do something wrong, we didn't tell anyone. Your mother was a tall woman with bigger bones than you. No one could tell she was pregnant yet. We made it through the first trimester and had just found out we were having a boy. We were so happy. We planned to tell everyone at Christmas, but then she miscarried."

Anna gasped, covering her mouth with her hand, but her father didn't look sad. He looked at peace.

"There was no medical reason why it happened, it just did," he went on, looking pensive as though he'd given this lots of thought. "I couldn't understand why or how that could happen to us. We were good people. What had we done to deserve this heartache? We couldn't bring ourselves to share the news with anyone. As if not talking about it made it like it had never happened. Your mother got pregnant again right away, and then we were blessed with six beautiful girls." He smiled tenderly. "Things got better, but neither one of us ever forgot about him."

"Oh, Dad." Anna squeezed his hand, feeling that bond between them grow stronger, knowing he truly did understand how she had felt. "H-How did you go on?" she asked, her voice breaking, hoping for some nugget of wisdom that would help her live again.

"Life goes on whether we want it to or not, kiddo." He stroked her cheek. "Your sisters were just like your mother. I never worried about them. But then came you." He chuckled and shook his head, his eyes filling with love as he looked at her. "You were special. So tiny. Wild and free, just like your aunt. I adored you so, and I worried. It was then that I finally understood why your brother was taken from us. He was meant to be your guardian angel. I have always felt his presence, and I know in my heart he is always with you." He looked her in the eye and nodded with conviction. "You will go on to be a wonderful mother, Anna."

That was the first time he had called her by her new name,

as though fully accepting who she was, which made her sniffle all over again.

"I don't know how I know these things; I just do. Just as I know little Clay will be watching from above, spreading his wings right beside his crazy Aunt Annabeth."

Anna laughed out loud at that, smiling over the picture he'd just put in her head. Thinking of her aunt and her son together made his passing just a little easier. "Thank you, Dad."

"Thank *you*, kiddo." He held the journal to his chest. "For everything. What do you say we go join the world of the living?"

"Wherever that journey may take us?"

"Wherever that may be." He smiled in resignation. "But that doesn't mean I'll stop worrying. Spread your wings, kiddo. It's time."

~

TWO WEEKS LATER, Anna stood on her front porch with Sarah and Bobby and Drew and Tess, saying goodbye. They all looked so sad, she wanted to make them understand that her going away was a good thing. She was leaving in search of happiness, determined to find her smile again.

"I'm going to miss you so much," Sarah said, giving her a big hug.

"I'm not going away forever," Anna replied. "I just can't live in this house anymore. There's too many memories. Besides, it's perfect for you and Bobby."

"It's too generous," Sarah said. "No one has ever done anything like this for me before." She shook her head. "I don't know what to say."

"You've already said thank you. That's all I need. You deserve this. And I like thinking at least one good thing will come from Erik's money." Anna winked at her.

The truth had come out like it always does, and Erik was mortified. People didn't care that he was sterile, but they were horrified over what he had done to Anna. He'd lost all respect at work, and his own family had shunned him. Even his new wife had divorced him, taking him for everything he was worth. Karma had a way of getting even in the end.

Bobby threw himself against Anna's legs, wrapping his arms around her and holding on tight. "I don't want you to go, Aunt Anna."

She rubbed his back. "Oh, honey, I won't be gone for long. I just need some time away. Some fun."

He looked up at her with big eyes full of excitement. "On a grand adventure?"

She laughed and ruffled his hair. "Yes, I plan on having a very grand adventure."

She turned to Drew and he walked right up to her with tears in his eyes, not caring who might see him. He pulled her into a big bear hug. "I'm going to miss the hell out of you, Anna Wilks. Who's going to take care of you now?"

She pulled back and looked up at him with a determined smile. She still felt like there was something missing in her life, but things were getting better, just like her father had said they would. "Me. I think It's about time, don't you? I'm going to be okay, Drew. You'll see."

"Don't worry, Anna. I'll keep him in line while you're gone." Tess joined Drew and wrapped her arms around him. "Isn't that right, Officer Jones?"

"Whatever you say, Chief." Drew smiled tenderly at Tess, planting a kiss on her lips. Anna's heart filled with joy to see them so happy. He still lived with his parents and Tess still rented, but they had both agreed to start looking for a place together.

Anna climbed into her SUV and waved goodbye as she set

out for parts unknown. She'd only packed a suitcase of clothes, deciding to send for her things once she knew where she was going to settle. Right she didn't have a clue where she was headed, but she was excited for the first time in a long time. She just had to make one stop before she set out in search of what was missing in her life. She needed to see her son's grave just one more time. She pulled into the cemetery and cut the engine, staring straight ahead in disbelief.

Sully.

She hadn't expected to see him here. He'd tried for a while to speak to her, but she just didn't have it in her to hear what he had to say. He was on his knees in front of their son's grave. Getting out of the car, she walked slowly toward him. Her anger at him had diminished to sadness over all that they could have been. If only he had been there. He still took her breath away every time she saw him. So big and strong and rugged, like a bear of a man. Yet he looked different somehow. Maybe it was the hunch of his shoulders, the rumpled look of his clothes, or the fact that he needed a haircut. She wasn't sure what it was exactly, but he looked vulnerable.

The part of her heart that would forever be his softened.

Anna didn't know why, but something made her approach him quietly. She didn't want to see him hide behind his walls. For once, she wanted to see inside his heart to the real Clay Sullivan. To know what he was truly thinking. To know if the man she'd fallen in love with still existed or if it had all just been a dream. Because she suddenly understood that right or wrong, the part of her life that was missing was him.

It had been him all along.

SULLY STARED at the small headstone on top of a grave that was way too tiny. *Clay Henry Sullivan, angel from above.* He hadn't allowed himself to cry over the loss of his son, even though it had eaten him alive, tearing him apart on the inside day by day. He had thought a man's tears made him weak. He had thought a lot of things.

He had been a damn fool.

Anna was back. He'd thought maybe he could finally make amends. Somehow make things right. But she hadn't agreed to see him. She had said nothing he could say would change the way she felt. She didn't want anything to do with him. It broke his heart to think about the way he'd hurt her. In trying to stay away, thinking that would be better, he'd made things so much worse.

He couldn't go back or change time. All he could do was move forward, but to what? His life had no meaning anymore. Not without Anna. He pulled the weeds away from the stone and adjusted the flowers and teddy bear he'd placed in front. It wasn't enough. It would probably never be enough. His shoulders started to shake, and he couldn't stop the sobs. Right there on a sunny day in June with the sounds of nature all around him, he broke down for the first time in years and poured out his heart.

"I'm so sorry," he said in a voice filled with agony. "I only hope one day you can forgive me." He stroked the stone. "I loved you so much. From the moment I heard about you, I loved you, but I thought I would do you more harm than good. I was so scared to be a father. When I felt you move beneath my hand, I was a goner. I wanted you so badly to be mine, but I was a stupid fool. I never told her I loved her. God, I love her so damn much my heart aches. She'll never know how much now, because I ruined everything."

He dropped his face into his palms and cried quietly.

When he could talk again, he said through his tears, "When she called and said she was in labor, I drove to the hospital immediately." He looked back at the stone. "I promise you I was there the whole time; I just couldn't bring myself to go inside. When I heard her scream, I nearly broke down the door to get to her. Made quite a ruckus that brought half the hospital staff out into the hall. Then they told me what happened. A piece of me died right then and there. When they brought you out of the room, I was the last one to hold you in my arms." His voice broke. "You were so perfect. I'm so sorry. I was there, son. I was there, I promise... just not enough to count."

"Clay Sullivan, you are such a fraud," said a voice from behind him, making his heart skip a beat. "You have been grieving as much I have. How dare you let me think you didn't care?"

He swiveled around on his knees and gaped at Anna, quickly wiping his eyes. She looked good. More than good. He ached to hold her in his arms just one more time, but knew that would never happen now. He couldn't deal with the pain that brought, so he jumped to his feet and tried to walk away. "I'll be going now," he said. "I'm sure you want to be alone with him."

"Not so fast," she said softly, with tears shining bright in her own eyes. "You can't hide from me anymore. I heard you. I heard it all. Why didn't you tell me you were there?"

He turned around and faced her. "I didn't think it would change anything," he said quietly. "I screwed up so badly."

"Not as badly as you might think. The fact that you were there changes everything."

"But I couldn't save him. I let you down. I let us all down."

"Doc Burns said they tried. They all tried. It just happened."

"But not our son. He was your miracle, my second chance. It's all my fault."

"It's not anyone's fault. To know you were there. That you got to hold him. That you loved him. That means the world to me. As much as I wanted to, I never truly gave up on you. I couldn't. You and me forever, remember?"

Her words made him open his arms. She threw herself against him. He was in shock, but he quickly wrapped his arms around her and held on tight, silently vowing to never let her go again. He leaned his head back and let the tears fall again, not ashamed for her to see. Then he kissed her for a long time, letting everything he felt show through that single kiss. When he pulled away, he cradled her face in his hands, drinking in the sight of her looking at him with love. Something he didn't ever think he would get to see again.

"I knew I loved you long before the day you told me you were pregnant. I was going to tell you that night, but then I let my stupid fear ruin everything. I never stopped loving you, and I loved him, too. I really did." His voice broke.

"I know you did. I think I always knew. And so did he. I'm sure of it." She ran her hands through his hair. "He looked just like you." She smiled. "I'm glad."

"Please don't go," Sully whispered, holding her tight. "I need you. I can't lose you, too, baby, I just can't."

She kissed him softly. "Oh, I'm still going."

"You are?" He tried not to show how crushed that made him.

"Yes. I need this trip. I wanted to get away to find what was missing in my life, but now that I know what that is, you're coming with me."

"I am?" Hope surged through him once more. Could she really be willing to give him a second chance after everything he'd done? If she did, he would spend the rest of his life making it up to her.

"You're what's missing in my life, Clay Sullivan. I forgive you, I love you, and I want you in my life forever, but on two conditions."

"Anything," he said immediately.

"You have to forgive yourself, and I want another baby."

He looked floored, and he waited a beat, but his usual panic didn't come. Then he surprised both of them by smiling. His heart filled with a joy he hadn't expected or ever thought he had needed. "I can't believe I'm saying this, but I want that too. More than I ever imagined possible. I'm still scared as hell, but after holding him in my arms, I fell head over heels. I want that feeling again. I want that with you."

"I never understood why he was taken from us until I talked to my father." She looked reflective, like she'd really given this a lot of thought. "I truly think he was meant to be a guardian angel."

"You really think so?" Sully latched onto that thought. The hope that his son was taken for a reason. That his short little life had a purpose. It somehow made it a little easier to deal with.

"I know so." She bit her bottom lip in the way that he loved, looking adorable as she grinned up at him. "Someone has to look out for our daughter."

He raised a brow. "How do you know it will be a girl?"

"I just know." She kissed him. "Now, let's go make a baby, and bring your pitchfork."

"Right now?" His body responded immediately.

"Oh yeah, and I know exactly where I want to go."

"The cabin." He kissed her back. "A magical place where dreams really do come true."

EPILOGUE

Nine months later, on a gorgeous sunny spring day, Anna grabbed Sully's hand. "It's time," she said.

They were standing in the kitchen of their brand new two-story contemporary house with a big back yard on the outskirts of town. It had just been built, and they'd just put the finishing touches on the baby's room. She'd given her ancient colonial house to Sarah and Bobby, while Sully had sold his old Cape Cod to Drew and Tess. The four of them had gotten married in a double wedding just as soon as Anna and Sully had returned from their magical weekend at the cabin, much to the delight of the entire town. True to his word he had forgiven himself for Cindy, and for Anna, and for Clay, and he'd even forgiven his father. He'd made peace with himself, and he'd become the man she'd always known he could be. Strong and loyal and loving and...

Fiercely protective.

"Okay, don't move." He jogged around her, then doubled back. "Wait, what do we do? Oh, God, I'm calling 911."

Anna smiled gently and grabbed his shirt because it was all she could reach past her mammoth belly, pulling him to a stop and making him bend down from his tall height so she could kiss him. "Calm down, Daddy. We're both fine." She patted her belly, not afraid in the least. She couldn't explain it, but she knew for certain everything was going to be fine this time.

Her sweet guardian angel Clay would make it so.

"You're sure?" Sully asked, and she smoothed out the wrinkle on his forehead with her fingertip as she nodded. "Okay," he said, and then repeated it three times.

"Grab my suitcase, and I'll call Doctor Burns to let him know we're coming. And then I'll call my parents. I think my dad is even more excited than you are." Her parents were all packed and ready, and had planned to come spend the week with them to help out after the baby was born.

"That's not possible. No one is more excited than I am." Sully looked at her so adoringly, Anna's heart filled full of love as she counted her many blessings. "All right, let's go, Mama." He winked. "I'm ready to meet my baby girl."

They had found out what she was having after a bet. Sully was sure his loins would only produce big strong sons like him, while Anna was positive right from the start that they would have a daughter. She had enjoyed him cooking dinner for a month after proving she was right. He didn't mind. He fussed over her constantly. For someone who had refused to help her when they first met, he wouldn't let her lift a finger now.

He was more terrified than ever over the thought of having a daughter, yet Anna could tell he was secretly thrilled. While Bobby had announced he was going to make the best big honorary brother, and he would even let her go on some of his adventures, but she was the only girl who would be allowed. Ever! They all laughed, knowing one day not too far off that he would eat those words. Life went by way too fast. All you could do was enjoy every second of the wild ride while it lasted.

Aunt Annabeth had taught her that.

Anna's contractions picked up as they arrived at the hospital. Doctor Burns had once told her she was lucky. She hadn't believed him, but she did now. Like her father always said, children were gifts from God, no matter what. Her labor came slower this time. Not as out of control as the last time. And this time her baby hadn't stopped moving. Quite the opposite, in fact. All her vitals looked great on the monitor.

"She's in too much pain, Doc," Sully kept saying, agonizing every time Anna had another contraction. "There has to be something more we can do for her."

"I'm fine," she gasped as another contraction hit her hard. They were getting close now, she could feel it. "I want to feel everything. I want to be able to push."

Doctor Burns checked her and came up smiling. "You're lucky. She's crowning and ready to meet you. You ready to do this, Mama?"

Anna grinned back. "I was born ready. Let's get this show on the road, Doc."

No one had been more thrilled for her than Doctor Burns when she found out she was pregnant for the second time. He had taken the loss of Clay hard as well. This was his way of helping to restore the light back in Anna's eyes, and she couldn't imagine anyone else by her side. He was also relieved and happy to see she had a support system this time.

After an hour of pushing, Anna and Sully's baby girl entered the world, kicking and screaming every inch of the way. Anna had never heard a more beautiful sound. A lump filled her throat as she looked up at Sully who let the tears fall freely from his eyes. He'd held her hand the entire time, not leaving her side no matter how scared he was, and encouraging her every step of the way.

He bent down and kissed Anna on the lips as he whispered,

"We did it." He kissed her again. "I love you so damn much, baby."

"I love you, too," she whispered back. "Of course, we did it. Don't you know we can do anything?"

"Come here, Papa," Doc said to Sully over the wails of the baby.

Sully stood up, eyeing the doctor warily. "Okay," he said as he walked over. "What now?"

"Care to do the honors?" the doctor asked and handed him the scissors. "She's got a set of lungs on her, that one." He laughed, probably trying to make Sully relax.

Anna thought for sure Sully would faint, but he didn't. He swallowed hard and took the scissors in his big hands, looking terrified. But when he looked down into the face of his daughter for the very first time, he melted. A fierce expression of love and adoration settled over him. He would never let anything happen to her, and she would know how much she was loved every day of her life. Anna was sure of it. After Sully cut the cord, the doctor wrapped the baby in a blanket and handed her to Sully.

The moment he held her in his arms, she stopped crying.

"Well, I'll be damned," Doctor Burns said.

Sully didn't look afraid anymore. He looked calm and confident and happy. He walked over to Anna and placed their daughter into her arms. Anna sucked in a breath. Her baby girl had fiery red hair and sparkling green eyes just like Anna's Aunt Annabeth. The baby stared back at Anna as though she could see clear through to her soul, and Anna felt the connection immediately.

"What should we name her?" she asked. They had gone round and round, unable to decide on a name.

"I was thinking Beth sounds about right," Sully said immediately with a smile, as though there were no question.

Anna didn't think her love for him could grow any stronger

than it already was, but it did. "Beth Deloris Sullivan," she said
—Deloris after his mother. "It's perfect."

"You're perfect," he said, gratitude clearly evident in his
stormy gray eyes.

"*We're* perfect." She kissed him, feeling invincible... *Like she
could do anything she damn well pleased...* and for the first time,
one hundred percent sure, she believed it.

ABOUT THE AUTHOR

Kari Lee Townsend is a National Bestselling Author of mysteries & a tween superhero series. She also writes romance and women's fiction as Kari Lee Harmon. With a background in English education, she's now a full-time writer, wife to her own superhero, mom of 3 sons, 1 darling diva, 1 daughter-in-law & 2 lovable fur babies. These days you'll find her walking her dogs or hard at work on her next story, living a blessed life.

ALSO BY THE AUTHOR

Sleeping in the Middle